HOSTILE TAKEOVER

DAVID BRUNS

CHRIS POURTEAU

SEVERN RIVER
PUBLISHING

Severn River Publishing
www.SevernRiverBooks.com

ISBN: 978-1-64875-545-3 (Paperback)

ALSO BY BRUNS AND POURTEAU

The SynCorp Saga

The Lazarus Protocol

Cassandra's War

Hostile Takeover

Valhalla Station

Masada's Gate

Serpent's Fury

Never miss a new release! Sign up to receive exclusive updates from authors Bruns and Pourteau!

severnriverbooks.com/series/the-syncorp-saga

For our canine companions
Katie, Lucy, Sydney, and Tricksy
Who warm our feet and help us walk off writer's block

1

CORAZON SANTOS • OUTSIDE FORT HOOD, TEXAS

From a high point on the interstate overpass, Corazon Santos squinted through the ripples of heat coming off the concrete for her first glimpse of their destination. It wasn't much to look at, just a blur of buildings in the distance.

Fort Hood, Texas. Home for herself and the hundred thousand plus refugees who streamed out behind her in a two-kilometer-long accordion of people. She shot a quick glance over her shoulder. A sea of swaying, bobbing head coverings stretched as far as the eye could see.

All following her. Just the thought of it made her stomach roil.

The temperature indicator in the corner of her data glasses told her it was 110 degrees Fahrenheit—the measurement had shifted automatically to Fahrenheit when they crossed the border from Mexico—but under her own head covering she was cool and comfortable thanks to the chill collar she wore. Everyone in her migration had one, she'd made sure of that. The loose-fitting collar cooled the blood in her neck just enough to keep the rest of her body comfortable.

"Is that it, Corazon?" asked Maria. Her acolyte's slim body was lost in a huddle of loose-fitting robes.

Cora studied the height of the morning sun. "We should be there by midafternoon. Let's call a ten-minute rest period, Maria." *Only a few more hours until I meet the one on whom rests the fate of the Child.*

The girl hurried away to pass the word. It wasn't easy to stop a group that large, but eventually the mob ground to a halt and spread out in the dust on either side of the interstate. Civilian aircars passed overhead, some of them swooping lower to catch a glimpse of Corazon Santos and the great Neo migration.

The newsfeeds called her the leader of the migration movement, but the reality was nothing so grand as that. One day, after services at the local Temple of Cassandra in Panama, where she was living at the time, she started walking north. She was the medic at an orphanage, and she took a few of the young men and women with her, staff and children alike.

She had no money, no transportation other than her own two feet, and no destination other than north.

But she had conviction. In retellings, the story grew to say she'd had a vision from Cassandra that inspired her to start the migration, but that also was not true. The visions started later.

Cora halted in place and sank to the ground. The heat from the concrete roadway radiated through her robes into her backside, soothing the aching muscles. For the last six months, she had walked at least thirty kilometers every day, hardening the flesh of her thighs, calves, and back into ridges of muscle.

A three-year-old boy ran to her and threw himself into her lap. His smile was bright and his dark eyes danced. "I walked the whole time all by myself, Corazon," he said.

She tweaked his nose. "I saw you, Juanito. You are such a big boy now."

He responded by snuggling deeper into her layers of robes and dragging Cora's arms around him. She was doing this to give the children a better life, she told herself. But the truth was harder than that. Corazon Santos's life was not her own. She was in service to a higher cause.

Visions compelled her. It was all she could do not to scoff at the absurd thought. She was a nurse, a mother, a sensible woman, not some magical mystic caught in the throes of religious fervor.

And yet, she walked. She followed the signs north. To him who would lead her to the Child.

"Excuse me, Corazon." The two men who approached were twins, Chaco and Lito. Together they formed the head of her security team. She hoisted young Juan off her lap and took the proffered hand from Chaco to get to her feet. The identical twins were dark-skinned, with straight, coarse black hair and quick eyes. They were shorter than her by a head.

"Has the spy moved?" she asked.

Chaco was two minutes older than his brother and usually served as the designated spokesman for the pair. "Yes, Corazon."

The US military had placed a young man in the migration just before they crossed the border. He looked and spoke like a native, but he was clearly a military man and asked a lot of questions. Further digging had shown him to be a United States Marine and close to General Graves.

"He disappeared about an hour ago," Chaco continued.

Cora blew out a breath of exasperation. She had yet to make up her mind how she should think about General Graves. He had put a spy in her ranks, but he was supposed to help her save the Child. Cassandra worked in mysterious ways, but that combination seemed a stretch even for Her.

"So you think he left to report in to his superiors?" Cora tried to keep the impatience out of her voice. The twins were just doing their job.

"Yes, Corazon," Lito spoke, probably trying to emphasize to her how important the request was to them. His voice was lower than his brother's and husky from lack of use. "We think it is wise to have security near you at all times now."

Cora chuckled. "There is no way you can make me safe, Lito. No matter how hard you try. If the Americans want me dead, I will be dead. I serve Cassandra. If it is Her will, then it is so. The spy will tell his superiors we are a peaceful migration of poor refugees."

The brothers exchanged glances. There was something they weren't telling her.

"Has the spy seen any weapons?" she asked. It was easy to hide a few dozen small arms amidst a hundred thousand people. Another look flashed between the brothers and Cora drew in a sharp breath. "The jamming device."

"It is a hunch only, Corazon," Chaco said. "The spy was seen near the bus where we have the device. It may be a coincidence, but we are being cautious."

Cora cursed to herself. Weapons they could steal, but the jammer was irreplaceable. Without it, any attack would be a bloodbath—on her side. They'd searched the spy's belongings on multiple occasions. If he had a scanner with him, it was tiny, and he would have to be close to the power block of the jammer to detect it. Still, if the jamming device had been discovered...

"Maria," she called out. The acolyte appeared at her side. "We'll stop here for lunch. Bring up the buses."

A caravan of ancient, mismatched, gas-powered buses followed the migration. They carried the infirm, the very young, and the supplies needed to feed a hundred thousand mouths twice a day.

"Yes, Corazon." Maria raced off, already issuing orders.

"We planned for this," Cora snapped at the twins. "Disassemble the device and spread the pieces among the designated carriers. Bring the power block to me."

"As you wish, Corazon." Lito held out his hand. On his opened palm sat a black cube about three centimeters to a side. When Cora picked it up, it was much heavier than it looked and slightly warm to the touch. The bottom side held an array of bright gold contacts.

"How close does someone need to be to detect it?" she asked.

"In this deactivated state, less than a meter," Chaco said.

Cora nodded. "I will keep it safe."

Chaco looked at his brother. "One of us will stay with—"

"I will keep it safe," Cora repeated, more gently this time. "They will not search me."

Reluctantly, the twins walked away. She could hear the buses moving closer now, the roar of their diesel engines breaking through the white noise of a thousand conversations.

The cube weighed heavily in her hand. She had refused air transport from the US–Mexico border all to conceal this tiny power source, the key to her entire plan to take over the army base. She looked at the smudge of a town on the wavering horizon, feeling the tension growing in her shoulders. There was a reckoning coming. She could feel it.

If I am worthy, take me, Cassandra, she prayed. She had lost so much already. Her husband, her child, her free will. Some days she just wanted to lie down on the hot pavement and never get up.

Even the visions, once so sharp and clear, had faded as she grew closer to her destination.

Faith. The word rang clear in her head. She was the anchor for these people and the millions—billions—of Cassandra's followers the world over. She had been chosen to show them a new path to the future. If she lost her faith, what about them?

"Juan!" she called out.

The little boy with the bright eyes was at her side in a flash. She knelt down to his level, taking one hand in hers while the other worked open the zipper of his yellow and red backpack and slipped the cube inside.

"Yes, Corazon?" he said, his mouth parted like a puppy. He danced with energy, making her laugh.

"How would you like to walk with me this afternoon?"

"Yes, Corazon!" His sandaled feet did a patter of excitement on the pavement.

Cora stood, still holding his hand. "You have to promise to stay right next to me for the rest of the day, especially when we get to the army base. Do you promise?"

2

WILLIAM GRAVES • FORT HOOD, TEXAS

The drone feed gave General William Graves a bird's-eye view of the incoming refugees. The uneven column stretched on for miles under the hot Texas sun. The people looked like ants from this distance, but the field of view showed the scope of the problem.

Situation, Graves reminded himself. This was a situation, not necessarily a problem. Yet even in his own head he emphasized the qualifier *necessarily*.

The dark shape surged and ebbed along I-35, moving north at a snail's pace. They spanned both lanes of traffic, guardrail to guardrail, and spilled into the dusty median. An endless caravan of yellow school buses, pickup trucks, tractors pulling wagons, semitrailers, and all manner of private vehicles followed them at a snail's pace, like camp followers in some ancient crusading army. Every day the refugees grew in number.

"Crowd size estimate?" he said to the room of uniformed army personnel wearing regulation data glasses and manipulator gloves.

"One hundred and six thousand, sir," replied Captain Cho, a slight Korean woman whose frame was all but lost in her pressed fatigues. "Looks like they picked up a few more last night."

Picked up a few more was the story of this migration. The nucleus of the movement formed in the immediate aftermath of the destruction of the New Earth Order space station, nearly six months ago. Graves should know; he'd personally set the charges that destroyed the station's fusion reactor. He turned to Sergeant Estes, another veteran of the Neo station destruction.

"Any word from Ortega?" Graves asked.

Estes, despite his Hispanic surname, had grown up in Iowa and didn't speak a word of Spanish. His shorter partner, Ortega, had a mahogany complexion, a noble nose that dominated his profile, and spoke fluent Spanish, so he'd been assigned to infiltrate the Neo migration. The only special request Graves had made following the heroic raid on the Neo Temple of Cassandra space station was for the two US Marines to be transferred to his staff. The Joint Chiefs, anxious to keep the attack on the Neos quiet, had agreed. The pair of marines had made their separate peace with working in an all-Army environment.

Estes shrugged. "He says they're quiet, sir. No signs of hostile intent ... just a shit-ton of them. He hears talk of weapons but hasn't found any as of yet. Still, that many Neo fugees in one place, sir? Kinda gives me the willies, you know?"

Graves's face darkened. "That'll be enough of that kind of talk, Sergeant. These people are not fugees, they're not illegals, they're not aliens—they're guests of the United States government. Is that clear?" He raised his voice so the rest of the room could hear.

Graves had his own reservations about President Teller's new open-borders plan, but his job was to follow orders to the best of his ability—and stay out of Teller's way. Since the Haven ships had departed Earth—without Graves telling the president the true nature of the Havens in advance—he and Teller had been incommunicado. Graves received his orders via the Joint Chiefs and he executed them, which was fine with him. He'd had enough of politics and side deals and secret plans to last a lifetime. If the Havens had been the last gasp of humanity, then so be it. He'd spend his last days helping people and meet his maker with a clear conscience.

Graves turned his attention back to the main screen. "Where is she?" he asked. He didn't need to say her name, they all knew who he was talking about.

Captain Cho answered again. "They're on the move again, sir. She's right up front." She stabbed at the air with her manipulator glove. "Putting her on-screen now."

Graves nodded as the image changed. Corazon Santos was a tall woman, draped in colorful robes, with a plain cloth drawn across her face to block the dust and dark sunglasses to protect her eyes. A little boy with a red and yellow backpack walked at her side, holding her hand.

For all the vaunted intelligence capability of the United States, Graves knew surprisingly little about this woman. Somewhere between mid-thirties and mid-fifties, she was of possible Brazilian descent and a devoted follower of Cassandra and the New Earth Order. She had zero social media presence, and until Panama, had been completely unknown to the Your-Voice community.

And if his intel reports were to be believed, she had single-handedly brought together a Neo diaspora to march north from South America. His instincts rebelled at the idea of a new Neo leader. He had destroyed Cassandra's seat of power, he and Estes and Ortega—and Remy Cade, he reminded himself. The station had gone up like a Roman candle ... and now, back here on terra firma, was he witnessing the threat reborn?

There was only one way to find out.

"Tell me when they reach the camp. I'll greet Ms. Santos in person," he said.

Graves decided to forgo the air transport down to the camp, settling instead for a solar-powered jeep driven by Sergeant Estes. The Texas afternoon sun beat down on his beret like a molten hammer. It had to be well over a hundred in the shade.

By the time they reached the refugee tent city, the streets were clogged with people. Estes laid on the horn and inched the vehicle forward. Graves put a hand on his arm.

"I'll go the last bit on foot, Sergeant," he said. Estes's face was pinched with worry. Graves knew the young man considered Graves's security his responsibility. "It'll be fine," he assured Estes.

Graves queried Captain Cho back at HQ for the exact location of Corazon Santos.

"She's at the center of the camp, sir," Cho replied. She dropped a pin at the coordinates. "Looks like they're setting up a building of some kind ... a church, I think."

Great, Graves thought. We're starting right off with the religious mumbo-jumbo. He stepped out of the jeep, dust puffing out from under his boots. A walk would do him good. He needed to get the lay of the land before confronting the Neo leader.

"Excuse us," Estes barked at a wall of backs in front of them. The people parted, dark eyes peeking out from under head coverings, brown hands pulling children out of the way. There were a lot of children, Graves noted. At least a third of the refugees he passed looked under the age of twelve.

He trudged behind Estes, nodding and smiling, meeting glares with what he hoped was a friendly demeanor. The sheer number of people was overwhelming, and he worried about their ability to keep them supplied with basic necessities indefinitely. To him, Teller's solution of opening the borders felt like a temporary political move, although to what end, he had no idea.

Graves tamped down his frustration. He was done with all that. His job was to keep these people alive and healthy. That was it.

The temporary structure described by Cho turned out to be an elaborate tent, like something out of an old movie about desert-dwelling Bedouins. Emblazoned on the side of the dwelling was the sign of Cassandra. The enigmatic woman, her face half hidden by the Earth, seemed to glare at him.

You, she seemed to say. You destroyed my temple. How dare you approach me?

"That's inviting, General," Estes muttered.

"Steady, Marine, we're about to enter the lion's den," Graves replied. Two young men swaddled in robes and head scarves nodded at Graves and pulled aside the tent flap. They motioned for Estes to remain outside.

"It's okay," Graves said.

The tent was large enough that he could walk through the flap without bowing his head. The interior was dark and surprisingly cool. He found himself in a spacious anteroom, complete with comfortable chairs and throw pillows. At the far end of the room was another doorway, this one guarded by a single young woman. She was dressed in a paramilitary uniform with a beret and the symbol of Cassandra on her shoulder. She eyed him as he approached. Although he saw no weapons, Graves suspected this woman knew how to handle herself in a fight.

"I'm here to see Corazon Santos," he said.

"The Corazon will see you when she is ready, General," came the surly reply.

The Corazon, Graves noted. Maybe that was not her given name? A useful piece of intel.

A muffled call from behind the curtains interrupted his intelligence gathering. The young woman parted the doorway material and a short conversation in rapid-fire Spanish followed. He cursed not putting on his data glasses before he'd entered. He could have used the translator function.

The young woman held the curtain open for him. He imagined her hissing at him as he brushed past her.

The interior room was spacious and simple. A rough altar faced the door, with a golden image of the New Earth Order gleaming in the soft light. The room was bare of any furniture, but thick rugs covered the floor and a pile of pillows was stacked in the corner.

A woman knelt in front of the altar, her back straight, head bowed. When Graves cleared his throat, she stood to acknowledge him. For a woman who had just walked 4,500 kilometers from Panama to Fort Hood, she moved with surprising ease and grace. She held out her hand. "I am Corazon Santos. Thank you for meeting me, General Graves."

Her voice was soft and musical, but with an unmistakable timbre of command. Graves was unable to distinguish if her accent was Spanish or Portuguese, but it had an exotic quality to him.

Corazon Santos was nearly as tall as Graves, with flowing silver hair and skin with the color and luminosity of beaten copper. She was lanky, with broad shoulders and angular features that softened when she smiled as she was doing now. He guessed her age to be about the same as his own fifty years.

"Welcome," Grave said, "on behalf of the United States government."

"Her blessings be upon you, General. She forgives you for what you have done. She knows it was necessary."

Graves froze. Although the destruction of the Neo space station had been visible from the planet, the UN had adopted a cover story of an industrial accident that the media had bought.

Maybe not.

His face tightened in a smile and he said nothing.

"You are surprised I am not angry?" Corazon said.

"I'm surprised about a lot of things, Ms. Santos."

"Call me Cora, please."

"So Corazon is your real name?" Graves pressed.

"It's the name I've taken—is there a difference?" She winked at him. In spite of himself, Graves liked her.

"We don't know much about you," Graves said.

She walked to the pile of pillows and selected two of the larger ones, dragging them back to the center of the room. "I am merely a servant, a handmaiden to Cassandra." She studied Graves's face, her gaze suddenly intent. "You know about the baby?"

"Yes, of course." He knew Elise Kisaan was pregnant and under the protection of Anthony Taulke's council, but how that tied back to the Neos was anyone's—and everyone's—guess. Since the announcement of Kisaan's pregnancy more than half a year ago, more digital time had been spent on the nature of the pregnancy than on any other topic he could remember. The second coming of Cassandra, the beginning of the end, the end of the beginning, every angle had been examined in the minutest detail.

"She came to me in a vision, you know," Cora continued, her demeanor serious. Her gaze strayed to the altar and the golden image. "The original Cassandra was a construct."

A construct? According to his intel reports, the original Cassandra wasn't a person at all. She was an AI, a program developed to control the minds of her followers through tattooed implants. Graves should know—he was the one who had killed the bitch.

But a pregnant Elise Kisaan had escaped. Graves's thoughts flashed to the final image of Remy Cade's last stand in the reactor room of the Neo space station. He'd given his life to free his beloved Elise.

"So I've been informed," Graves said finally.

"The child is Cassandra made flesh. She will live again."

Graves decided he'd had enough religious doublespeak for one sitting. He started to rise. "It was a pleasure meeting you, Cora, and my troops will do everything we can to make your stay with us comfortable—"

"You were in my vision."

Grave sat back down. "Pardon?"

Cora reached across the distance between them and took Graves's hand. Her fingers were long and thin, thick with calluses, but gentle.

"I came here to find you, General."

Graves snorted. "You and a hundred thousand of your closest friends, you mean."

Her fingers tightened. "The moment is coming when you will choose, William. You will choose to help me, to protect me and all that I believe in."

Graves's throat went dry and he jerked his hand back. He struggled to his feet. "I assure you, Ms. Santos, my allegiance is to the United States government and no other institution."

Cora kept her seat, her legs curled up under her haunches, her teeth white in the shadow of her face. Her dark eyes locked with his.

"Her will be done."

3

ANTHONY TAULKE • MARS STATION

If he ever remodeled the council chamber on Mars Station, he would make sure that seating for the chairman—his chair—was elevated above the others so as to give him a slight psychological advantage over visitors to the council—and the other council members too.

First among peers. That's how it should be.

He glared down the long table at the United Nations ambassador, a portly Spanish man with a pencil-thin mustache and an annoying habit of rolling his *r*'s unnecessarily. "What do you mean declaration of independence?" Anthony demanded.

Over the course of the last few minutes, the ambassador's initial haughty demeanor had evaporated, leaving only a sweaty man in an ill-fitting black suit. "LUNa City has put forth a declaration of independence. They claim they deserve status as a separate nation in Earth's government, not as a UN-run colony." The *r* in the word *run* trilled, grating on Anthony's nerves.

"And this has what to do with the He-3 shipments I need for my freighters?" Anthony said.

"They claim the He-3 is theirs to sell on the open market. They see it as a bargaining chip." He offered a weak smile.

Tony Taulke, seated at Anthony's right hand, sat up from his normal insolent slouch. "Let me handle this, Pop. I think we need to inject some reality into this situation." He grinned as he said it, as if they shared some secret joke about the term *reality*.

Anthony pursed his lips in thought. Decades of corporate maneuvering told him the LUNa City He-3 embargo was only a symptom of a much larger problem. He needed that fuel for his fusion reactors and everyone knew it. Someone was targeting his interests, someone who wanted him to fail. The same someone he suspected was behind the New Earth Order.

Possibly someone in this very room, on this very council.

He scanned the faces, looking for a clue.

Viktor Erkennen, the scion of the R&D giant Erkennen Labs and his oldest friend in the world. Viktor was too busy playing with his latest gadget to care about corporate politics. Elise Kisaan, swollen with pregnancy. Her past connection with the Neos made her the obvious choice, but Anthony had her under constant surveillance. Besides, with her due date drawing near, why start this fight now?

Xi Qinlao and her niece Ming, the two halves of the Qinlao family. Xi had her own Earthside issues to deal with—that was next on the agenda, in fact—and Anthony doubted she had the juice to pull off this kind of maneuver.

Ming. His eyes stopped on the young woman slumped in her maglev chair and sought out her vacant gaze. She stared back dully. In many ways, Ming had been responsible for forming the current council structure by bringing in Elise Kisaan as a prisoner, but at great cost to her own health. The radiation poisoning she'd endured in capturing Elise had left permanent damage to her body. In the intervening months, her hair had grown back in patches and the skin grafts on the right side of her face had slowly merged with her real flesh to make her look presentable. But she was a far cry from the beautiful, vibrant young woman he'd once thought of as a surrogate daughter. These days she mostly whirred around the halls of Mars Station in her maglev chair, slumped to one side and staring straight ahead in complete lack of interest.

His heart went out to her. He owed her much and she owed him her seat on this council.

The traitor certainly was not Ming.

And that left Adriana Rabh, the matron of interstellar finance and another longtime business associate of Anthony's. Her dark eyes regarded him coolly as her red-tipped fingernails rapped a light tattoo on the tabletop.

Yes, Anthony thought, if anyone in the room—besides Anthony himself —could pull off this kind of political maneuver, it would be Adriana. A punch required a counterpunch.

"Adriana," he said. "I think we have a problem that only you can fix."

Her carefully sculpted eyebrows hitched. "How so?"

"We have an opening for ambassador to Earth."

The Spanish man heaved a sigh of indignation. "Mr. Taulke," he began.

"You're fired," Anthony said. "It's time the council protected our own interests with the UN and stopped this silly game you are playing with my plans."

"Might I remind you, sir, that I am a duly elected representative of the United Nations—"

"I accept," Adriana said, her cool voice cutting through the ambassador's bluster. "Might I suggest we delay any sort of public announcement until I have made the trip back to Earth? The former ambassador can make the trip with me."

The motion received unanimous approval, and Anthony pulsed a quick message to station security to put the former ambassador in a secure room with no access to communications.

"I think that will do nicely," he said to the room at large as the protesting Spaniard was escorted out of the chamber. Strangely, he no longer seemed to be rolling his *r*'s.

Anthony waited until the door had closed and his retinal display told him the room was secure again before he energized the holographic display in the center of the council. The solar system in miniature sprang up from the center of the table.

The first MOAB units, mining operations in a box, were just reaching the Kuiper Belt and had targeted their initial asteroids for samples. Another exploratory mission was operating on Titan. The Callisto colonization team was in training and designs for the orbital ring to be installed over the Jovian moon's colony were almost complete. Here on Mars the three domes were complete and manufacturing lines up and running, but they lacked enough skilled engineers to run all the lines for all shifts.

Their expansion plans were well underway, but to Anthony's mind, the holographic image showed the weakness of the council's strategy: their very long supply lines.

Without food, fuel, and skilled labor from Earth, all his grand plans for the outer planet projects would wither on the vine. First the LUNa City He-3 supply issue starved his growing fleet of spacecraft, then the typical foot-dragging by the UN on personnel quotas for his Mars Station.

And that line of reasoning brought him to his least favorite topic: the weather back on Earth.

The loss of control of his Lazarus weather nanites still stung. He turned to Elise Kisaan, his gaze automatically falling to the cryptokey bracelet she wore. She was the failsafe, a living firewall against Anthony Taulke taking action on his own creation.

Separate Elise from the key and the weather on Earth would spin out of control. He could have challenged her when she'd come to him as an offering from the mysterious Cassandra, but he'd chosen to follow the oldest of business rules: keep your friends close and your enemies closer.

He invited Elise to join the council—and the decision to cede a modicum of power to this fanatical religious zealot had haunted him ever since.

She carried a child of which he knew nothing. He'd heard the rumors, of course. The Neos claimed the child was the second coming of Cassandra, a messiah figure. If the first Cassandra had been destroyed in the space station explosion, she had made plans for her return—so the reasoning went. Elise was Her vessel, the YourVoice commentators said, always emphasizing the holy She.

Cassandra was not dead, the Neos claimed, the baby was Her will made flesh.

Anthony eyed Elise. The pregnancy had not been easy for Elise Kisaan. Her tall, lithe frame was hunched and swollen with the child, and her face was haggard. Her light brown skin formed into dark bags under her eyes and her cheekbones poked painfully from her drawn face. Straight black hair showed streaks of gray and hung listlessly over her shoulder.

"Our weather patterns are holding?" he asked finally.

Elise nodded. "Her will be done. The expected migration is already beginning."

Anthony stopped the smirk that threatened to crease his face at the use of the religious phrase. These Neo fanatics were a joke—a joke that had managed to outwit him so far, he reminded himself sternly.

"And when will She deign to enlighten us as to the long-term plan?" he asked in as neutral a tone as he could manage.

Elise's enigmatic smile infuriated him. "All will be revealed in time," she said.

The expected answer, but galling nonetheless. He and Viktor had generated a model based on the initial weather changes already. Their best guess was that Cassandra had put in a program to organize the planet Earth into zones by latitude, but the true nature of the reshaping of Earth still escaped them.

In the end, it didn't matter. He was planning his own takeover of the weather well before Cassandra's long-term plans went into effect. But to do that, he needed the assistance of Qinlao Manufacturing.

He zoomed in on the holographic display to show Earth. A regularly-spaced pattern of red dots surrounded the planet. "That brings us to our next agenda item. Xi, please update us on the communications satellite network."

It was much, much more than just a new comms network. Anthony had secretly contracted with Xi to produce a next generation of weather-altering nanites and the satellites to deploy and control them. Rather than broad weather patterns, he would be able to make it rain on a single city block with pinpoint accuracy. The United Nations would finally see the real benefit of working with a genius like Anthony Taulke. With his new technology, he would finally bring home his long-sought promise of true climate control for the benefit of humanity. He would be the savior the Earth had needed for so long.

And Elise Kisaan and her blasted Neos would be cut out of the picture—for good.

Xi Qinlao's holographic image shifted in her chair. Her voice projected over the speakers. "I'm sorry to say, we are behind schedule due to some unexpected manufacturing delays."

"Delays?" Anthony let his frustration show. "What sort of delays?"

"There was a fire in one of our manufacturing facilities. The entire structure was destroyed."

Tony leaned over to his father. "Pop, shift the manufacturing up here. No matter what it is, we can manage—"

"No," Anthony cut his son off. No one else on the council besides Xi and Viktor knew of the true nature of the project Qinlao was handling for him and they needed to keep it that way. He couldn't risk Elise and her Neos finding out. Or Adriana and Tony, for that matter.

"What will it take to get back on schedule?" he asked Xi.

The woman's elegant face wrinkled in a scowl. "There is no more 'on schedule,' Anthony. That was my premier manufacturing facility and it is gone. The backup site needs a complete upgrade. That's a month of work, at the least."

Anthony took a deep breath to calm his nerves. He didn't have that kind of time. Viktor met his gaze and gave a little shrug of his heavy shoulders.

"Very well," he said, growling to show it was anything but. "Let me know the revised schedule as soon as you have it. I think that concludes our meeting—"

"I have another issue," Xi said. Her face in the holographic image sharpened, and there was a slight mismatch in the synchronization between her lips moving and her voice that Anthony found irritating.

"I move that we remove Ming Qinlao from this council," Xi said.

"I second the motion," Elise said immediately.

Anthony sat dumbfounded. In her current condition, Ming was unable to add much to the proceedings, but she was a reliable vote for Anthony when he needed it. And she was under his protection. They all knew that. "On what grounds?" he asked finally.

"She has no real role here," Xi continued. "My dear niece needs to recuperate properly from her ordeal. She needs rest."

"I am the rightful CEO of Qinlao Manufacturing, Auntie." Ming's quavering voice did not help her case.

"Then you should come back to your home and claim your office." Xi's challenge held an edge of contempt. "Or are you afraid of that vote, too?"

"I am not afraid of you," Ming said, but to Anthony her tone suggested otherwise.

"I demand a vote," Xi replied, her words directed at Anthony.

Anthony did a quick vote count. Xi and Elise wanted Ming gone. It was settling a score for both of them, plain and simple. He could rely on Viktor to side with him and Adriana and Tony would follow his lead.

"Very well, Xi," Anthony said. "I call a vote for the motion to remove Ming Qinlao from the council." He accessed his retinal display.

"I demand a voice vote," Ming said. When she looked at Anthony, her eyes were glassy with unshed tears. His heart went out to her again. Her injuries were his fault. He was the one who sent her on the mission with Viktor's tech that had so damaged her body. "It is my right," she added.

Anthony swallowed the lump in his throat. "A voice vote then. I vote against the motion."

Xi and Elise voted for it.

"Against," Viktor said. He crossed his pudgy arms for emphasis.

"For," Adriana said. Anthony's head snapped in her direction. Never before had she voted against him. He tried to read her face and gave up.

"That makes the vote two in favor and two against," Anthony said. He turned to his son. "Tony, you have the honor of casting the tie-breaking vote."

Tony's normal nonchalance was missing as he sat up straight in his chair. His gaze cut from his father to Ming, who stared at him without expression. Anthony could see his son gripping his thigh muscle.

Tony looked out the window at the Mars landscape. "For," he said.

Anthony gaped at him. His son knew what Ming meant to his father. He knew Anthony had personally promised Ming's seat on the council to protect the young woman from her relentless Aunt Xi.

And his son had voted against him.

A hundred reasons sprang to mind—none of them flattering to Tony—but one stood out to Anthony: jealousy. His son was jealous of Ming Qinlao.

Anthony cleared his throat and addressed the council. "By a vote of three to two, the motion is carried. Ming Qinlao's seat on the council has been suspended. I would like to say how much..."

His voice trailed off as Ming reversed her maglev chair away from the table and headed for the door.

4

MING QINLAO • MARS STATION

Ming heard the door of the council chamber boom closed behind her before she allowed herself an inner smile.

Well played, Ming! said the voice inside her. She had taken to calling the voice Echo.

Ming nodded in acknowledgment. There was a time when the voice had seemed foreign, a personality apart from her, but those days were gone. Technically, the voice was a remnant of MoSCOW, one of Viktor's inventions, but Ming had long ceased to think of the voice as something distinct from herself. The voice was as much a part of her as her arm, and every bit as important. She made no decisions now without consulting her inner voice. It was always there, waiting, helping, supporting her when no one else cared.

Tony Taulke had played his part well, a born actor. The indecision on his face just before the vote had probably torn Anthony's conscience to shreds. Good, she needed the old man vulnerable for the next step in her plan.

She thought of the rest of the council and their transparent faces. Echo had long ago taught her the art of reading expressions. The furrow of a brow, the tightening of a lip, the flutter of a jaw muscle were all signs she could read like an open tablet. Auntie Xi's motives were obvious enough.

Elise Kisaan hated her for separating her from her beloved Cassandra. Viktor still felt guilty for ruining her health and Adriana had seen an opportunity to gain more power within the council.

But what they all had in common was how they underestimated Ming Qinlao. They would come to regret their mistake. Every one of them in their own special way.

She reached her quarters and swept her maglev chair through the doorway. When she heard the door close behind her, Ming stopped the chair and let it settle to the floor. She probed the carpet with her toe, then set her right foot firmly on the floor. The left foot followed and she hoisted herself upright. She took a series of tottering steps to the wall, then turned to settle her back against the cool plastic.

Her legs shook with the effort, but she locked her knees and gazed out the window at the Martian sunset. Dusky red, fading to indigo, crept across the rocky landscape. The dying light etched the shape of a distant mountain range in the night sky.

Like a toddler finding her balance, Ming staggered back to the chair and collapsed into the soft cushions. She grinned in triumph through the sweat. She would miss this place. In a way, Ming Qinlao had been reborn here.

The old Ming, the Ming before she met Anthony Taulke, had been a serious woman who played by the rules and expected the best person to win. Sying, her stepmother and lover, had taught her to think bigger, take calculated risks, see the entire battlefield of business. To think like a queen. Sying taught her that the world of business was not a competition of commerce, it was a battle of wits and skill that was fought behind the scenes. Alliances, marriage pacts, disinformation—these were all skills of a queen.

Ming had taken Sying's guidance to heart. She had learned and loved—and lost.

Discovering the murder of her father had been the real turning point for her, the crystallization of her mission. Like these unsteady steps, she had embarked on a journey of revenge and redemption. She would take back control of Qinlao Manufacturing because it was rightfully hers. Nothing would stand in her way.

She had faced adversity, to be sure. The supercomputer MoSCOW nearly finished her. The prolonged integration left her broken in body and shattered in mind.

And then something remarkable happened: Ming Qinlao put the pieces back together. Shard by shard, she refashioned her mind with the help of Echo, rebuilding her sense of self in the process. Her body ... that took longer. Viktor Erkennen had given her a strict physical therapy regimen, which she followed, but that was not enough. To fulfill her mission, Ming needed to return to her roots. Ming needed to return home.

Her breathing had calmed again and she wriggled to an upright position in her chair. The gravity of Earth in her condition would be bone-crushing, but there was no way around it. The pain would be worth it in the end.

She met her reflection in the dark glass without flinching. She was ugly, her skin a mismatched mess of shifting shades of color, her hair—once long and silky—a patchy, ragged mat that barely hid her scalp.

Time enough for a complete makeover later. For now, the "poor, damaged girl" image fit her needs. Let them pity her. Let them underestimate her. Let them push her aside. Her day was coming.

She blinked her retinal display on and sent a pulsed message to Lander. *"Get the ship ready."*

Sunrise on Mars was a gradual event. The light of the distant sun reflected in the dusty atmosphere, creating a hazy light long before the tiny disk of Sol appeared. Even after many months on Mars, Ming had never quite gotten used to seeing the sun that small.

She paused in the hallway outside Anthony's office to compose herself. For months she had played the weakling, the damsel in distress. In her final hours on Mars, there was no need to break that image for Anthony.

She needn't have worried. Anthony Taulke was as distraught over her ousting from the council as if he'd been attacked personally. Echo confirmed the emotions were genuine. Echo's affirmations were second nature now, involuntary responses to any interaction.

"We can fight this, Ming," he said in a heated tone. "I can bring Adriana and Tony around—I'm not sure what got into them. They've always supported me before."

You're going to start seeing a lot more of that kind of behavior, old man.

Ming whirred her way across the close-cropped carpet of Anthony's spacious office. The floor-to-ceiling windows revealed a stunning view of the Mars landscape, lightening now, but with a sweep of stars still looming overhead. She pretended to study the scene, letting her head droop like it did when she was tired.

Anthony stood beside her, his hand resting comfortably on her thin shoulder. She wanted to pull away in disgust, but Ming allowed the intrusion. It was all part of the show for the next few hours.

"It's time for me to go home, Anthony," she said in a soft voice.

"Home?" He seemed startled by the word. "I promised to protect you, Ming. This is your home."

"No." Ming shook her head gently and swung her chair so it dislodged his hand. "My real home. China. Shanghai."

Anthony's face clouded and Echo confirmed the conflict in his features. *He's worried about his "secret" project with Xi.* The transparency of his machinations made Ming want to laugh in his face.

"But, your aunt..." he said. "Is it safe?"

Ming waved a limp hand. "Do I look like a threat to you?" She studied his reaction in the window.

"That's not what I mean. Xi is a vindictive woman ... are you sure it's safe?" Echo registered more warring emotions as the older man sought to phrase the real issue.

"It's time, Anthony," she said in as firm a voice as she dared. "I hoped you would see that. I can't live under your care forever."

"And what about the company? Do you intend to make trouble for your aunt? You are technically a CEO in exile, after all."

Ah, there it was: the real issue had finally surfaced. A flash of anger threatened to blow Ming's persona as a fragile weakling.

"I hadn't thought of it like that," she said. "Does that worry you?"

Anthony backtracked hastily. "Of course not. We've always been in lock-step in how we see the world, Ming. It's just that there are some dynamics that you might not be aware of..."

"You mean your plan to release new nanites into the atmosphere? To take over weather control from the Neos?"

The older man froze. If she hadn't been playing a part, Ming might have laughed out loud at his expression.

"You know about that?"

"Of course, Anthony. I've known for months."

"Who told you? It was Viktor, wasn't it?"

"No, Viktor has been the soul of discretion. I figured it out all on my own."

He looked at her now, really looked at her, as if he might have underestimated her after all. Ming felt a sudden stab of apprehension that she'd gone too far, but Echo's voice assured her.

Respect. Surprise.

Ming relaxed. "It's what I would have done, Anthony. Elise is a wild card on the council. She serves a purpose in the short term, but her agenda is unclear. You need to reduce her power if you want to stay in control. She's a threat."

Another knowing nod. "Agreed. I will miss you, Ming."

"Yes, you will."

He laughed, a genuine expression of delight according to Echo. Then he turned serious again. "If your aunt should fail me, can I rely on you to do the right thing?"

Ming felt the laugh bubble out of her. "Of that you can be sure, Anthony. I will always do the right thing." *For me.*

She left Anthony's office feeling as if she were floating on a cloud. Echo cautioned emotional restraint, but Ming chafed at the advice. She'd planned this day for months, it was impossible not to feel a growing sense of satisfaction.

But Ming had one more stop before she was free of Mars.

The door to Viktor's lab was open when she arrived. As always, the room showed the Russian's eclectic creative process. A painting by an old master hung next to a wallscreen displaying the schematics of a new weapon, which was next to a bench filled with the innards of a disassembled surveillance drone.

"Viktor?" she called.

"Back here," came the muffled response from the rear of the lab.

Ming whizzed past the scattered lab tables. Viktor liked to leave projects in plain sight so he could work on them whenever inspiration struck him. It led to a very crowded and chaotic work space, but the man did produce some of the most innovative designs in the known universe—easier to do when money was not an object.

He raised a pair of VR goggles from his eyes when she rode up, pinning billows of flyaway gray hair in place. His face lit up when he saw her. Ming's smile in return was genuine. Of all the council members, Viktor was her favorite—and the only one who had never lied to her.

The old man's eyes brimmed with tears. "This is it, then?" His native Russian accent always thickened under stress and she could hear it plainly now.

Ming nodded a reply. She was feeling oddly nostalgic herself.

Viktor shifted his feet and thrust his hands in the pockets of his lab coat. "I will miss you, Ming." His expression brightened. "I have a gift for you." He hustled past her to a lab bench and scooped up a flat box with a red bow. "For you. Maybe it will make your transition to Earth's gravity a little easier."

Ming hefted the box. It was about the size of a dress box, but heavy. "Can I open it?"

Viktor feigned indifference, but Ming could see he was anxious for her to see the gift. She tugged the bow apart and lifted the lid from the box.

She froze for an instant. Inside was a MoSCOW suit, the same type of suit she had worn during the attack on the Neo space station. Did Viktor know her secret? That a piece of the MoSCOW supercomputer lived in her brain still? Slowly, she met his gaze, searching for an answer to the unasked question. Echo reported only affection, with not even a whiff of deception.

"I wondered if the same type of suit could interact with your implant and provide you with some better mobility than ..." His voice trailed off as he gestured at the maglev chair.

"I love it," Ming said.

It was not the same one, she could see that now. This garment was a newer version, lighter, with a more finished appearance. It also had a hood. She held up the ebony suit and noticed how it changed in the light. "You got the camouflage feature working," she said with approval.

Viktor dipped his chin. "*Da.* I know you will have no use for it, but you never know."

Ming clasped the suit to her chest. "I love it," she said again. "Thank you so much, Viktor. You are a true friend."

The old man bent over her chair and bussed her cheek with a goodbye kiss. His whiskers scratched at the grafted skin on her cheek. "Take care of yourself, Ming. And I am sorry for all that has happened to you."

In spite of herself, Ming felt tears spring to her eyes. Echo rebelled at the sudden rush of emotion, chastising her lack of control. She didn't care. Ming kissed the old man back and then swung her chair toward the door, the open box still in her lap.

Lander was waiting for her at the docks, pacing the tarmac outside a space yacht, a gift from Anthony. They would be heading back home in style on this trip. His sharp gaze took in the MoSCOW suit on her lap and his expression darkened. "Is that what I think it is?" he asked.

Lander had been there when Ming linked with the MoSCOW system last time and done untold damage to her body. The sight of the suit clearly made him uncomfortable. Ming hurriedly replaced the lid and tucked the container next her hip.

"It's no concern of yours, Lander," she said sharply. "You're just the driver for this trip."

He offered a mock salute. "Yes, ma'am." His tone was cheeky but his radar was up. Ming cursed to herself. Her emotional goodbye with Viktor had made her sloppy. That was unacceptable.

"I'm sorry, Lander," she said. "It's just a bit harder to leave than I expected."

His eyes weighed her words. Echo reported he didn't quite believe her.

Ming drove her maglev chair past him and up the ramp of the yacht. The interior was tastefully appointed, but with a few too many Taulke company logos for her liking. The ship had staterooms for four passengers and berths for three crew, but for this trip it was just her and Lander.

She locked her chair in place next to the viewing window and waited while Lander ran his preflight checks and got clearance to depart. The clamshell doors of the launch bay opened to show the red-orange landscape and the stars beyond the horizon.

She touched the comms circuit. "Take us up slow, Lander, and then do a flyby before we leave orbit."

"Roger that." Lander was a soldier by training. He knew not to ask for reasons why.

The ship moved beneath her, pressing Ming's body deep into the cushions. She let her breath leak out of her. At altitude, the ship made a long, slow banking turn, angled so that Ming could get a final view of the Taulke complex on Mars.

Three domes gleamed in the weak sunlight like bubbles of water on the rust-colored terrain. Tracks of vehicles streamed away like spokes of a wheel and drones crisscrossed the skies beneath them.

"You good?" Lander called over the intercom.

Ming nodded to herself. She keyed the intercom. "All good."

They lifted higher, the domes shrinking to pinpoints then lost to distance. Still Ming stared at the Red Planet.

Step one complete.

5

ADRIANA RABH • EARTH ORBIT

It was good to be home.

Adriana stood at the windows overlooking the vista of Earth from orbit. She caught a glimpse of the Amazon emptying like a coffee-colored stain into the slate blue of the Atlantic Ocean. Not a red rock in sight and that was just fine with her.

She had directed the captain of her space yacht, *Staff of Isis*, to take his time in the transit from Mars to Earth, keeping the gravity at a half-gee or so most of the time. While glad to be back in the culture of Earth, she did not relish the thought of readjusting to full gravity and the continual ache in her bones for the next month until she acclimated.

But comfort wasn't the reason for her leisurely voyage home. She needed time to think, to reflect on how best to turn her new position as ambassador to her advantage. If the last year with the council had taught her anything, it was the changing nature of power. In this post-Earth age, her traditional source of advantage—money—was less useful. Everyone on the council was fabulously wealthy by traditional measures, so they essentially canceled each other out.

The new currency was assets and she needed to make better use of hers.

Anthony and Tony Taulke had their expanding space fleet and a beachhead on Mars. A growing army of mercenaries was also now a part of the

Taulke portfolio—another sign of Anthony Taulke's future designs on power. The Qinlaos had their manufacturing prowess, which would only expand with the council's off-planet business. Viktor had his marvelous brain and endless inventions to keep his place at the table and Elise Kisaan had the double benefit of her family's agricultural strength and her emotional connection to the Neos. Elise's path was not without risk, of course. The identity of the Kisaan child was a closely guarded secret, and new rumors swept daily through YourVoice with the speed of light. If the child was a hoax, there would be hell to pay.

In the old days, Anthony and the rest of the council needed Adriana for her money, but those times were long past. In this post-wealth world, what were her real assets? What did she possess that no other family could bring to the council?

Information, she decided. Connections. That would be her new currency. She would adapt her vast business network to her new position as information broker. She would be the spider at the center of the web, sharply tuned to any tremors in the individual strands of silken data.

Adriana smiled at the analogy. She liked the image of herself at the center of the universe. She would need all of her considerable skills if she wished to displace Anthony Taulke one day. In her opinion, he was a leader gradually losing touch with his mission in life. Tony saw it too, of that she was sure. Part of her reason for voting against Ming Qinlao at the last council meeting had been to test Tony—and he had more than met her expectations. There was an alliance to be cultivated there.

She put aside any thoughts of a coup for now. It was far too early to consider such actions. First, she needed to build her base of spies.

All during the voyage home, Adriana had connected with her people on Earth—and the result was less than encouraging. The catastrophic weather conditions that had occurred immediately after the Lazarus launch had faded, but the damage was done. Beijing was still a sand dune, the highlands of Scotland still blighted by the deep freeze, and coastal cities all over the globe swept away by the ravages of rising sea levels.

The governments of the United Nations were anything but united. On most days, the general assembly more resembled a barroom brawl than a gathering of diplomats. No wonder the demands of the council were not being met promptly.

In the civilian population, the New Earth Order was seeing a resurgence despite the lack of a new leader. The mark of Cassandra had gone from the brand of a traitor to a badge of honor in just a few months. In South America, a mysterious woman known as the Corazon had gathered hundreds of thousands of followers and marched on the US border. Behind that backdrop, rumors spread of a third way, a military option that transcended both politics and religion.

It was chaos, pure and simple. Anarchy on a global scale.

And the answer to chaos was order, discipline. What the planet needed was a unifying cause to rally behind, something all sides could agree on as a viable path forward. Even more important, it had to appear to be a plan developed by Earth governments for the benefit of Earth's citizens.

For days in her cabin on the *Isis*, Adriana pondered the question, probing her network for ideas. One idea came up again and again.

"Ms. Rabh," the captain's voice on the intercom interrupted her thoughts. "We've got a shuttle hailing us, requesting permission to dock."

"Permission granted, Captain. I'll receive the president in my personal dining room."

United States President Howard Teller III strode into her dining room moments later, hand extended, disarmingly warm smile at the ready. She kept her expression stern as she shook his hand and invited him to sit.

Teller had decided to age gracefully. He had allowed his close-cropped curls to go full gray and deep lines carved his mahogany facial features. His smile was still full and bright, though, and his handshake firm and reassuring.

"Ms. Rabh," he said with a slight bow, "may I be the first to address you as ambassador?"

"You may, Mr. President," she replied, liking the sound of the new title in her own ears.

They sat across from each other at a table that would seat eight, an expanse of snowy white linen between them. Her manservant populated their place settings with bowls of creamy red soup.

Teller took a spoonful and his eyebrows arched with surprise.

"Fresh tomatoes," Adriana said, enjoying his reaction. "Anthony grows them on Mars now by the truckload." An exaggeration, but first impressions were important.

They worked through a pasta course as the orbit of the *Isis* crossed into darkness. The room lights adjusted automatically. Teller nodded at the window. "You can see it clearly from this vantage point. The bands, I mean."

It was true. Whole bands of latitude, each one probably hundreds of miles across, were dimmer than narrow strips between them.

"The weather patterns do it," Teller said, the lines on his face deepening even more. "Storms drive people out of what were once populated regions into these narrow habitable bands. Whole cities are being abandoned in places, displacing thousands of people at a time. The refugee problem is enormous."

"The UN? Can they help?" Adriana asked.

"The weather is not a political problem, Ambassador. The wind knows no borders."

Adriana rested her fork on her plate and indicated for the servant to take it away.

"Have you seen Elise Kisaan?" Teller asked her.

She thought about the pregnant woman with the sunken eyes and the bemused expression that passed for a smile. "I have."

"Is it true? The Neos claim she carries the second coming of Cassandra." Teller looked her at her directly. "That could be a problem. For all of us."

"So the Neos are organizing again?"

Teller's face twisted. "A third of the world's population belongs to the New Earth Order. They don't have to organize to be a force we need to reckon with." He caught her eye again. "A force that *you* need to reckon with, Ambassador."

Adriana felt a slight chill. Her network had been more sanguine about the effect of the Neos on her position than Teller's dire warnings. More digging was required.

"But you have brought me a proposal, Mr. President?" she said.

Teller nodded. "I have, Madam Ambassador. I believe this current political crisis is also a political opportunity. The world governments are not being responsive to their people and are not unified in solving the problem. In many ways, the United Nations has outlived its usefulness as a governing body."

Adriana signaled for the wine to be poured. Before responding, she took a sip, savoring the crisp taste of chilled fruit. "So you're attempting to eliminate my position before I even start, Howard? How ballsy of you."

"Not exactly. I'm proposing we look at our history. After the devastation of World War Two, the United States launched a massive rebuilding program to reinvigorate Europe called the Marshall Plan. That move cemented America's place as the leader of the free world for nearly a century. With the devastation caused by climate change, I see a parallel situation."

"You mean the Lazarus Protocol that you personally unleashed on the world, Mr. President?"

Teller flushed but kept his cool. "I mean the weather changes wrought by Cassandra and her band of fanatics."

Adriana listened as he described his vision of the Teller Plan, a massive worldwide rebuilding effort targeted at the most devastated regions of the globe. Adriana found herself agreeing with his conclusions. No wonder this man had managed to convince his own countrymen to reelect him after the Lazarus debacle.

"So what do you need from me?" she asked after he had finished.

"From the council," he said. "Funding, of course, and political support. This will not be a slam dunk in the general assembly or even in the security council."

Adriana eyed him over the rim of her wineglass. There was a missing piece still. "What's in it for you?" she asked. "Why now? Why not have the former ambassador present this to the council and seek funding?"

Teller shrugged. "This is only the first step." He got to his feet and strode to the window. They had been talking long enough to make a complete orbit and the *Isis* was passing into darkness again. Teller pointed at the globe.

"Boundaries set by governments and ethnicity are dissolving. I'm positioning myself for the next step in the political evolution of Earth—a world government." He turned to her, his eyes shining. "I know about the expansion plans of the council, the outposts on Titan, the exploratory missions to the Kuiper Belt and Callisto. Earth may be our birthplace, but this planet will soon be only one star in the constellation of the council. A world government will need a world governor."

"You're volunteering for the job?" Adriana chuckled.

Teller gave a self-deprecating shrug. "If and when it becomes available."

Adriana drained her wine. Maybe she'd underestimated Teller. This was an ambition that needed some controls put on it.

"And who did you envision would run this organization you are proposing?" she asked.

Teller looked surprised. "Why me, of course. With my staff."

Adriana pursed her lips. "I'm not sure you have the background to pull that off. It will look like a political stunt, not a serious effort. After all, your historical precedent was called the Marshall Plan, not the Truman Plan after the president that signed it into existence. No, I think the council will insist on someone with an operational background to lead the effort. It is our money, after all."

Teller nodded gamely. "I'm sure I can come up with a list of acceptable candidates—"

"What about the general who did that heroic raid on the Neo space station? What's his name?"

"Graves," Teller muttered in a voice reminiscent of crushed glass.

His reaction told Adriana all she needed to know.

"That's the one," she said. "I want him."

6

WILLIAM GRAVES • SOUTHERN CALIFORNIA

Graves let his eyes roam over the gray hills surrounding the shallow valley. It was strange how the ash softened the edges of the destruction, almost like a frosting of snow. Twenty-four hours ago, this area had been a neighborhood of close-packed single-family dwellings and row houses centered around an area school.

Now it was a featureless landscape of soft gray.

The place smelled like the inside of an incinerator, a complex mix of burnt plastic, wood, and something softer, organic in nature.

Graves pointed to the flat fields next to where the school had stood. A few spikes of metal poked out of the ground. What was left of a backstop for a baseball diamond, he realized.

"There," he said. "Land the aid package there."

Behind him, Estes called in the air transports. There would be three ships landing in the next fifteen minutes with food, shelter, and a medical team. They would take away any bodies that remained. Not usually an issue in this kind of natural disaster.

A few solitary figures trudged along the ridge, kicking up billows of dusty gray. The sun peeked through a smoky cloud, ready to irradiate the planet for another day.

"This town wasn't hit so badly, sir," Estes said. "Most of the people either had fire shelters in their homes or managed to get to the community shelter in the city hall. Looks like eighteen dead, twenty-seven missing."

Fire shelters ... when he was growing up, his grandfather used to talk about bomb shelters to protect against nuclear attack. Now citizens used shelters to protect them from fire attacks. Graves sometimes felt like people today spent more time sheltering than living.

"What's the name?" he asked.

"Sir?"

"The name of the town, Estes. Or what used to be this town."

The sergeant consulted his tablet. "San Garafala."

"Never heard of it," Graves said. And he probably never would again. Once these people got a night or two in the government shelters and ate a few meals of field rations, they'd decide to take what little they had left and move inland. Denver, maybe, or Bend, Oregon, or Chicago. Anything but wildfire country.

But those inland cities harbored a different kind of fire danger. Political fire. Masses of people pushed to the edge and more joining them every day...

Graves drove that line of thought from his head. He was here to help people. Politics was not his problem.

"Let's get a move on, Estes," he said, turning back to the command ship. Once inside, he passed through the compact ops deck comprised of a central holographic map display and ringed by half a dozen workstations.

"At ease, people," he called. They had standing orders to stay working when he transited the ops deck, but there were always a few rookies who leaped to their feet every time a general appeared.

Graves entered the cramped restroom and splashed water on his face. The smoke had pinkened the whites of his eyes and his eyelids were raw and red. He wiped the water away and studied his reflection in the mirror. "What are you doing?" he muttered.

On days like this, depression lurked around the corner. His job felt hopeless, like he was trying to heal an amputated limb with a Band-Aid. There was so much need out there and growing by the hour.

After a final stern look at his reflection, Graves snapped open the washroom door to find Estes waiting for him.

"You have a visitor, sir. She's waiting in your office."

"Well, who is it, Estes? And why am I receiving visitors in the middle of a relief op?"

Estes shifted his feet. "She said her name is Olga."

Graves's head snapped up. "Olga, you said? Make preps to reposition the command ship to the next site and don't disturb me."

Estes ghosted a smile. "Yes, sir."

Graves whipped open the door to his office. Major Olga Rodchenkov stood when she saw him. Her blonde hair, with streaks of silver now, was drawn back into a thick braid and she was dressed in jeans and a fitted khaki shirt. He kicked the door shut behind him and enveloped her in a tight hug.

She barely reached his shoulder, but her former gymnast's body was all muscle. He buried his face in her hair and breathed deeply. It was her smell he remembered the most. A warm scent, like vanilla sugar and jasmine. Delicate and intoxicating.

"You smell great," he said.

She pushed him away. "And you smell like someone pissed on a campfire." She laughed and kissed him on the cheek. If he listened very carefully, he could still hear a trace of her native Vladivostok in her voice.

Graves tried to check the rush of emotion that threatened to overwhelm him. There was a time when he'd almost abandoned the United States Army for this woman and seeing her brought back a flood of memories of stolen nights together in Germany.

They'd been younger then—and stupid. There was no way on earth for a Russian FSB officer and a US Army officer to have a life together. They'd ended it before it ended their respective careers, but Graves sometimes wondered what his life might have been like if he'd just married this woman when he'd had the chance. He certainly wouldn't be delivering aid to victims of wildfires, that's for sure.

"You're thinking about me, aren't you?" she teased him.

Graves grinned sheepishly. "Can you blame me? You look amazing."

Olga's cheeks colored slightly. She reached out and brushed a lock of hair out of his eyes. "You look like a man with the weight of the world on his shoulders ... I heard about the Neo space station. That was a brave thing you did, Will."

Graves shook his head. "It was a suicide mission and I'm lucky to be alive. We lost a lot of people that day."

Olga pulled her chair close to his and took his hand. "It needed to be done. You were the right man for the job."

Graves twisted his fingers into hers. Recalling the attack on the Neo station sobered him, which was probably Olga's intention. She knew how to push his buttons.

"You're about to get another job, Will. A much bigger one."

"Really? You're spying on me, Olga?"

She withdrew her hand. "I'm not with the FSB anymore, Will. I'm free-lancing, you could say."

Graves studied her. The woman would not meet his gaze, unusual for her, and she seemed to have drawn back into herself.

"What is it?" he said.

Instead of responding, Olga reached into her hip pocket and drew out a slim disc. She placed it on the edge of the desk next to her elbow and pushed the center button. It glowed a soft blue. Graves looked at her incredulously.

"You brought a personal jamming device into a US Army command ship?"

Olga gripped his hand again, the pressure of her fingers insistent. "Please, Will, listen to me. I represent a group of like-minded people—military people, professionals. We think there's a war coming. Not with the Neos, but with Anthony Taulke's council. We'd like you to keep an open mind, and when the time comes, make a decision."

Graves's first reaction was anger. He reached for the jamming disc, but Olga held him back. "You know me, Will Graves. I'm not some cockeyed reactionary. The Sentinels are serious. All of the major world militaries are represented, even a few brave politicians. There's a war coming, and no one sees it yet. We will be ready."

"The Sentinels? That's the name of your organization?" Graves tried to make a joke out of it, but Olga was having none of it.

Olga moved so close he could feel her breath on his cheek and lowered her voice. "I volunteered to come because I know you trust me. I'm asking you to trust me." The crystal blue of her eyes would not let him go.

"Fine. For you."

Olga whispered, "Do you still wear that Saint Christopher medal?"

Graves grinned in spite of the tension between them. "Always. Why?"

She pressed a silver chain and medal into his hand. "Wear this one instead. It's got an emergency implant inside. If—when—you need me, I'll find you."

Olga turned off the jamming device and slipped it back into her pocket. He stood with her and was surprised when she kissed him again. On the lips this time, and she let it linger. "I never found anyone after you, Will Graves. Part of me still wonders what might have been."

Graves just nodded.

She smiled. "If we never see each other again, I guess that means I'll never know for sure."

Fort Hood, Texas

It was good to be home. That's what Fort Hood felt like now: home. In his nearly three decades in the army, Graves had learned to use that term loosely. For him, home was where the work was.

He stepped off the transport into a wall of late afternoon Texas heat. The stifling humidity seemed to push against him as he made his way to the command center. A shower, an update on the disaster mitigation efforts, and some grub. That was the plan for the evening.

Sergeant Ortega was waiting for him, his crisp BDUs already starting to wilt in the heat. He returned the young man's salute. "How are our guests, Sergeant?" he said, referring to the Neos and Corazon Santos.

"The well on the south side of the camp ran dry, sir, so we're trucking in water. We received another eighty thousand refugees yesterday."

Graves whistled. Eighty thousand new refugees put the camp well past the planned limit of one fifty. He hoped again Teller knew what he was doing with this new open-borders policy. "How are we doing on logistics?"

Ortega shook his head. "Barely keeping up, sir. The last food shipment came in late and we're already looking at half rations later in the week. But that's not why I needed to see you, General."

Graves stopped. The heat settled on him like a wet blanket. "What's the issue, son?"

Ortega hesitated. "She found me out, sir. When I was in the refugee column."

"Corazon." They both knew who she was.

Ortega nodded.

Graves shrugged. "Marines don't exactly blend in, Sergeant."

"She called me in today, sir, to see her."

Graves raised an eyebrow. "And?"

"She wants to meet with you, General. Soon. Says she has information she needs to tell you."

Graves thought of his meeting yesterday with Olga. For a confirmed bachelor, he was getting an awful lot of attention from the fairer sex these days.

"And she didn't say what kind of information?"

Ortega shook his head.

"Fine. Schedule her into my morning calendar somewhere for fifteen minutes." He turned to go.

"You want her to come here, sir?" Ortega gestured at the command center building looming behind them.

"Yes, I want her to come here. Is that an issue, Sergeant?" Graves felt the three days on the road and his lack of sleep making his tone sharp.

"I—I think she meant for you to come see her, sir."

Graves turned on his heel. "Tell Corazon Santos to call my office and schedule an appointment like the rest of the free world."

He stormed into the building and climbed the steps two at a time, already regretting losing his temper with Ortega. The kid was a marine, not a goddamned secretary, and he knew how Cora could get into someone's head.

With a sigh, he closed the door to his quarters and rested his back against the wall, fighting the urge to lie down on his bed in his dirty uniform and just take a nap. He removed his uniform shirt and stripped off the T-shirt underneath. The silver Saint Christopher medal unstuck from his sweaty chest and swung free.

Olga ... it had been good to see her after all these years, but the circumstances were troubling. She was a bright woman with a hardheaded intellect, not one given to flights of fancy. But the idea of a transnational military corps ready to protect the planet? He considered reporting the contact. The idea seemed beyond farfetched, and she hadn't actually asked him to do anything specific. Maybe he'd just wait and see what developed.

He scanned his fingerprint for his three-minute ration of shower water. Technically, as commander of the Disaster Mitigation Corps he didn't need to install a water rationing device, but he'd insisted. It was the little things that let the troops know he followed the same rules as they did.

He cleaned his body from the top down, making liberal use of the valve to temporarily stop the flow of water so he could soap up the next part of his anatomy. He pinched some excess flesh around his beltline and resolved to restart his daily PT regimen. Olga had aged well. She was just as fit as she'd been back in Germany.

He let his mind wander as he rinsed off and reached for a towel.

Graves and Olga had met at an embassy party of all things. Such a spy novel cliché. He had been a captain on thirty days temporary duty to the US embassy in Berlin and she was a low-level staffer at the Russian embassy. He noticed her across the bar. Her blonde hair was short then, cut in a severe bob that showed off the defined muscles of her neck and shoulders.

Before he knew it, Graves was standing next to her, asking her name in terrible Russian and her replying in much better English. She told him she was an FSB agent their first night together and he said he didn't care. They spent his three remaining weeks sneaking around Berlin, screwing their brains out in a different hotel every night.

They both knew it was stupid. They both knew it couldn't last. Neither of them cared a whit.

Graves stood in the center of his apartment. Naked, dripping water on the floor, towel slung over his shoulder, lost in his past.

Now he was a gray-haired general packing a few extra pounds, reliving his glory days with the one who got away. He shook his head at his own foolishness.

As he turned back to the bathroom, he spied his data glasses in the breast pocket of his dirty uniform on the floor. The message light blinked. He wrapped the towel around his waist and retrieved the glasses.

The message was from Helena Telemachus, better known as H, special assistant to the President of the United States. General Graves was to report to the United Nations headquarters in New York City immediately. A White House vehicle was en route to retrieve him. No further details were provided.

Graves sighed, remembering Olga's caution about a new job.

He knew one thing. If H was involved, then Teller was involved, and if Teller was involved, this job was not going to be the kind of job he wanted.

7

MING QINLAO • SHANGHAI, CHINA

If the weather was any indicator of what she could expect as a reception from her family, Ming realized she was in for a disappointing homecoming. Their shuttle broke through the cloud cover over Shanghai into sheets of rain and gusting winds. The familiar buildings of the city moved in and out of view behind walls of moisture.

Only the most daring—or foolish—pilots were willing to fly in this kind of weather, so the traffic patterns were mostly clear. Lander eased back on the controls, letting the craft glide as he tried to get a visual on their destination. As usual, he said little, and Ming was glad for the silence.

She caught a glimpse of the Qinlao building through a break in the rain, the stylized red QM shining like a beacon over the dimmer lights of the city. The logo was yet another change by Auntie Xi, a nod to her Western customers.

Ming let the emotion pass through her. The time for outrage was long gone. This was the age of action. But first, there were things that needed to be done.

"Locked on the landing beacon," Lander called back to her.

Ming nodded, not bothering to reply. She would miss Lander. He was probably the closest thing to a friend she'd had in the last year. Although she had never shared even the most basic details of her plan with him, he seemed to realize she was on a trajectory that he was not a part of. There were times when she caught him watching her and Echo read the micro-emotions in his face.

Concern, apprehension, even a shade of tenderness.

Ming's thoughts hardened. How quaint, she chided herself. The next moves were the most critical of anything she had done thus far. There was no room for error. Too much was riding on the outcome of the next twenty-four hours.

The ship spun and nosed up into a landing attitude, rocking gently as the pads touched down on the roof of Marcus Sun's office building, her lawyer and most trusted confidant. Even he didn't know the full details of what she was planning. The roar of the rain hammering on the exterior of their ship ceased as the roof shell closed over them.

Lander stood and stretched. "Welcome home."

Ming toggled the exit ramp down so she could disembark with her maglev chair. "Stay close, Lander. We're not staying long."

Marcus Sun's office smelled of old books and ink, a false scent he deliberately cultivated since all the walls were skinned with the trappings of a nineteenth-century English library. Her lawyer was a short, spare man with round glasses that gave him an owlish look. But his smile was genuine. He took Ming's hand in both of his own.

"Ming, it is so good to see you. Welcome home."

Authentic, worried, sympathetic, Echo whispered.

She didn't really need Echo's coaching anymore, but the sound of another voice in her head was oddly comforting.

"Marcus, thank you for seeing me on such short notice."

He waved his hand. "For Jie's daughter, anything is possible. Let me get the contracts."

Ming navigated her maglev to the back of his office, where a box of clear glass jutted out into space. The lights of the city were smeared and wavy from rain running down the glass. She peered over the edge of her chair into the blackness below. She felt nothing, no fear, no clenching of her gut, just ... empty.

Marcus came up behind her but stopped at the edge of the glass. He grinned at her nervously.

"You remember what your father said about this space?" he asked.

Ming stared down, squinting to make out the lights of the city below. Echo told her the street was eighty-nine stories down. "He said it gave him perspective. There was a time when I agreed with him."

"What about now?"

Ming spun her chair and drove past him to the table in the center of the room. "I think right now I have all the perspective I can handle, Marcus."

The revision to her will took only a few minutes. Ming pressed her thumb into the slot for the DNA confirmation and that was it. She was leaving everything to Sying, except for one small piece of property in one of the outlying provinces. Too minor even to garner a mention in the main document. It was captured—or, more accurately, not captured—in one of the many addenda and exhibits to the main document. A clerical error, nothing more.

"You're sure you don't want her to know about this change?" Marcus asked for the third time. Echo was registering his increased concern at her erratic behavior and Ming resolved to show more empathy in her responses.

She touched Marcus's hand, giving the old man's withered paw a gentle squeeze. "I'm sorry I'm so short with you, Marcus. I'm just tired. Not used to full gravity, you know."

To her surprise, the old man teared up. "I can't help but feel like I pushed you too hard, Ming. I was responsible for what happened..."

Ming squeezed his fingers again. "The other document, Marcus? I'm starting to run out of energy."

The old man bustled to his chair and looked up the next document, the light of the desk screen reflecting on his glasses. He spun the tablet to face Ming.

Petition for Divorce, it read.

"Have you told the boy yet? Or JC?" Marcus asked.

The boy was Ken Han, a young man who was about to get his first divorce at the tender age of sixteen. His father, JC, had agreed to the match for business reasons. The family would justifiably feel used, but Ming's severance payment on their prenup would ease the pain. The Hans had served their purpose; it was time for Ming's next act.

She didn't need to respond for Marcus to know the answer was no.

"Ming," he said in an anxious voice, "I advise against this course of action. As soon as this document is filed, JC Han will know. You should tell him first."

She pressed her thumb into the DNA slot. "I know what I'm doing, Marcus. File it."

The lawyer did as he was told. "What's next for you, Ming?"

"I'm going home.

Her father's apartment in the Qinlao headquarters building had been left empty since her departure almost a year ago. No wonder. Although convenient to the office, it was not the kind of luxury accommodations her Auntie Xi was used to.

The empty rooms saddened her a little. She and Sying had made a home of sorts here—along with Ming's contracted husband and Sying's son, Ruben—an odd home, but a home all the same. Now it was an empty shell.

She motored into her father's office-workshop. No, not quite empty.

Ming's mother sat in the center of the room, holding a 3-D picture, waiting for her daughter. "Welcome home," Wenqian said. Her voice was a wheezy whisper without the aid of her amplifier, but it carried in the still room.

"Marcus told you," Ming said.

"Marcus told me."

Her mother had deteriorated since the last time Ming had seen her. The skin of her face was mottled with age spots and her cheekbones seemed to stretch her skin to the breaking point. Her eyes were bright but rheumy, and dried tracks of moisture ran down her cheeks.

"We're two of a kind now," Wenqian said, dragging her nerve-impaired hand up to stab at Ming's maglev chair.

"I'll get better."

"I don't think so," came the wheezy reply.

Ming navigated her chair alongside her mother's and plucked the picture from her hands. Her breath caught in her throat. It was a picture of Ming with her father when she was about seven years old. She'd accompanied him to a job site, and the picture showed her chasing a butterfly. Young Ming, bobbed hair tousled and dirty, reached up for the butterfly as her father looked on with a grin. It was her favorite picture.

"Keep it," her mother said. "It will remind you of who you are."

"What is that supposed to mean?" Ming said sharply. Echo was unable to read her mother's emotions from her nerve-damaged face and failing voice. The lack of backup unnerved Ming more than she imagined it would, reminding her how much she had come to rely on her internal friend.

"I wanted you to know the truth about your father's death, but nothing you can do will ever bring him back."

Ming said nothing in reply, but clutched the picture. In the final moments before she fled Shanghai, her mother had given Ming a data file that showed the murder of her father. From that fifty-nine second video, the course of Ming's life changed.

Auntie Xi had lied about his death. Auntie Xi would pay for her lie. It wouldn't bring her father back, but in Ming's mind, the lie deserved an answer and she intended to deliver it.

"Good night, Mother."

Wenqian shook her head as much as her illness allowed. "I'm just glad Ito wasn't here to see this."

"Where is Ito?" Ming said.

"Retired." The old woman used her amplifier now and it gave her voice an odd mechanical property. "He said he was going on a pilgrimage."

When she left, Ming breathed in the smell of the place. Her father's scent was diminished but still there. Pipe smoke, motor oil, ozone. She sat in the dark, watching the 3-D picture cycle over and over again.

No matter how many times she watched it, young Ming never caught the butterfly and her father always smiled.

8

WILLIAM GRAVES • UN HEADQUARTERS, NEW YORK CITY

After a full day of briefings in a windowless conference room deep in the bowels of the UN headquarters building, Graves was more than ready for a drink.

He had been instructed to wear civilian clothes to the gathering. He hadn't worn the suit in months and the jacket felt tight in all the wrong places—another sign he needed to spend more time at the gym and less time at the chow hall. Graves paused in the doorway of the ballroom, acutely aware he was mingling with some of the top political leaders of the day.

He spied the President of Russia across the room, a jowly man with carefully combed gray hair, speaking with the leader of Brazil. Germany, Australia, the United Kingdom, and Saudi Arabia, leaders and diplomats stood ready to attack him from all sides.

"May I buy you a drink, General?" The woman who spoke to him was tall and elegant, with exquisitely knotted hair and red-lacquered finger-nails. Graves knew he should recognize her, but his memory failed him. Putting on his data glasses for facial rec would be too obvious.

"Adriana Rabh," she said in a low voice, extending her hand.

Graves smiled back as he shook her hand. "I think a drink might be a good idea, Ms. Rabh."

She took arm. "Please, call me Adriana."

Adriana Rabh ... Graves was escorting the richest woman in the known universe and a member of Anthony Taulke's Council of Corporations. People peeled away to leave a clear path as he led her through the crowd.

"You know how to make an entrance, Adriana," he said in a low voice.

"I'm sure they're looking at you," she whispered back with a giggle.

At the bar, he secured drinks for them both—vodka tonic for her and a whiskey for him—and started to move away. She put a hand on his arm.

"Please, General, stay a moment. I want your opinion on something."

Graves awkwardly sipped his drink and tried to ignore the stares of the other people at the reception. Surely there were more interesting people in this room to talk to than him?

"What do you think of President Teller's plan, General?"

Graves reflected on the back-to-back briefings he'd received throughout the day along with a group of assorted NGOs and other disaster mitigation professionals. The Marshall Plan for the twenty-first century, it was being called after the plan of the same name put into action after World War Two. A more apt description might be a Marshall Plan to ensure they'd be here for a twenty-second century. Graves wondered if she realized she was asking him to critique the signature project of the commander in chief and Graves's boss.

"Ambitious," was all he said. In truth, Teller's plan was too little, too late. Graves would have set up the logistics completely differently. They were being arranged by country of origin, not by need. Africa needed far more support than South America, but they had the same number of supply depots and transport ships for each country. Political considerations, no doubt.

"Oh, come now, General," Adriana chided him. "A man of your experience can certainly offer a less diplomatic answer. Since I'm paying for it, I think I have a right to know if my money's being spent wisely."

"I think there are some opportunities for improvement." Graves explained the differences in need between the two southern continents.

Adriana nodded. "I see. You know, he wants to name the plan after himself?"

Graves suppressed a grimace. "I didn't know that."

She dropped her empty glass off with a passing waiter. "Absolutely. I'm surprised he didn't tell you that."

"I haven't met with the president in some time, Adriana."

Her eyes sparkled. "Really? Then this should be an interesting evening." She walked away before Graves could say anything else.

He moved back to the bar and ordered another whiskey, nodding to a woman he vaguely recognized as one of the attendees from the Marshall Plan briefing earlier that day. When she made a move to speak with him, he pretended he was meeting someone else and walked away.

Graves moved like a slow-motion pinball through the crowd, careening off various clusters of talking people, never stopping, never engaging, just walking as if he had someplace to go.

He gauged the wisdom of trying to sneak out early. There was a presentation after the cocktail party by President Teller, probably an empty thank-you-for-coming speech. Graves glared at the glass in his hand, frustrated by the inanity of it all. Millions, maybe billions of refugees in the world tonight were going to bed hungry, or maybe not even going to sleep at all because it wasn't safe to close their eyes. Yet all around him in this room, their leaders and diplomats and people of power laughed and made witty remarks about the weather.

A stirring in the crowd made him turn. President Teller had arrived with his entourage. The man of the hour. The brains behind the Twenty-First Century Marshall Plan—some wag on YourVoice had already dubbed it the Martial Plan because it relied so heavily on the military.

He hadn't seen Teller in person in nearly a year. The man had changed his look, opting for a statesman gray. Graves had a strange flash of compassion. Whatever his motives, at least Teller was talking about the problem, which was more than the rest of this room was doing. He needed better advisers to be sure. The mismatch in aid to Africa was the kind of mistake a politician made, not a real expert in disaster mitigation.

Graves craned his neck to see if H was with him. She stepped from behind the president and swept her gaze across the room. Helena Telemachus's vivid green eyes found his and her face twisted into a smile, at least her version of one. That woman made him more than a little uncomfortable. Teller he could figure out. The man wanted the kind of power that made other men fear him and envy him. The kind of power that made legacies. Teller was a history junkie, he wanted nothing more than to be remembered for eons as a great man.

But H ... what she wanted was a mystery to Graves. She seemed content to be the woman behind the man, but somehow that simple explanation never satisfied Graves. She had power and lots of it, but a different kind of power than her boss. The kind of power that wasn't written about but changed the world all the same. The kind of power that lived in the shadows.

A woman's carefully modulated voice came over the speaker. "Ladies and gentlemen, please join our host, President Teller, in the De Gaulle Room for a short presentation."

The wall opposite Graves slid apart and the crowd shuffled in that direction. Graves dropped his drink on a passing waiter's tray. If he wanted to duck out, now was his chance.

"General." Adriana Rabh appeared between him and the exit, taking his arm. "I saved a place for you in the front row."

Graves plastered a tight smile on his lips. "How kind of you, Ms. Rabh."

She patted his arm. "Adriana, dear, please call me Adriana."

The second whiskey had been a mistake, Graves realized as they moved to the front of the presentation room. He felt a lightness in his head and a looseness in his bearing that made him extra careful as he walked. The room was set up with a lectern on a dais and three chairs behind it. Teller was on the stage, chatting with the secretary-general, a dour Brazilian woman with raven-black hair that made her look young next to Teller's new gray look. To his surprise, Adriana left Graves in the center of the front row and made her way to the dais.

He did his best to put the alcoholic buzz behind him by focusing on the details of the room. They were on a high floor and the windows overlooked the brilliant lights of New York City at night. The room was set with well-cushioned chairs for a hundred people or so from the cocktail party, but what caught Graves's eye was the overly large press pool. There had to be almost as many press as there were attendees, and clouds of tiny newsfeed drones, each the size of his thumbnail, buzzed overhead, held back by an

EM barrier. A quartet of string instruments provided a melodic backdrop to the white noise of the crowd.

The music ramped up to a crescendo, then stopped, the signal to the crowd that they were about to get started.

Teller took the podium and waited for silence. He had his serious face on, Graves noted. The one that usually delivered portentous news. Not the usual trust-me face of a politician in full persuasion mode.

He took his time thanking the delegates for their attention and the secretary-general for her cooperation. Teller's deep voice had a hypnotic effect on Graves's mood. He felt his breathing evening out as he relaxed.

"More than one hundred fifty years ago, when our planet was devastated by a world war, the United States had a choice. We could retreat behind the safety of our borders and let the rest of the world recover, or we could take a leadership role in that rebuilding. Make the world a safer, stronger, more robust place for all people. We chose the latter. The Marshall Plan poured millions of dollars and countless resources into rebuilding a shattered world. In my mind, the Marshall Plan goes down as the single greatest achievement in US history." He paused.

Graves wasn't sure he agreed with Teller's historical ranking, but he certainly had the attention of his audience.

"Today," Teller continued, "we face an even greater challenge: a world devastated by weather. Weaponized weather has destroyed our cities, gnawed at our borders, and made millions of people homeless." Graves gauged the mood in the room. Teller—and Graves, for that matter—had been at least partially responsible for some of those events, but the room seemed to be buying what Teller was selling.

"We have tried to solve these problems as individual countries with mixed success. Weather recognizes no borders and it threatens the very livelihood of every person and every country represented in this room. We need a better solution, a more comprehensive solution, a Marshall Plan for our time. The briefings you received today are just the beginning. The Council of Corporations, represented here by Ms. Rabh, has agreed to match every dollar raised by your governments. Tonight, I am announcing a three-trillion-dollar commitment by the United States to the new Marshall Plan."

The room erupted in applause and the news drone cloud shifted as their handlers angled for the best shot of whoever they were following. Graves stood dutifully with the rest of the audience, clapping along as Teller smiled for the cameras. He waited for the noise to die off before he continued.

"But the Marshall Plan had a leader, former US Army General George C. Marshall, a hero of World War Two and revered by his country. Under his leadership, the plan was a resounding success. We need that same kind of leadership today, which is why I am naming General William Graves as the leader of this Twenty-First Century Marshall Plan!"

Graves imagined he'd misheard the last part. It was the second whiskey, he told himself. Teller had not just named him to run this entire operation, that hadn't happened.

But it had. H appeared by his side as if by magic and pulled him to a standing position, pushing him toward the dais where Teller and Adriana Rabh and the secretary-general were all standing, applauding.

Teller reached down and hauled him up to the dais, then he pumped his hand.

Graves stood slack-jawed, still numb to the announcement. He didn't want this, didn't need this. He already had a job.

Then he looked at Teller and he saw the reason: Graves was being set up.

Teller's lips were smiling but his eyes were cold. He pulled Graves close and whispered in his ear. "You screwed me over on the Havens, Graves, but let's see you wriggle your way out of this one. When you go down in flames, I'll be right there to pick up the pieces."

He stepped back and Graves was alone next to the lectern.

Adriana took his hand, squeezing gently. "Congratulations, General." Her eyes flicked to Teller, then back to Graves. "I just want you to know you have my full support."

Graves mumbled his thanks.

She gestured at the lectern. "I think you should say a few words."

Then Graves stood all by himself.

9

MING QINLAO • SHANGHAI, CHINA

The next morning, when Ming drove her maglev chair into the Qinlao boardroom with Marcus at her side, she heard the collective gasp of the room. She didn't need Echo to read their expressions: pity, disgust, sorrow, anger ... not a shred of decency in the room.

Ming approached her aunt. The older woman did everything but sneer at her. "Back so soon, Ming? You were not missed, Niece."

She started to turn away when Marcus spoke. "Ms. Qinlao would like to add an item to the agenda for the board meeting."

Her aunt's green eyes might as well have been carved jade. "The agenda is closed, Marcus. You can put forth a request when we get to new business."

"As CEO of Qinlao Manufacturing," Ming said in a clear voice, "I will adjust the agenda as I see fit, Aunt."

The buzz of the room stopped to watch the dance of the lionesses. Ming could feel their eyes on her—Sying, her mother, JC Han, Danny Xiao—and they all had reasons to vote against her. For a fleeting moment, a twinge of unease filtered through her defenses. She was taking a step that was not easily undone.

Xi backed down, just as Ming had known she would. "Very well."

Ming displaced Xi at the head of the table, enjoying the scarlet flush that crept up her aunt's neck as she forced the rest of the board to slide down so she could still be close to the chairman's seat. Ming engaged Echo as they shifted their seats and Marcus called the roll.

"Xi Qinlao." Her aunt was flustered and angry. Perhaps she had expected Ming to make a subtler attack, not this direct assault on her base of power. But she was also confident. Her aunt had long prepared for this day.

"Jong Chul Han." JC's square face was ruddy with anger beneath his oiled gray pompadour. In the elevator, Marcus had reported the old man was furious about the divorce and her betrayal of his trust.

"The Xiao family." Danny Xiao, her former boyfriend whom Ming had dumped in a spectacularly public way, acknowledged his presence. He slouched in his designer suit, cuffs rolled up to his elbows, eyes surveying Ming. Danny might be a pretty boy, but he knew how to play the game. He was watching and waiting to see which side he should support.

"Sying Qinlao." It pained Ming to look at her former lover. Sying's beauty had only ripened in Ming's absence and looking deep into her eyes did nothing to lessen the impact of her presence on Ming's emotions. She had dreamed of this moment for so many nights, but it was not to be. She hardened her gaze and looked away as Marcus called out the rest of the board.

"We have a quorum, Madam Chairwoman," Marcus said quietly. The room was still, tense, watching every move she made, trying to divine meaning from nuance.

"My aunt has failed to follow the course set for this company by my father and by me," Ming said. "As Chairman and CEO, I call for an immediate vote to remove her from the board." The whooshing of the air conditioning was the only sound.

Marcus cleared his throat. "We have a motion. Do we have a second?"

There was none. Marcus waited as Ming challenged each board member with her gaze. Echo reported anger, resentment, and frustration, but no fear and no trace of pity now. Certainly no agreement with her motion.

As she had expected. Ming let the coldness of reason settle on her. *Focus.* This was the only way.

"The motion to remove Xi Qinlao does not pass," Marcus said, making a note in his tablet. "Moving to the next item—"

"We're not finished, Marcus," Xi said.

Ming feigned surprise as she turned to her aunt. "You have something to say, Xi?" Using her aunt's given name infuriated the older woman, Ming knew.

Careful, Echo cautioned, *her anger is barely under control.* Which was exactly where Ming wanted her aunt's anger level.

Xi rose from her seat and posted her fists on the tabletop. "In the last year, we have created more wealth for our shareholders than in any one-year period in the last three decades, despite the global economic slump caused in part by the rash actions of my niece."

"That's all a result of council money, Xi," Ming said. "Have you delivered anything yet? Do you even know how to deliver what you promised?"

"That is enough!" Xi crashed her fist onto the table. A strand of hair slipped from the clasp on her nape and draped across her face, giving her a wild look. "I demand a vote of no confidence in our newly returned CEO. She is clearly unwell and needs rest."

"Seconded," Sying said.

Ming met her eyes for a split second, then let her gaze slide away. *Focus.*

"We have a motion before the board," Marcus said in an even voice.

The vote was unanimous. Ming let tears she didn't feel run down her face as she pushed back from the table and headed to the door.

Step two complete.

Ming sat at the window of her father's apartment, watching the sun set. Burnt orange on a muddy brown horizon. The rain from the night before had washed Shanghai clean and deep reds gleamed on the buildings and the aircars flashing by.

Lander let Marcus into the office. He stood by her at the window. "I can still smell those vile pipes your old man used to smoke in here."

Ming rested her head against his narrow hip. "It's almost gone," she said. "The smell, I mean."

"Eventually, we all move on, Ming. Even you."

The sun slipped below the horizon, changing the city from solid buildings into arrays of pinpoint lights. "That was quite a show you put on today," he continued. "If I didn't know better, I'd say you were trying to get fired."

"It's time for a change, Marcus. I'm going away."

Marcus chuckled. "That's good, because your aunt wants you out of this apartment by tomorrow morning. I've arranged for security to take you—"

"That won't be necessary. I have my own security."

"I hope that's enough."

Ming had had enough. "Goodbye, Marcus."

She waited in the dark for her next visitor, studying the patterns in the city lights, enjoying the anonymity of her position. Lander pulsed her when the visitor showed up.

"Send her in," she sent back.

As the door opened, Sying's lithe form stood silhouetted in the light of the hallway. Ming caught a glimpse of her face, then darkness again.

Sying stood beside her in the same place Marcus had stood. Her hand trailed across Ming's shoulder and Ming felt a shiver of anticipation.

"Why didn't you tell me you were coming home?" Sying asked.

Ming ignored the question. "How is Ruben?"

"He's a boy in a man's body," she said with a laugh. "Hormones, muscles, and the attention span of a mosquito. Makes me glad I was born a woman."

Ming tried to reconcile this description with the kid she had protected for months, until he was bartered away by Anthony Taulke. She felt her hands clench and she twisted away from Sying's touch. She was wasting time.

The woman's fingers followed her. She stroked the line of grafted skin. "Does it hurt?" she asked.

"I don't feel anything anymore," Ming replied.

Sying knelt so she was at Ming's level. Taking Ming's face in both hands, she said, "I don't believe that." She kissed her, and the touch of her lips was a rush of pure energy in Ming's head. She pulled back. This was not the plan. She needed to stay on track.

"What's the matter?" Sying's hands pushed Ming's regrown hair behind her ear. It was all Ming could do not to rub her head into Sying's arm like a cat seeking affection. "Come home with me," she whispered, her breath hot on Ming's cheek. "We can be together again. That's what you want, right?"

Her plan was all mixed up now, all twisted in her head. Up was down, left was right.

Echo, help me...

Icy calm descended on Ming's consciousness. She reversed her chair, leaving Sying kneeling on the floor. A flash of annoyance crossed the woman's face, then she stood.

"It doesn't have to be like this, Ming. You don't have to be alone."

Ming spun the chair. As she passed the desk, the 3-D picture of young Ming and the butterfly caught her eye. On impulse, she picked it up and tucked it next to her hip on the chair seat.

"I was just leaving," she said.

Sying followed her into the hallway. "Wait, Ming, don't leave like this."

Lander was waiting for her at the aircar dock. "Ready to leave whenever you are, Ming." He eyed Sying, trying to puzzle out what was going on between them. His expression told her he wasn't buying that the only relationship between them was stepmother to stepdaughter.

"You can take my stepmother home, Lander," Ming said coldly. "I'll drive myself." Without waiting for an answer, she moved her maglev into the waiting shuttle that had been modified for her chair.

Lander shrugged and reached for Sying's elbow. "Ma'am, if you'll come this way. I'll get you back to—"

Sying shook him off. "I'm coming to see you tomorrow, Ming." She strode into the shuttle and threw herself in a chair.

"I'm looking forward to it," Ming said without looking back. Her voice did not break.

Lander's shuttle dropped away from the dock and made a broad turn away from the building.

Ming took a deep breath and used the arms of her chair to stand. Her legs shook, but they held her weight. She extracted the small bundle containing the MoSCOW suit from the storage compartment under the seat and tucked it under her arm. As she turned to make her way out of the shuttle, she spied the picture on the seat. Young Ming grasping for the butterfly. She snatched it up and tucked it into the bundle.

In the hallway, she used her retinal display to access the shuttle's remote-control feature and program a course due east. She made sure the transponder was working and dropped the craft away from the dock.

The brick of explosives under the seat of her chair would detonate in one hour.

The air on the street level was stifling and thick with the heavy smells of close-packed humanity as Ming navigated the foot traffic on stiff, aching legs. She found a cab, an electric model illegally siphoning a charge off the Qinlao power meter. Ming pulled her cap lower on her face and hugged the bundle close to her chest as she negotiated with the driver to take her to an address in the old city.

The van had quaint, hand-sewn curtains covering the windows. Ming opened them a few centimeters to watch the Shanghai night scenes. It had been years since she'd spent time on the street level in the city. Through the driver's open window, the scents rode in on the humid air. Street vendors, baked concrete, barely functioning sewers.

When they crossed the river into the old city, the roads narrowed even further, alleys grew darker, and the odors intensified. She could smell the river clearly, the mud, the rotting vegetation, and who knew whatever else the Han drew in from the countryside.

Her retinal display alerted her that the explosives timer in the shuttle had reached the final countdown. Ming twisted in her seat in a vain attempt to see the explosion. Buildings blocked her on all sides and the shuttle was miles away, but she looked east anyway.

The timer ran to zero.

Ming Qinlao was dead.

Too late, she realized the cab had stopped. She checked her position and saw they were at least two hundred meters from her destination.

"Why have we stopped?" she asked in Mandarin.

The driver twisted in his seat. "I miscalculated your fare," he said with an evil leer. He spoke in Shanghainese, the local dialect of the area. Ming cursed to herself; using Mandarin had pegged her as an outsider and now she was paying the price. She didn't need Echo to tell her she was in trouble.

Ming fingered the wad of cash in her pocket. If Ming Qinlao was dead, there was no way she could make a credit transaction.

"We had a deal," she snapped, switching to the local dialect and surprising the man as she did so. Good, she had him second-guessing himself. Ming pulled out some cash and counted out the bills for the original fare, adding one more to the pile. "You take me where I want to go and I'll forget this ever happened."

The man's eyes flicked from the cash to her face.

He's not going to take the deal, Ming, Echo said.

She held out the cash tentatively and the driver reached for it. Ming dropped the money, gripped his wrist and twisted as hard as she could. With her free hand, she jabbed her fingernails into his eyes, then levered his arm over the seat until she heard something pop. The driver screamed in rage and pain.

Ming pushed her door open, still clutching the bundle with the picture and the suit. She swayed on her feet in the alley. She could barely walk, much less run. If this guy made it out of the vehicle, she was in real trouble.

The driver's side door started to open and she saw his face, a blotchy mass of wild hair and wilder eyes. Ming seized the door and yanked it open. The driver, suddenly off-balance, began to fall out of the car. Ming slammed the door shut on his body again and again. He slipped lower and his head fell into the path of the doorframe.

She kept going until he stopped screaming, then gave two more wet, mushy slams of the door for good measure. His limp body slid to the ground. He did not get up.

Ming staggered down the empty alley toward her destination. Each step was a jolt of pain through her legs and hips and all the way up her spine, but she kept going, the dot on her retinal display slowly drawing closer to the dropped pin of her destination.

She hadn't chosen this part of town for its safe neighborhoods. If the driver woke up or someone decided to take advantage of the strange wandering girl, it was all over for Ming Qinlao.

The warehouse was deep in an alley, but there was a dingy light over the doorway. Ming collapsed against the wall and slid the cover off the security panel. Her handprint opened the door and she fell inside.

Automatic lights came on, but she kept her face pressed against the cool concrete. Just a short nap, she told herself.

No rest, Echo said. *Keep moving.*

Ming startled awake. A quick check of her retinal display showed she had been asleep for seven minutes. Between the fight with the cabbie and her nap, she was almost thirty minutes behind schedule.

She drew her knees up under her chest and came to a kneeling position. The pain moved through her like a wave and a surge of nausea threatened to overwhelm her. A few deep breaths later and Ming stood on unsteady legs. Another handprint to another room revealed her destination: a one-seater aircar racer, unmarked, matte black, and equipped with a spoofed transponder.

Ming stowed her now-dirty and blood-spattered bundle under the seat, then lowered her body into the cockpit. The conforming cushions hugged her aching body like a lover and she sighed with blessed relief as she strapped into the harness. Her retinal display connected with the controls and started the preflight check automatically. The destination was preset, she noticed, and she smiled at his thoroughness.

When the craft was ready, Ming ordered the roof retracted. The aircar made a fast vertical ascent and entered the Shanghai air traffic patterns, just one of millions of vehicles buzzing over the massive city.

She ascended swiftly through a series of traffic loops until she entered the transcontinental lanes heading westward and Shanghai was a glow on the horizon. Blots of light showed cities in the dark velvet carpet beneath her car. These thinned as they moved farther west.

A drowsy hour later, Ming felt it in her stomach as the craft dropped rapidly out of the traffic lane. The aircar slowed and settled at a few hundred feet off the ground, engaging the terrain-following feature. In the dimness, Ming could make out shapes of trees and a few buildings as they flashed by. Up ahead, she spied the silver of a lake and knew she was close now. She saw a pattern of cultivated fields and the geometry of a white building looming out of the night as the aircar slowed and dropped to a landing.

She popped the cockpit top and sat for a moment in the night. Sweet air passed over her, carrying the scent of cut grass and turned earth, taking her back years to her childhood. Crickets sounded and the wind soughed through the trees bordering the property.

A light from the building pierced the night, making Ming squint. She clambered out of the cockpit, her legs like formed rubber beneath her, but somehow still holding her weight. A doorway opened on the building and more light spilled out. A silhouette, short, blocky, but still light on his feet despite his years.

Ming drew herself up and walked toward the man.

They paused a few steps from each other, as if by mutual agreement. Ito's voice was older, but still strong, still comforting.

"Are you ready to begin your training, Little Tiger?"

Ming tried to bow to her former sensei but nearly lost her balance. "Not so little anymore, Ito."

His chuckle was like a warm bath to her senses. "It is not the size of the tiger that matters, it is her will to hunt." He reached for Ming. "Welcome home, Ming."

She leaned into his sturdy frame, then sagged against him. Her breath caught, her eyes burned.

Step three.

10

ADRIANA RABH • NEW YORK CITY

Adriana studied the man across the coffee table from her. Short and bowlegged, with a belly that obscured his beltline and blocky facial features. Her dossier on him said he was native Chinese, but she doubted the accuracy of the file. His size and dark wavy hair spoke of some strain of a South Pacific nation. His face was placid, almost vacant, but she knew there was a sharp intellect behind this benign exterior.

He looked as unlike a spy as one could imagine, which is probably why he was so good. His day job was as a middle-manager bureaucrat in the Chinese Unit 8200, the notorious hacker corps of the Chinese People's Liberation Army. While the hotshot young engineers did the sexy cyber work, he kept the lights on and made sure the garbage got taken out every night. Over the years, he had developed his own tools to monitor what was going on inside the Chinese military and he sold the fruits of his labors to the highest bidder: her.

Adriana winced as her guest slurped his tea, years of breeding rebelling against his lack of social graces. She cleared her throat, anxious to get the meeting over with. She had gone to great lengths to bring him here, to her Park Avenue penthouse, to deliver his intelligence report in person because he refused to divulge it to anyone but her.

"Perhaps we can...?" Adriana began.

The Chinese spy, whose name was Wen Liu, grunted and took a cookie from the silver tray on the table. He chewed with his mouth open.

"There is a coup coming," he said.

"A coup?" Adriana replied. "You mean in China?"

"I mean in the world." He took another cookie. "The Chinese are tracking two military leaders, one army, one navy, for possible crimes against the State. They've been meeting secretly with Russian and European military leaders."

"The State? I thought you said it was against the world."

The man grinned, bits of crushed chocolate cookie clinging to his teeth. "That's why they haven't picked them up yet. For every action, there is a reaction—the action might be in China's favor. They want to see what happens."

"Do they have any association with the New Earth Order?" she asked.

Liu pulled a face as if he was considering the idea. "Possibly," he said finally.

Adriana resisted the urge to snap at him. Liu had always been a reliable source, one of her best, but this was the first time she'd met him in person. She needed to tread carefully. "What does *possibly* mean?"

"One of the officers is a Neo, the other is not, but they work together. There is no other connection that I know of."

Adriana got up and strode to the windows overlooking the city. She could see the UN Headquarters from here, even see her office window near the top of the gleaming building. She made an appearance at least once a week, but she preferred to work from her own apartment.

The UN office was adequate as far as government offices went—better than most—but she had grown accustomed to a higher standard of living. Her own quarters offered comfort, privacy, and security that the UN building did not. As for access to her colleagues, that was not a problem. Anyone from the UN who wanted to see her in person seemed happy to travel the half-mile to her penthouse to pay their respects to the Council of Corporations' only representative on Earth.

"How long do you need to verify that the Neos are behind the coup attempt?" she asked him without turning around. She could hear him masticating another cookie and she wasn't sure her stomach could handle it.

"We don't know if that is true or not," he said.

"I know it's true," she said back. "I need you to bring me the proof."

The Neos were on the move, of that she was sure, but their end game was less clear to her. Intel from all over the world showed Neos congregating in population centers and refugee camps. Some of it could be explained by population displacement, but not all. Local leaders were getting established, as if they had shifted their strategy to one of decentralized management. The most persistent voice on the newsfeeds was the woman in Fort Hood, Corazon Santos. Even the name made her sound like a revolutionary. And now she found that the Chinese knew about subversive activity and sat on their hands. What did it take to exercise some good old-fashioned military might? Instead of feeding the would-be terrorists, why not lock them up?

But Liu's report was the first to connect Neos with a potential coup. The fact that China was willing to sit this one out gave her pause. Her inclination was to stamp out the first sign of a Neo insurrection, but maybe drawing them out first wasn't a terrible idea either. Perhaps she should invite the Chinese ambassador to the UN for dinner...

"Who else knows about this?" she asked.

"No one. The party is keeping this closely held."

Adriana studied his face. The problem with spies was that she never knew if she could trust them. Her mind ran through the permutations of who else could gain from forcing her to act on this new intel. "Keep me posted," she said. "And prove a link with the Neos."

He seemed about to object to her request, then thought better of it. She heard him take another cookie on his way out.

She folded her arms and surveyed the city—her city—again. From this vantage point, the metropolis was a beautiful piece of miniaturist art. The weather stains on the building across the way looked beautiful at a distance, and the cars and people all merged into a never-ending flow of unified movement. Exactly the way she liked it.

Her virtual queried her about an unscheduled visitor. President Teller.

She allowed an inner smile as she accepted the request. Even the very mighty made the trek to see her.

Teller had apparently checked his political charm in the elevator. He stormed into the room, his face a deep red, and stalked toward her at the windows. It was all Adriana could do to hold her ground.

"What have you done?" he hissed at her.

His normally coiffed hair was mussed from where he'd run his fingers through it and his body seemed to quiver with emotion. "Don't tell me the council is not behind this because it's got your stink all over it!" Teller shouted.

"Calm down, Mr. President," Adriana said in a neutral tone. "Tell me what you're talking about."

Teller looked wildly around the room. "Don't you watch the fucking newsfeeds?" He found a wallscreen and connected to it. The YourVoice commentator was a breathy young blonde dressed in a jumpsuit that was sized just small enough to mold to her figure. Behind her was a mob of coveralls-clad people in a narrow hall celebrating. The chyron said: "LUNa City elects governor from opposition party."

Adriana frowned. "Since when is there an opposition party on the Moon?"

Teller threw up his hands. "There isn't! That's the problem." He changed channels rapidly. All of them carried the LUNa City takeover as their lead story. Members of the United Nations were already reacting to it, and not in a positive way. She could hear Teller's teeth grinding together.

"Calm down." She said again, pointing to the couch recently vacated by her Chinese spy. "Sit."

Teller held his face with both hands. "I put myself on the line for you. Go along with the council, I told them. We can work this out with them. They'll fund the Marshall Plan and we'll get things back under control." He glared at her. "And the very first thing you do is lose control of the Moon! You can buy all the He-3 you want, why do you have to take over the supply?"

Adriana didn't bother to answer the question. The council didn't want to buy the He-3, they wanted to take it. All of it. But Anthony wouldn't be that bold, not yet, anyway. He was still trying to save the world, not destabilize it.

"Who is this opposition leader?"

Teller's eyes defocused as he consulted his retinal display. She felt a pulse as he sent her a data packet. "Young guy," Teller said. "Total unknown, no political experience. Used to drive an extraction rig, for God's sake, now he's in charge."

Adriana ignored his chatter. She could read. Her eyes scanned the dossier for one fact. There, under religious affiliation, she found what she was looking for.

New Earth Order.

"It's a coup," she said, her blunt pronouncement shutting down Teller's rant.

"What?" He stared at her.

"It's a coup. The Neos are launching a coup."

"That's ridiculous," Teller said. "The opposition party ran on only one issue: alignment with the council. They're in your pocket."

Adriana shook her head. "If this was the council's doing, I'd know it. I give you my word, we had nothing to do with it. This is the first step in a global takeover, and if you don't get ahead of the problem, you'll get run over, Mr. President."

Teller's face showed a war of emotions. He had no reason to believe her, even she could see that, but politics makes strange bedfellows.

"What do I need to do?" he asked.

"Get one of these Neo organizers. Question them." Adriana thought frantically for a name. "The woman in Fort Hood, the one that's always on the newsfeeds spouting her refugee bullshit."

"Corazon Santos?"

"That's her. Bring her in and get to the bottom of this mess fast."

Teller got to his feet. "I can do that. What are you going to do?"

Adriana stood, meeting his gaze. "I'm going to get my own house in order."

Teller left with less anger than he'd had when he entered, but he'd transferred that negative energy to her. She felt a slow burn of anger in her belly, the kind born of being used by another person.

If the Neos were behind this—and they were—only one person on the council was responsible.

Elise Kisaan.

She called up her retinal display. "Get me Anthony Taulke on the line. Immediately."

11

CORAZON SANTOS • FORT HOOD, TEXAS

Corazon Santos spent the afternoon in the Shrine of the Child. Through the insulated walls of the tent, she could hear the muffled sounds of the crowded camp around her. She could imagine the blinding sunlight, the closeness of the heat and the smell of dust and bodies in the air.

But inside, it was cool and dim and smelled faintly of the sage and incense her acolyte liked to burn in the morning service.

She did not kneel, she did not pray, she just sat in a comfortable chair in the half-light, alone with her thoughts.

Corazon thought about sleep. It might encourage a vision like the one that had set her on this path in the first place, but she did not expect one. It was not needed. She didn't require a vision to tell her that the taking of LUNa City by the Neos would exact a response from the Earth governments. She had made herself the lightning rod of the New Earth Order on the planet, so it was natural to expect them to come for her. It was the logical conclusion.

She studied the golden symbol of Cassandra. The curve of the globe, the slope of the half-hidden eye of the mysterious woman.

She wondered if they would send Graves to take her. No, that would be too easy. Cassandra would want Cora to be tested more than that. Besides, she suspected Graves would refuse the order anyway.

Cora knew she should hate him. There were those in her following who wanted him dead for destroying the Temple of Cassandra. How could she explain to these people that it was all part of Her plan? From the ashes of Her demise would rise the Child, Cassandra made flesh, and Graves had a role to play. An important role, but the future was not clear to her anymore. She needed to trust her instincts.

She liked Graves. He knew his heart, that was what she liked about him. He did not see himself as strong, but he also did not let his doubts stop him from doing the right thing. He grieved for the lives he had ended. She saw all this in his face, and this made her glad Cassandra had chosen him to share her burden.

Will I grieve the same way for the blood I am about to shed? Do I have that same capacity for sorrow?

It didn't matter. The test was nearly upon her, there was no way but forward.

There was a flurry of action in the anteroom to the shrine and Maria slipped through the flap. "Pardon me, Corazon, but they are in the camp. I have Valeria." She stepped aside to let an older woman enter the room. She was dressed identical to Cora and bore a striking resemblance to her.

"Pass the word to begin the attack," Cora said.

Routine is the enemy of vigilance. That was not a teaching of Cassandra, but a line from Cora's own mouth.

In the months her people had been in camp, she had done nothing to arouse the attention of the United States Army. When their food shipments arrived late or short, she counseled her people to smile and say thank you. When the latrines overflowed, they fixed the problem themselves or helped the army personnel fix it and showered them with thanks. She encouraged the young men and women to strike up personal friendships with soldiers their own age. She organized groups of refugees to take exercise walks all over the army base and enter as many buildings as possible.

All for this moment. Cora stayed back from the group of a dozen young men and women who approached a side entrance to the command building.

One of the teenagers broke off, sauntering toward the pair of guards at the door. A dark-haired young woman followed. "*Que pasa,* Liam," she heard the boy say to one soldier as they bumped fists. The girl sidled up to the second soldier in a way that said they knew each other. The larger group waited for them, just as they did every morning.

The pair of young refugees slipped Tasers out of their sleeves and attacked both soldiers. By the time their bodies hit the pavement, the rest of the refugee group was inside the building. In the hallway, two of the young men stripped the soldiers of their uniforms, while a girl hacked into the security station to disable the cameras in that zone. By the time the replacement soldiers were back outside at their post, a second group of a dozen refugees was inside the door.

If all was going to plan, the same assault was happening at two more side entrances to the building. A truck containing a full platoon of armed fighters was backing up to the loading dock. Their plan ignored the heavily guarded main doors in the front of the building.

"Take control of the armory," she ordered.

"Yes, Corazon." The young team leader took six people and raced off down the hall.

As she had waited outside, watching the team launch the assault, Cora's heart had hammered at her rib cage. But now that the action had begun, she felt a freedom of movement, like her actions were preordained.

"Who has the jamming device?" she asked.

A girl wearing a heavy backpack, who looked no older than fifteen, raised her hand. "I do, Corazon."

We fight this war with children.

From deep inside the facility, she heard the rattle of small arms fire. It had begun.

She smiled and held out her hand to the girl. "Stay with me."

Her team moved swiftly through the tiled halls of the building, headed for the heart of the complex, the command-and-control center. All base operations, communications, and tactical support ran through this digital nerve center. They rounded a corner to find a soldier in uniform sprawled across the floor. A spatter of blood decorated the wall behind him.

Cora heard the girl take in a sharp breath and she gripped her hand tighter. A few yards on, they passed two of their own slumped against the wall. The wide steel double doors at the entrance to the ops center were flung open and she could see rows of empty workstations facing a pair of immense wallscreens. A mix of two dozen uniformed and civilian personnel were kneeling along the back wall.

"Over here, Corazon," one of her people called. "I have the core open." Cora took the silver case from the girl's backpack and handed it to her technician. Another tech joined him and they argued in low tones.

"What's the holdup?" she hissed at them. She heard another distant burst of gunfire and thought of the dead men in the hallway.

A scuffle broke out behind them and Cora turned to find that a group of the hostages had jumped two of her men. The soldier kneed her man in the gut and wrenched his rifle away.

"Drop it!" Cora's weapon was in her hand and she was advancing toward him. The rifle muzzle wavered and she pulled the trigger twice. Two blots of red appeared on his light green uniform shirt and the soldier crashed to the floor. She swung her aim to the second fighter. "Get back!" she screamed. "Now!"

The row of workstations behind her winked out and she saw the people kneeling on the floor look up as their retinal displays went blank.

"Jamming device activated," said one of the techs.

Cora turned her attention on the man who had lost his weapon. She hauled him to his feet and dragged his face close to hers. "Pick up your weapon and get these people locked up in one of the offices."

"Yes, Corazon."

She stepped back between the rows of desks, wanting nothing more than to steady her trembling legs against something sturdy. The heat behind her eyes threatened to spill over into hot tears.

She had killed a man in cold blood—and he might not be the last one this day.

Cora offered up a silent prayer to the man's soul. She had sworn to protect the Child. She had vowed to lay down her life for the Child. *Her* life. But instead she had taken another's.

These were acts that would not be forgiven. There was no act of contrition she could make to wash away that stain.

Cora clenched her jaw until she heard ringing in her ears, then she relaxed.

It was done. Forward was the only way.

"Set the charges," she said.

12

WILLIAM GRAVES • SOMEWHERE OVER THE ATLANTIC OCEAN

Graves dozed in the cavernous cargo bay of the logistics transport aircraft. He could have taken the diplomatic aircar back to the UN—a much nicer ride, to be sure—but he'd begged off. He'd had enough of policy meetings and diplomatic negotiations and the people who went along with those functions. Though he didn't doubt their necessity, he did doubt his own ability to actually make a difference in the meetings.

Instead, he focused on making the trains run on time. A few hours ago, this transport had been packed to the ceiling with food, tankers of water, tents, and educational supplies for local schools. Graves had been able to witness aid getting to where it made a difference. When he closed his eyes, he could still smell the dust of the Nigerian aid station in the air.

The drone of the big transport's engines translated into a steady, comforting vibration under his backside. He dozed.

"Sir?" a familiar voice tried to penetrate his peaceful shell.

"What is it, Jansen?" he mumbled back.

"Sir? It's Estes."

Graves opened his eyes to find Sergeant Estes crouched next to his seat, the light from above angling down so his face was in shadow. Graves felt a pang of regret as he wondered where in the universe Captain Jansen was now. Wherever it was, he just hoped she was safe.

"Sorry, Sergeant. I used to have a right-hand woman who ran things for me."

"I heard she was good, sir."

"She was the best, Estes. The very best..." Graves unsnapped the harness and stood. "What've you got for me?"

Estes's expression was troubled. "I'm not sure, sir, but Ortega contacted me via private comms that there's trouble at home."

"Home? You mean back at Hood?"

Estes nodded. "Orders came from Washington to take Corazon Santos into custody."

Graves was all the way awake now. "Orders? From who?"

"He doesn't know, sir. A squad of MPs showed up and told the base commander they were there to take Santos. He let them ... and all hell broke loose."

"Get me Maxwell on the horn. Right now." Graves clenched his eyes shut in frustration. After the LUNa City fiasco, the best course of action was to negotiate with the Neos, not attack them. They all had enough on their plates without adding another crisis.

"That's the problem, sir. I can't raise them. That's why Ortega contacted me by private comms."

Graves stared at him. "It's an army base, Sergeant. What do you mean you can't raise them?"

"I mean they're not online, sir. Ortega thinks the fugees—sorry, sir, the refugees—might have done something—"

"Tell the pilot to divert to Fort Hood and make best possible speed."

The familiar swelter of the Texas summer did nothing to ease Graves's mind as he strode down the ramp of the transport ship to the waiting aircar. Inside, Ortega sat with Colonel Maxwell, the base commander, a barrel-chested soldier whose pale, aquiline features were a marked contrast to Ortega. Neither looked eager to brief Graves.

"What's the situation, gentlemen?" Graves said. "Let's hear it."

"A squad of MPs were sent from Washington to pick up Corazon Santos.

They arrested a woman who claimed to be her, but it wasn't. While that was going on, the Neos took the command building," Maxwell said. "Commando style. Neat as could be. Just overwhelmed us in one move. They're pros." His voice had a measure of respect.

"Casualties?"

"We don't know, sir."

"You don't know if there were casualties?"

"They have them inside. The place is locked down with some sort of EM shield. Drones don't work and any attacks have been rebuffed. She's got hundreds of civilians in there—theirs and ours. I'm afraid if we go in hard, it'll be a bloodbath."

Graves thought about taking a stim and rejected the idea. What he needed now was a clear head.

"Good call. What about the media?" he asked.

"They're here, but we're keeping them off base for national security reasons. The rep from the White House is here, though."

Graves sighed. "Let me guess: white lady, dark hair, elf ears?"

Maxwell and Ortega exchanged glances, then the colonel nodded.

"Fucking great," Graves muttered.

"We have an assault plan ready for you to approve, sir." Maxwell went on to describe a classic feint maneuver. Launch an open, noisy assault from the south while a small team entered the complex from the maintenance tunnels underneath the base.

The aircar stopped at the temporary ops center set up in a hangar a half mile from the perimeter of the base command building. Graves put his game face on before he entered the space. These people needed a confidence boost, not a show of anger. Hell, *he* needed a confidence boost. Graves had the distinct impression that the Neos knew exactly what they were doing and he was the one playing defense.

The holographic display of the base was on the tabletop. Graves looked around the room, realizing he was operating with all new people. The regular command center team were all in the building taken by the Neos. These replacements might be good, but they'd never operated as a team before today. Meanwhile, the Neos had control of his resources and a plan they'd been working on for who knew how long.

Corazon Santos had effectively cut the head off the snake—and he was the snake.

"We're being jammed on all frequencies, sir," Maxwell was saying. "Drones are useless, so—"

"So we're going in blind," Graves finished for him. "How many of our people are in there?"

Maxwell nodded at a young lieutenant. "On a typical day, we'll have about two hundred people in the building, a mix of civilian and military. Because of the jamming device, we can't access their implants for an exact census. There's something else. Visuals show us these boxes are in the windows." She passed Graves a tablet with a blown-up picture of an office window and a box sitting on a windowsill.

He studied the picture, then zoomed out, looking for more of the boxes. He found them right where he expected to find them. "Son of a bitch," he said. He passed the tablet to Maxwell. "You never had combat engineer training, did you?"

Maxwell shook his head.

"They're explosives," Graves said. "Set on all the structural points of the building. If we attack, they blow it."

Maxwell handed the tablet back. "Maybe they're bluffing."

"Maybe they're not," Graves snapped back. "Are you willing to take that chance?"

A familiar voice came from behind Graves, confidence laced with the slightest sneer. "We need to contain this situation, General Graves. You know they're bluffing, and we can't let a few pissant refugees take over a US Army base." Helena Telemachus stepped into the ring of people around the tabletop holo. "It's bad for your image."

Graves knew she was trying to provoke him, and it was working. "Clear the room," he barked, his eyes never leaving H's gaze. "Now."

"Why?" he said when they were alone. "Why did you try to arrest her? She's done nothing to us."

"Wrong," H shot back. "The Neos took LUNa City. What's next? The White House? The UN? An army base?" She stabbed a finger at the holo of the command building. "A third of the world's population are Neos. Today it's an army base. What happens when they start taking over cities? This

Corazon woman knows something. We use her as a bargaining chip. Figure it out and shut this attack down." She leaned in closer. "Or I will."

Graves stormed out of the command center and found Maxwell. "I need to talk to your prisoner. The one they thought was Santos," he said to Maxwell, who led him quickly to an office door at the end of the hall guarded by a young airman.

Graves put his hand on the door handle. "I've got it from here, Max."

The woman behind the desk had Cora's long silver hair, luminous skin, and upright posture, but it was not her. Graves sighed and took the chair across from her. The woman smiled pleasantly.

"Why am I not surprised?" he said.

"The Corazon speaks highly of you, General."

"The Corazon has made me look like a fool, ma'am—what is your name?"

"Valeria," she said. "She wants you to know she had nothing to do with the LUNa City takeover."

The woman—Valeria—had another trait in common with Cora, Graves realized. She was cool under pressure, as if this interaction was insignificant against her larger mission. A true believer.

"So Cora thinks the Neos are being framed?"

Valeria's look reprimanded him. "This is not a game to us, General. We took an oath to Cassandra. It is how we live our lives."

"By taking over army bases?"

"We react to the circumstances at hand."

Graves rubbed his eyes with the heel of his hand. He could use that stim now. "What does she want?"

Valeria smiled again. "You should ask her yourself, William. She's waiting for you."

13

WILLIAM GRAVES • FORT HOOD, TEXAS

Although he'd made the walk at least a thousand times, under the glare of floodlights and the eyes of a few hundred soldiers and civilians, the walk from the edge of the road to the front entrance of the Fort Hood command center felt much longer this time.

The news media was on the base now. Someone had smuggled one outlet in, and Graves made the decision to let them all in rather than risk a charge that the army was hiding the truth from the public. The cynical part of him knew he'd be accused of something anyway, but why play into their hands like that?

The calls with Washington had been brutal. The Joint Chiefs looked at him with something akin to scornful pity as he explained how the refugees had taken the command center and he had no idea what was going on inside their own building. His request to enter the compound alone was denied outright, but he kept at it until his bosses relented.

And here he was, walking into the lion's den all by his lonesome to see a woman who had screwed him over on the world stage. But for some reason he still trusted her.

Go figure.

He kept his hands in plain sight as he walked—as if he'd be dumb enough to draw down on an entire building—and sweated into the body armor they insisted he wear. Graves knew they weren't really worried about his safety, just the appearance of not looking weak in front of all the cameras.

He chuckled bitterly to himself. That ship had sailed, as far as he was concerned.

Somewhere above him, Adriana Rabh was watching this drama, undoubtedly from the comfort of an obscenely expensive aircar. H told him she was "in the area," watching to see how he managed to defuse this very tense situation. Her attitude toward Adriana was scornful.

Another data point: Graves had been placed in his new job because of Adriana Rabh. He'd suspected as much and H's attitude confirmed it.

Layers within layers, schemes within schemes. That seemed to be the way these people worked. Maybe it would be better for all if someone just shot him now.

The automatic doors opened when he reached the building and he walked through, hands still out. The inside of the foyer was dark, and his eyes had not yet adjusted. Whispers, breathing noises, and shoe scuffs told him there were at least three people close by.

"I'm here," he said.

"Walk forward," said a woman's voice. "Get on your knees, hands on your head."

"I'm unarmed," Graves replied.

"Do it," said another voice. This one male, but just as young.

"No," Graves said. "I'm not getting on my knees. I'm unarmed and I'm here to see the Corazon."

Frantic whispering in the dark. Graves's eyes were adjusting to the gloom and he saw there were four of them. Two looking outside, two talking back and forth.

"I'm waiting," he said. The whispers stopped.

"Walk forward," said the man. "Slowly. And take the second right."

"I know where the ops center is," Graves said.

"How do you know that's where the Corazon is?"

"Because that's where I'd be."

Graves had never been in the ops center without the room buzzing with energy. He scanned the rows of empty, dead workstations and the blank wallscreens. "Where is she?" he asked.

His escort was a thin young man with a wispy goatee and shaggy dark hair. He pointed the muzzle of his gun toward the base commander's office, the glass front of which overlooked the watch floor from the mezzanine level.

Graves climbed the steps and stood in front of the glass. On a previous tour of duty, this had been Graves's office, and it hadn't changed at all. He took in the wide, government-issued desk with the interactive glass top that occasionally stopped working for no reason and the cozy chairs, couch, and coffee table that comprised the meeting area. Cora, her lean frame curled into a ball, occupied one end of the couch.

Graves knocked on the window and she opened her eyes. He pushed the door open and stepped inside as Cora dismissed the guard with a quick jerk of her chin.

"You came," she said simply.

Graves sat in one of the chairs. "Didn't leave me much choice in the matter."

"No, I didn't." Although her plan had worked perfectly as far as Graves could tell, she seemed sad. "They tried to arrest me, you know."

"I know." He tried to take stock of his feelings. The anger and self-righteousness he knew he should be feeling were just not there. Like her, he was sad that it had all come to this.

"How many?" he asked.

She looked away, and he could tell she knew he was talking about casualties. "Ten dead," she said finally. There was a break in her voice. "Three of yours, seven of mine. A few more injured, nothing too serious."

"I hope it was worth it."

"It was necessary."

Graves felt the missing anger creep up on him. "What is it you want exactly?"

"I can't serve the Child from a refugee camp. I need to be there for the birth." Cora's speech hesitated, but her eyes met his without reservation. "I —I've seen it in a vision."

Graves gaped at her. "A vision? You attacked an army base because of a vision? Was that the same vision that told the Neo crazies on the Moon to take over LUNa City?"

Cora lifted her chin. "They are not Neos, not real ones anyway."

Graves narrowed his eyes. "How do you know that? Is there a secret Neo network or something?"

"Every organization has people who use the group for their own ends. Even the army."

Graves decided silence was the best answer. He resisted the urge to touch the Saint Christopher medal around his neck. She was right. Why would the New Earth Order be any different from any other large organization?

"So a vision told you to take over an army base?"

"A vision told me to find you, General, and you would create the conditions necessary for me to serve the Child."

Graves let the reflexive flash of anger show. "I don't suppose your vision says what I'm supposed to do next, does it? Or what I'm supposed to say to the parents of the soldiers who are dead because of you?"

"That's not how visions work, William," she said. "They tell me what I'm supposed to do. The rest takes care of itself. The vision said I was to trust you implicitly."

"Why do you believe?" he asked.

Cora leaned across the open space between them and took his hand. Her grip was warm and strong, with a confidence that felt out of place with the turmoil in his own chest. His anger eased and he looked into her eyes. Deep brown, soft, caring. It had been a long time since he'd been this close to a woman, especially a strong, vibrant woman like Cora. Graves swallowed when she smiled at him. He noticed the right side of her smile hitched a few millimeters higher than the left side.

"I believe because it is all I have left," she said. "I believe because when my life was at its lowest point, She was there for me, and now I must be there for Her. When Cassandra tells me to trust a man I have no reason to trust, I listen to Her."

Graves realized she was pressing an object into his hand. He turned it over and saw it was a remote detonator. "The explosives?" he said.

Cora nodded. "I'm turning myself in to you and only you."

Graves sat back in his chair. "Under what conditions?"

"None. I trust you."

Graves got to his feet. "I need you to drop the jamming screen you've got over the facility."

Cora stood and walked to the door. "Alberto," she called. A young man dozing next to the cabinet that housed the main computer core startled awake at her call.

"Yes, Corazon."

"Turn off the jamming field."

He stood now, looking puzzled. He saw Graves behind Cora and his eyes widened.

"Alberto." Cora's voice was soft, but strong, with the tone of a mother speaking to a child. "Turn off the jamming field."

The young man nodded. A moment later, Grave saw the temple of his data glasses light up, showing a signal. He slipped them on and pinged Maxwell.

The colonel's square face filled his screen. "General Graves," Maxwell said. "I'm glad I got you, sir. The situation out here has changed. This whole thing has turned into a three-ring circus."

Through the transparent glasses, he saw Cora's eyebrows raise in query. "Changed how?" Graves said.

"He's landing in about three minutes, sir, and this place is a zoo. I really need you out here. We are not prepared for this kind of visit."

Teller. That was Graves's immediate thought. Somehow he was going to twist this thing into a win for the White House, probably at Graves's expense.

"Who's coming, Max?"

"Anthony Taulke, sir. The council is coming here."

14

ANTHONY TAULKE • ABOVE TEXAS

Apparently, size did matter.

Anthony fretted as the captain of his space yacht *Ambition* negotiated with the ground commander for a suitable spot to land his ship. He stood at the window as they circled Fort Hood again and again. The lights of the city looked pretty from this altitude, all smeary and twinkling from the humidity in the air.

In the room behind him, President Teller cleared his throat for the second time.

"What is it, Mr. President?" he said without turning around.

He had some grudging admiration for Teller. Since Anthony hadn't made his departure from Mars public, the man had an impressive intel network to be able to intercept the *Ambition* in orbit. If he was being honest with himself, he loved the fact that Teller was tracking him. With the president came more news coverage, and for this announcement he wanted all the coverage he could get.

Teller's reflection appeared in the darkened window next to his own. He began to open his mouth when a call came in from the captain. "Mr. Taulke, we have Ms. Rabh coming alongside in a shuttle. She's requesting permission to board, sir."

Adriana, better late than never. Since Teller had arrived first, he wondered if he should take that as a sign that his ambassador was slipping.

"Permission granted, Captain. Show her to the observation lounge as soon as she's onboard."

The captain signed off with a snappy "Aye-aye, sir," leaving Anthony with that glow that came from having a first-rate crew at his disposal. He peered out the window again. If he had a hundred men with a can-do attitude like his captain, maybe he could begin to tackle this fiasco of a planet for real.

Teller's reflection watched Anthony for a sign that he was again paying attention. "You haven't mentioned why you've come all this way, Mr. Taulke."

"No, I haven't," Anthony agreed. He smiled to himself as Teller's lips twitched in annoyance. He let him twist on the line for another moment. "I wanted to see how my investment was doing."

"Your investment?"

"The renewal project? The Twenty-First Century Marshall Plan, you call it?"

Teller's face cleared. "It's still early days yet. These things take time."

Anthony went back to gazing out the window. "Do they?"

If Xi Qinlao was able to finish manufacturing the last pieces of his satellite network to take over the Lazarus nanites, he would be able to solve this weather problem by dinnertime. Then he'd have the satisfaction of wiping that smug, pious look off of Elise Kisaan's face. He would be untangled from Cassandra's web of deceit, and he could deal with Elise Kisaan and the Neos without having the fate of the world hanging over his head.

The thought of the Qinlao family brought Ming to mind. The news of her death came as a hammer blow to Anthony's conscience. Apart from Viktor, Ming was the only one on the council he felt he could really trust. They had been through some rough times together, he reflected, but they'd made up in the end and she had forgiven him. When he recalled her resignation and helplessness at their last meeting, it nearly broke his heart. At least they'd parted as friends, he consoled himself.

For all her youth, Ming was twice the CEO of her aunt. The older woman seemed to only care about wealth, diversifying the company into all sorts of unrelated financial instruments. Xi had no vision. Money was the old metric of success. A true member of the Council of Corporations measured their wealth in terms of the number of people who depended on them. Sort of a modern-day feudal system.

Ming understood that. She knew how to build things. If she were in charge, the reinvention of the Lazarus network would have already been completed. Instead, Xi had announced just yesterday another delay.

Teller shifted next to him, clearly wanting to continue their conversation, but Anthony ignored him.

In hindsight, the timing of his decision to leave Mars for Earth was prescient. The Neo takeover of LUNa City was an unexpected and unwelcome surprise. Until the council's other He-3 mining operations were operational, the Moon was a single point of failure in their supply chain. And now this Neo uprising at Fort Hood.

To Anthony's mind, these setbacks were all symptoms of the same root cause: a lack of leadership. Specifically, a lack of his brand of leadership. The kind of hands-on involvement that got things done. After all, the world wasn't going to save itself.

The door to the observation lounge opened and Adriana Rabh strolled in. Anthony studied her reflection in the window, not bothering to turn around. From all normal appearances, his ambassador to Earth looked calm and collected. Her raven hair was held back by a platinum clasp and her chin angled upwards just enough to give one the impression that she was taller than she actually was. There was a time not that long ago when Anthony would have rushed across the room to greet her, mindful of her money and her connections to his success.

But that time was past. He allowed an inward chuckle at the tiny flare of her eyes at the slight. He noticed Teller took his cue from him as well, another confirmation of the new power dynamic.

He half-turned from the window. "Ambassador."

Adriana's reflection joined them as the *Ambition* made another sweeping turn in their racetrack loop over Texas. "I didn't expect to see you so soon, Anthony." She made no attempt to thaw the ice in her voice.

"I didn't expect to need to make the trip, Ambassador."

Adriana's posture stiffened. "What's that supposed to mean?"

"LUNa City, the Neos. My plans cannot sustain a delay in He-3 production."

"You mean the council's plans."

"Is there a difference?"

Teller sought to break the tension. "The Neo situation on LUNa is being dealt with through diplomatic channels—"

"It never should have happened in the first place," Adriana snapped at Teller. "You are supposed to prevent these things from happening."

"And you," Anthony said to Adriana, "are supposed to see them coming. Where were your spies when all this was being planned? For Christ's sake, Adriana, our He-3 supply? It's like the Neos were inside the council room."

"Maybe they are," Adriana said.

Anthony said nothing for a long time. "You suspect Elise." He didn't make it a question.

"You don't?' Adriana turned away from the window and strode back into the room. She threw her long frame into an overstuffed chair.

Anthony followed, considering if he should excuse Teller from the rest of the conversation. He decided against it. Watch his reaction. Take his counsel. See how he worked with Adriana. Maybe they would need a new ambassador at some point.

"We've monitored every possible emanation from Elise since she's been on Mars," Anthony said. "There is no possible way she's communicating to anyone off-planet."

"Someone is coordinating these events." Adriana was all but pouting now. "My money—and I have a lot of money, Anthony—is on her."

"Well, why don't you ask her?" Anthony said. "I can have her brought down, if you like."

Teller and Adriana gaped at him. "You brought her with you?"

"I subscribe to the keep-your-friends-close-and-your-enemies-closer school of management." He felt the ship losing altitude. Over the intercom, the captain said: "Mr. Taulke, we've got clearance to land."

"Very well, Captain." Anthony stood. A quick session with his cosmeticist before he greeted the newsfeeds was in order.

Teller's gaze had defocused as he received an incoming message. "It looks like our man Graves has handled the Neo uprising." He ignored the sneer from Adriana at the use of *our man*. Teller had fought tooth and nail against putting Graves in charge. "He's asking to meet you, sir, when you land."

Anthony rubbed his hands together. This was shaping up very nicely. Another problem solved just by him showing up... "Good, perfect. Tell him to bring the Neo top banana with him—what's her name again?"

"Corazon Santos," Adriana supplied. "Are you sure that's a good idea, Anthony?"

"I think it's an excellent idea, Ambassador."

15

ANTHONY TAULKE • FORT HOOD, TEXAS

Anthony could literally feel his complexion glowing. He pinched at the skin under his neck and titled his head in the mirrored reflection. The new facial treatment from his cosmeticist was truly amazing. No needles, no recovery time, just a personalized mask that covered his face for three minutes and shazam—what a confidence booster!

"Two minutes to ramp time, Mr. Taulke," his press secretary said, catching his eye in the mirror. Anthony flashed her a smile in response. "We've got bots diverting all traffic to this site. You should be hitting an eighty percent worldwide coverage level by broadcast time."

Anthony felt a shiver at the thought of billions of eyeballs focused on him. They would tell their children about this moment. Anthony Taulke vowing to save the world would go down in history as more important than JFK vowing to go to the Moon.

"You've seen the stage, right? It's per my design?"

The press secretary smoothed the lapels of his jacket and picked an invisible piece of lint from his sleeve. "Nancy selected the furniture herself, sir. How do you feel?"

Nancy Watson was a fixture of the YourVoice generation. While other reporters flitted on and off the network, the *Watson Report* had lasted nearly a generation. Nancy styled herself as the voice of YourVoice, the one reporter who had seen it all in an age of microscopic attention spans.

It had been Nancy's idea to use the *Ambition* as a backdrop for the show. She said it would project the image of a self-made man who had the resources to give his fellow citizens a generous hand up.

"She's ready for you, sir." The press secretary opened the door for him. "Break a leg, Mr. Taulke."

Anthony paused at the top of the ramp. The pumping beat of the *Watson Report*'s theme music was playing loudly enough that he could feel the bass in his chest. The darkness outside the *Ambition* was shattered by spotlights from all sides, leaving a bubble of brightness at the bottom of the ramp. Beyond, Anthony could see vague shapes of a crowd, scattered lights, but no details.

The ramp seemed very long and steep as Anthony walked forward. Head up, shoulders back, the Billion-Byte smile on full display. Clouds of news drones, their red recording lights like little angry stars in his periphery. He grinned wider. Nancy would block them all once they started the interview, he knew. This was an exclusive, that's why he'd gone with Nancy.

The woman herself stood to greet him, matching his greeting with her own characteristic disarming smile. She was taller than he expected, with a rangy frame and generous bosom. Her skin was a warm, creamy brown, the color of café au lait, but her hair was a shock of bright pink curls piled high on her head. Her most striking features—and real, if one believed the reports—were her mismatched eyes. One blue, one green. Anthony had done an interview with her years ago and he recalled now how the eyes seemed to register different emotions as she asked him questions. Her ever-present recording drones enveloped him like he was stepping into her cocoon.

Nancy threw her arms open like they were old friends and kissed him on both cheeks. Anthony dimly heard applause, but whether it was real people beyond the wall of light or some enhanced track, he did not know. His pulse raced from all the attention and he could feel his recent skin treatment glowing in response. His facial muscles ached from the intensity of his smile, but he also couldn't stop smiling.

The customized chair that Nancy waved him into held his ass in perfect form to create an erect, alert interview posture.

Nancy settled into her own seat. Her smile dimmed as she consulted her retinal display. "Mr. Taulke, welcome to the *Watson Report*."

"Thank you for having me, Nancy. When I want to speak to the world, I only want the very best at my side."

Nancy cocked her head, the pink curls quivering. "Well, that's very sweet of you, sir, but I think maybe the world might be just a bit skeptical of a man—a felon, mind you—who has done so much to change our lives."

Anthony put on his serious face. The whole line, except for the felon part, had been planned as their opener. Go for the big push on the guest right out of the gate to generate some drama.

He rubbed his jaw as if she was really putting the screws to him. "Nancy, that's exactly why I asked to speak with you and address the world tonight. I, more than anyone, recognize that with great power comes great responsibility. The fact is that we were facing a climate crisis before the Lazarus Protocol went into effect, and we are facing one now—"

"But your actions made it worse."

"The actions of President Teller served to remind us of the real climate danger we were not facing up to. Not then, not now. Did Lazarus make the weather worse? Yes, of course, but we needed to wake up as a species. The Council of Corporations stands ready to help."

"The council..." Nancy's blue eye skewered him with a shrewd look while the green one looked innocent. "Tell us about this council. I think most of us wonder what is going on in your mysterious hideout on Mars."

"The council is a group of concerned citizens, businessmen and - women from some of the most powerful corporations in the world—"

"Family businesses, you mean."

"Why does that make a difference, Nancy?" She was definitely off script now, and it annoyed Anthony. The spotlight was supposed to stay on him.

"Family concerns might have a narrower set of interests than a public venture."

"I don't think so, Nancy, we all want the same—"

"Isn't it true that your council has made unilateral demands on the UN for people and resources? How is that in the best interests of Earth?

Shouldn't we be having a broad public debate about the role of private companies serving the public good?"

"I think we're a little beyond that point, Nancy, don't you?"

Her head cocked again. "How so?"

Anthony should have seen the trademark head tilt for what it was, but he pressed forward. "The public good is not being served by the disorganized governments of the UN. If they had worked with President Teller in the first place, Lazarus would have been a massive success—"

"So you blame the president for the situation we find ourselves in?"

Anthony shook his head. "The president has been a public servant of the highest order. He has the best interests of the entire planet in mind. The Twenty-First Century Marshall Plan—his idea, mind you—is a great first step in fixing our climate crisis once and for all."

They were back on script now. Nancy had pulled back when he said the words *first step*. Now she leaned forward. "Say more about that, Anthony. Our audience wants to know what you mean by first step."

"The council and I feel that we need to do more. Earth is in trouble, plain and simple, and we need a relief plan worthy of the size of the problem. In three days, at the United Nations in New York, I will announce the Taulke Renewal Initiative. This is a multiyear recovery plan backed by the council that will provide a final solution to our climate crisis."

Nancy sat back, her blue-green gaze studying him in stereo. Anthony could feel the recording drones whirring softly in his peripheral vision, capturing his strong profile. He resisted the urge to look at them. Let them think he was looking into the future, a place they wanted to be.

"Is everyone included in this recovery, Anthony? The New Earth Order, for instance?"

Anthony resisted the urge to clench his jaw. "The Neos are a unique segment of the population, Nancy. They have a parallel agenda."

"Parallel? Just in the past few days, we've seen uprisings in LUNa City and right here at Fort Hood. Are they working for you or against you?"

"I think you'll find that General Graves has the situation here well in hand. He has resolved the Neo uprising without loss of additional life. I have complete faith in the general and his abilities."

Nancy's head ticked slightly as she sent a pulsed message. "I agree with you, Anthony, which is why I've invited General Graves to join us along with the local Neo representative."

Anthony stared at her. The Taulke Renewal Initiative was the centerpiece of the entire segment. *He* was the whole show.

General Graves wore his battle dress uniform with creases and sweat stains from where he'd shed his body armor. His gray hair was tousled and he wore no makeup. Anthony suddenly felt conspicuous about his facial.

He escorted a tall, thin woman with silver hair and beautiful brown skin that glowed naturally, not like his temporary cosmetic treatment. Her dark eyes darted about the stage, fastened on Anthony for a moment, then flitted away. She was obviously nervous. He could use that.

Two more chairs appeared, and Graves and the woman sat down. Nancy lasered in on Graves.

"General Graves and Corazon Santos, welcome to the show. We understand you've just reached a truce of sorts. The Neos had taken over the Fort Hood command center in response to President Teller trying to arrest Ms. Santos, but you two managed to work it out without additional bloodshed."

The pair exchanged glances and Anthony saw a personal connection. There was respect there, admiration, maybe even more than that. He could use that, too.

Graves spoke first. "I think Mr. Taulke said it right, Ms. Watson—"

"Nancy, please, General."

Anthony cursed to himself. He should have used the first-name thing when he met Nancy. It was a classy move, as if he was giving her permission to call him by his first name.

Graves ducked his head. "Nancy, then. Mr. Taulke has the right idea. We need to solve this thing together. The Neos need to be part of the solution, not working against us. Mr. Taulke's council has the resources to effect real change, and he has the technology to make a difference in..."

A sudden thought seized Anthony's attention. If Nancy wanted to try to upstage him, two could play at that game. He sent an urgent message to Elise Kisaan. He had the Neo trump card: the blessed vessel of Cassandra, or whatever those lunatics called her. And she was part of his council. He should have thought of that before, but he'd been so busy trying to keep the spotlight on himself.

He half-listened to Nancy's mindless banter with her other guests until she interrupted his thoughts. "Anthony? How does all this fit in with your announcement at the UN?"

Elise appeared at the top of the ramp. Instead of answering Nancy, he stood and held out his hand to Elise. Her pregnancy was well along now and her belly thrust out of her slender frame like a basketball. She took mincing steps forward, peering down beside her outthrust belly as if afraid she might fall. Anthony met her halfway down the ramp and linked her arm in his.

She was dressed in a simple cream-colored dress that outlined her pregnant frame and also gave her a saintly look. Nancy stood, and so did the general and the Santos woman.

A careful makeup job had erased the dark circles under Elise's eyes, leaving the viewer with the impression that she was bursting with life. She looked every bit the religious figure.

But what happened next sealed it for Anthony. As he drew Elise into the bubble of bright light that surrounded the stage, her loose dress exploded with reflected illumination. Corazon Santos stepped forward and sank to her knees in front of Elise. The recording drones flocked to the intimate scene of worshipped and worshipper, ignoring Anthony entirely. One of them whispered past his cheek and he tried to swat it away.

Elise used a long, elegant hand to raise Corazon's bowed head. With billions of people watching, the pair locked eyes. Corazon's fingers found the other woman's hand and Elise guided it to her belly. The thin material of her dress rippled as the baby moved inside her. Santos began to cry silent tears of joy and adoration.

It was beautiful and unscripted and would play fabulously well in ultra-high-def. Anthony let himself fall back from the action. Doing anything to distract from this touching scene would only make him look petty.

He kept his face still as he gazed at the pair. He did his best to work up a tear just in case any cameras were on him.

But inside, his heart was a battleground of raging jealousy.

16

MING QINLAO • WESTERN CHINA

Ming trained in the high-ceilinged gymnasium in the basement of the main house of her father's estate. Set on top of a hill, the main house offered a commanding view of the surrounding countryside. Rolling hills of neatly tended gardens and tea plants, the oval lake at the base of the hill, the stone house abutting the high stone where the caretaker lived with his wife.

Here, in this pocket of serenity, surrounded by the sights and smells of nature, Ming could almost forget the weather wars that raged only a few hundred kilometers away.

The house itself had the feel of a castle, with an imposing stone exterior and a flagstone courtyard with a landing pad. But inside the building, her father had spared no expense in making the place modern. It was inside that she felt closest to him. He was a minimalist: there were rooms with nothing but a simple chair and lamp sitting on the warm bamboo floors—except when it came to his workshop. There, her father's creativity reminded Ming of Viktor's hoarder style of working on multiple projects at once.

Jie Qinlao had come to this country house when he needed to be alone. And now it was Ming's fortress of retreat.

No, not retreat, she told herself. Rebuilding.

In the gymnasium, she could tell the time of day by the light coming through the narrow, horizontal windows high up on the walls. In the early morning, the windows facing east glowed pink, then a bar of golden light crept down the wall. In the afternoon, the process reversed itself in the western-facing windows. If the sun was especially strong that day, she could see a whirlwind of dust motes glowing in the shaft of clean light.

She trained with Ito in the early morning, when the sun was still high on the wall, perfecting his blended martial arts version of hand-to-hand combat. He'd started teaching her this style when she was just eight, the training tuned just for her size, speed, and strength. All her life, Ming's opponents had almost always been larger than her. Her opponent, the theory went, had more reach and more power than her, so her style must strip away those advantages. She must get close and work inside the enemy's range of motion. Hit hard, hit fast, hit often, and then get back out.

Balance was the cornerstone of Ito's style of fighting. Without the ability to control every micro-move such that she could stay on her feet, any opponent worth their chopsticks would kick her ass every time.

For the first week, Ito had her do nothing but balance on one foot. Lean forward, lean back. Raise the free leg and grasp the outstretched big toe. Between the gravity working on her weakened muscles and the damage to her inner ear from the MoSCOW integration, the first few days were both painful and humiliating. Ito caught her hundreds of times in addition to the hundreds of times she crashed to the mats when working on her own.

But she got better. The muscle-building drugs helped, as did the acupuncture to stabilize the nerves of her inner ear.

When Ito was satisfied, they moved on to light sparring. Even with the pads, her weakened body still bruised. More drugs, more ice baths, more massages. She relearned the basics of the style again as if she was eight years old and just forming the muscle memory by repetition.

She lost track of the days. Ming's complete focus was on herself. Echo was locked away in a room in her mind.

When she was strong enough, Ito sent her on a morning run around the stone-walled perimeter of the estate. The first day was a walk-run combination, mostly walking, but she reveled in the smell of the dewy greenery from the tea leaves. Within a few days, she was running the full perimeter.

Weekly visits from a cosmeticist rejuvenated her hair growth and blended the skin grafts so she recognized her reflection in the mirror.

They shifted to traditional sparring, full contact. Ming took a beating three days in a row but refused to move her training schedule backwards. On the fourth day, she bested her master in two out of three rounds.

Ito licked a trickle of blood from his split lip. "My Little Tiger has returned."

Ming grinned but said nothing. Ito beat her on the next bout, but she made him work for it. She parried his thrust, spun her way inside his reach, and nailed an elbow into his gut. But before she could make her escape, his strong hand locked on to her free wrist and twisted. Ming felt her feet leave the ground as her body followed the sudden movement. She tried to counter, but Ito had gravity on his side and the mat rushed up to smack into her face.

Suddenly Echo was in her head, twisting her body, sweeping Ito's legs. She felt him crash to the floor next to her and she leaped on his chest, her arm raised to strike downward in a finishing blow.

Ito's eyes widened with surprise. "How did you do that?"

Ming lowered her hand. In all her time at the estate, she had pushed Echo aside, focusing on her own independent health. In order to tame the voice in her head, she needed her strength first. She rolled off his chest and to her feet.

"A reaction, that's all. Instinct."

Ming experienced a surge of energy in her limbs, the tips of her fingers tingling. It felt as if she'd suddenly leveled up in her skills, allowing Echo to kick in like some kind of ninja afterburner.

Ito got to his feet. He beckoned to her. "Again."

His movements felt ridiculously slow and telegraphed. Parry, parry, kick-punch, parry, spin. She seized his forearm and slammed him to the floor with more force than was necessary.

He got to his feet more slowly this time, favoring his shoulder. "You've changed. What happened?"

Ming shrugged. A flush of embarrassment swept up her neck as she realized how much she enjoyed putting Ito on the mat. He was an old man, she realized. And one who had given up his own freedom to help her heal.

When she'd first set up this scheme to come home, she just told Ito she needed his help. Never asking, never assuming he would even consider refusing her demands. She'd never even told him why.

And now she was making him eat mat like some spiteful child.

"I'm sorry." The words came out of her mouth with the threat of tears to follow. Ming tried to rein in her emotions, but failed. What was the matter with her?

Ito rolled his shoulder. "I'll live. You worry me, Little Tiger. You are a knife without a sheath, I fear. A blade that cuts without meaning to."

Ming thought about his words on her run later that morning. A few months ago, she wondered if she would ever walk again. Now, Ming was throwing her old instructor to the mat with impunity. She was indeed a weapon again, a force to be reckoned with.

The integration with the supercomputer known as MoSCOW had given her abilities, she could feel them, but had it changed her? The ground flashed beneath her feet as she ran faster and faster. Her pulse thundered in her ears.

MoSCOW, as painful as it was, had made her stronger, given her skills she'd never dreamed of ... but had it made her better?

Better than what?

She skidded to a halt, a cloud of dust catching up to her now-still feet. Echo was silent in her head, another testament to the completion of her integration with MoSCOW. Ming Qinlao had been reborn into ... into what?

Ming told herself that her father's death was what compelled her, but that wasn't what had changed her. In the string of events leading to this moment, Ming never would have gone on the mission with MoSCOW were it not for Anthony Taulke's lies. Her life would be completely different but for that deception.

She never would have left Ruben alone. MoSCOW would still be an experiment locked in Viktor Erkennen's lab. Elise Kisaan would have died in the explosion of the Neo space station.

And her father would still be dead.

All but for the lies of Anthony Taulke. His deception had set her on this course. She would avenge her father's death, but then her path led her back to Anthony Taulke's doorstep.

She felt the sting of sweat in her eyes, the sound of her breath, the smell of fresh tea leaves ripening in the morning sunshine. And she felt clarity of purpose.

The old Ming Qinlao was dead, replaced by a version that was half computer, half woman, and all business.

A Qinlao aircar passed overhead and lowered over the landing pad within the walls of the house. Ming sprinted home.

From the anonymity of a second-story window, Ming watched her mother's maglev chair move slowly across the yard. Ito emerged from the house, still clad in his workout gear.

He bowed to Wenqian and spoke to her. If he had been facing Ming, Echo would have allowed her to read his lips, but his back was to her. Her mother, on the other hand, was facing in her direction.

The old woman was slumped in her chair, her body no more than a slack bag of bones and sinew. But her mother's lips said to Ito: "I will see her now."

So her mother hadn't been fooled by Ming's faked death and had tracked her here. Ming's gaze swept the small room where she stayed, alighting on the 3-D picture of Ming and her father and the butterfly.

That was the only possible answer. It was the only item she'd brought with her from Shanghai. In spite of the situation, Ming smiled at the craftiness of her mother. The old woman had deliberately shown the picture to Ming, knowing it would prove irresistible to her daughter.

Ming blew out a breath at the ceiling. For all her newfound strength and clarity, meeting with her mother filled her with a dread she could not explain.

Ito appeared at the door. He saw the picture in her hand and his eyes narrowed for a split second. "Your mother wishes to see you."

"You told her I'm not here, of course."

A ghost of a smile. Ito stepped back to let her pass into the hallway.

Her mother's lips twisted as her daughter walked into the room. The old woman had slumped over in her chair, her shoulder and the side of her face pressed against the cushion. Ming gently centered her and tucked pillows around her frame to keep her upright. Her ribs felt like a sack of loose twigs under Ming's fingers. Her mother nudged away the amplifier with her chin—the extent of her range of motion. She normally used the amplifier to conduct a conversation with someone more than a foot or two from her face. She could still speak, but it came out as a whisper.

Ming lowered the chair and sat on the arm. She stroked her mother's thin gray hair.

"It is good to see you," her mother whispered. "And unexpected, as well. Your funeral was beautiful."

"I'm sorry," Ming said automatically. She wasn't, and it showed.

"You're not."

"No, I'm not."

Wenqian started to slump again and Ming held her up. Her rheumy eyes locked with Ming's and held on.

"This is about your father," she said.

Ming nodded. "I've changed, Mama. I can't explain it."

"I never should have given you that video. I was afraid..." She took a break, wheezing slightly. "I thought I might not see you again."

Ming chuckled. "If I hadn't stolen the picture, you might not have seen me again."

Wenqian's laugh was a sputtering of breaths. "I know you, Ming-child."

"You knew me, you mean."

Her mother's chin wavered—her version of shaking her head, Ming knew.

"You are my daughter. That will never change, no matter the circumstances..." More wheezing. Ming found the old woman's oxygen feed and looped the tube under her nose. The old woman breathed with her eyes closed, then opened them again with an effort.

"I see things in you. Your natures are stronger now—and at war. You are half angel and half animal. One will win."

Ming let a flash of anger show through. "She killed my father, Mama. She deserves what is coming to her."

"It's not her I'm worried about, Ming. It's you. Which side will win?"

Ming scowled. "You started this, Mama. I will finish it."

"I was wrong. Nothing will bring your father back." She pressed a slim disk into Ming's hand. "A life taken cannot be restored." Her hand nudged at Ming's thigh, a signal to move.

Ming stood and her mother engaged the chair's drive.

"Goodbye, Ming." The old woman's amplified voice felt cold and impersonal as it echoed throughout the room. The chair disappeared out the door.

Ming stayed where she was until she heard the engines on the aircar hum into life. A shadow traversed the window as the vehicle took to the air.

She held her palm flat, held the disk up to the light. It was carved from green jade, a simple medallion in the combined teardrop shape of the traditional yin-yang symbol.

Half the medal was creamy white-green and carved with an angel's wing. The other half was a deep green jade, almost black in places, with the face of a snarling wolf.

Half animal, half angel.

The same crackle of energy and purpose she had felt on her run earlier surged back. Ming found a silver chain and attached the medallion. The disk hung heavy, centered over her breastbone.

Half animal, half angel. One will win.

It was time to decide which one.

17

ADRIANA RABH • NEW YORK CITY

From her perch on the Louis XV chaise, Adriana studied Tony Taulke as he stood at the window. He raised his drink to his lips and she caught him in profile. So much like his father as a young man—and so unlike him at the same time.

Young Anthony had been an unabashed optimist, as if he could will his projects into existence by sheer force of personality and enthusiasm. As an early entrepreneur, it was nearly impossible to say no to Anthony Taulke. There was a group of people still who said he built his ByteCoin empire on bullshit and bravado—and they were mostly right.

But they were the sour ones, the ones who had not drunk the Taulke Kool-Aid and tasted the sweetness of victory—and money. Lots and lots of money. But Anthony had proven to be more than just a pretty face when he also managed to exit out of the volatile secondary market at exactly the right time.

Accumulation of capital and preservation of capital. The foundational concepts of true wealth. He had managed both in spectacular fashion.

But Anthony Taulke, then barely thirty years old, had not rested on his laurels. He sought out new frontiers. Space elevator in Darwin, Australia. The Mars project. The weather control experiment. Not all of them worked out, but no one ever accused Anthony Taulke of thinking too small.

Adriana nursed her own drink, enjoying the cool bite of the bespoke gin in her cocktail. Tony could have been her son, she mused. She was older than Anthony by a few years—not enough to matter—and they had flirted in the same circles, but never connected in a meaningful way. That was her fault. The Rabhs were old money; Taulke was nouveau riche, and his wild moves in the market by no means ensured he would retain his riches. When it came time to start a family, Anthony had settled on a commoner and the result of his coupling was Tony Taulke.

The subject of her thoughts turned from the window just then and she caught him in an unguarded moment. He was not like his father. There was no enthusiasm there, no optimism. But there was energy and plenty of intelligence. His father might secretly mourn over the young man's lack of certain qualities, but the ones he did possess were exactly the ones Adriana needed right now.

She used her retinal display to turn on the wallscreen. A clip of Anthony's interview played without sound. The elder Taulke smiled at Nancy Watson and said something witty. This was at the beginning of the interview, before that disastrous part at the end where Tony's father lost control of the narrative.

"You can turn it off, Adriana," Tony said. "I've seen it plenty of times already."

Indeed, it was hard not to have seen the interview. Anthony had managed to direct almost every commercial channel on the planet to the live interview, and the following days were nothing but a nonstop commercial and pundit fest of speculation over the details of the Taulke Renewal Initiative. At least he'd managed to regain part of the narrative by announcing General Graves and Corazon Santos would be his special guests at the UN ceremony this evening.

She chuckled to herself as she wondered how Graves liked being a prop at one of Anthony's media spectacles. Her decision to put him in charge over Teller had proved prescient. She now had Teller at bay and a conduit into the inner workings of Anthony's new endeavor. But she needed more. She needed to insulate herself from Elise Kisaan's meddlings on the council. She needed an inside man.

"We've never really gotten to know one another, Tony," she began.

Tony drained his drink. "It's a little tough when I'm stuck in the old man's shadow." He crossed the room in a few loose strides and took a seat across from her. "Still, I'm always willing to make new friends."

"And what is your opinion of the New Earth Order?"

Tony shrugged and slouched in his seat. "The Neos? Religious crackpots that will burn themselves out eventually."

Not the answer she expected. "You don't see a linkage between LUNa City and the Fort Hood fiasco?"

"Such as?" Tony was challenging her, she realized too late. He was daring her to name another council member as a traitor. Maybe she had underestimated him after all.

"The Neo space station was destroyed," Adriana began, "but Elise Kisaan managed to escape and secure herself a place on the council and maintain the loyalty of the Neo masses. You saw the same spectacle I did of the Santos woman touching her belly and weeping on the newsfeeds, right?"

Tony propped an ankle on the opposite knee and waggled his foot as if he was already bored with this topic. "You're trying to connect dots between a few unrelated incidents. Elise is a symbol to a few diehard zealots, nothing more. She's harmless. Easily dealt with."

Adriana sniffed. This was not the answer she expected from the son of the man whose fusion reactor fuel supply was being threatened. Or maybe he was bluffing.

"So you'll have no issue if I take some action against her?"

Tony's lips thinned. "I would think a woman in your position would be loath to 'take action,' as you call it. If anything were to go awry, you'd be the obvious suspect."

"You have another idea?"

Tony's eyes defocused for a second and then there was a knock on the door. "That's for you," he said.

The young man who entered was mid-twenties, medium height, with brown hair that was already thinning. She wondered why he didn't get some cosmetic work done to fix that. He had a wiry frame that made his every move a study in efficiency. His dark eyes swept the room, taking in everything at a glance.

"Eugene Fischer, meet Adriana Rabh," Tony said without bothering to get up. "I think Eugene can offer the kind of services you might need on an exclusive basis. He has many talents."

Adriana rose and shook his hand, feeling every tendon and muscle in the young man's grip, and felt his quick eyes measuring her. She realized now why he hadn't bothered with the cosmetic treatment. He looked ordinary, completely unremarkable—and that was a gift in his line of work.

Eugene Fischer was a hit man.

"Pleasure, Ms. Rabh," he murmured. An unremarkable voice for an unremarkable man.

She pointed to the book stuck under his arm. He saw her looking and offered it to her. It was a hardback volume of *The Sun Also Rises* by Ernest Hemingway. She hadn't bothered with reading an actual paper volume in decades, but when she passed it back, Fischer carefully tucked it back under his arm.

"Yeah, about that," Tony chimed in. "Eugene is an old soul, born in the wrong era, I think. He's not a big fan of technology. No implants, no integrated tech. He likes to keep a low profile. Reading is his only vice. He's good at what he does, so I keep him around for special assignments."

"I see." Adriana nodded at Fischer and pulsed a message to her staff to arrange for Mr. Fischer's security clearance. Eugene read the room and left as unobtrusively as he came. "You seem to have come prepared, Tony. I don't know what to say."

Tony came alive. In an instant, he went from slouching insolence to seated upright at attention. "Then perhaps I can put words in your mouth, Adriana. Young Eugene is a master, an artiste, if you will, in the finer aspects of corporate problem-solving. As it so happens, I have needs of my own that you can help me with."

Adriana took her seat, arranging the fold of her dress over her knee with extra care. She *had* underestimated this young man. Tony had not only anticipated her needs, but arranged a very high-risk solution and pressed it on her. She was now implicated with Mr. Eugene Fischer, hit man.

She pushed those thoughts aside. "What can I do for you, Tony?"

"I want the GEMDrive tech. I need you to squeeze Teller until his cotton ball head pops off or I get some answers." So that's what was sticking in his

craw. The tech that powered the mysterious Haven ships. That stunt had
caught them all by surprise. The ships were on their way to another solar
system and the secret of their superfast drive with them.

Adriana regarded him coolly. "You know Teller says he had no knowledge of the GEMDrive program. It was started three decades ago and
buried in the depths of the black operations budget."

Tony launched himself out of his chair and paced to the window. "I
know what they say, but there has to be a record somewhere. I refuse to
believe that not a single scientist exists who can replicate the drive."

Adriana suppressed a sneer. For all his hipster cool, Tony was just like
his old man. He'd been bested and all he could think about was getting
even. A family flaw, it seemed. One she could play to her advantage.

"I'll do my best," she said.

Tony whirled. "I just gave you a weapon, Adriana, I expect more than
just an effort. I need results."

She stood slowly and walked to the window, never breaking eye contact,
always advancing. He stood his ground, but his gaze softened.

"I said I would do my best, Tony. I mean what I say."

He squinted at her, then nodded. "Okay. I need your help on this, Adriana. It's important."

She air-kissed the space next to her ear and watched him leave. He had
swagger, that one. The question was, did he have the balls to make the big
calls, the life-and-death, bet-the-company kinds of calls that left you empty
inside but also launched you into the realm of business genius.

Adriana shaded her eyes as she peered into the late afternoon sunshine.
There was more smoke in the atmosphere today from the Canadian forest
fires. The sun was a hazy disk that turned the cityscape below her
blood red.

She had made those kinds of choices before and she would make them
again. The issue with Elise Kisaan was shaping up to be one of them, a
choice that could go either way.

The way that woman—Corazon Santos—had dropped to her knees at
the sight of Elise. There was a disturbing aura of sainthood there. If she
went after Elise directly, that would only turn her into a martyr. No, she

needed to find a way to break Elise, crush her spirit without killing her outright.

Adriana sighed. The red engulfing the city sprawled beneath her deepened.

As a mother, she did not make her decision lightly. As a woman of power, she knew it had to be made.

Elise Kisaan would live. Her child needed to die.

18

WILLIAM GRAVES • UN HEADQUARTERS, NEW YORK CITY

Graves pressed his back against the column in the center of the United Nations ballroom and clutched his glass of seltzer water. The last time he'd been in this building, Teller and Adriana Rabh had hoodwinked him into a new job. That was *not* going to happen tonight.

He surveyed the assembled guests. The women in brightly colored gowns and the men in tuxedoes, their happy chatter filling the air with a noisy drone. His own dress uniform with the row of miniature medals felt gaudy and pretentious.

It was times like these that made a man seriously reconsider his life choices. These elites were worlds apart from the common man. The brilliant pearly shimmer of the gown on a woman a few meters away probably cost more than Graves's annual salary and the bar bill for these guzzling people could run a small city in Africa for a month.

And somehow he was in the middle of it.

It was the property of inertia, he decided. He'd entered West Point at eighteen and tackled every challenge put in front of him without ever asking if the challenge was right or was even what he wanted for his life. From a wet-behind-the-ears infantry officer to a commander in the Sinai to leading the Disaster Mitigation Corps to this ... whatever this was. He'd just followed the dots until someone told him to stop.

But no one ever did. And so he was here, locked in a room full of glad-handing politicians and their plus-ones, each sizing up the other as their next meal on the ladder of upward mobility.

The setting sun, red with atmospheric haze, blazed through the floor-to-ceiling windows. A pair of security drones shot past, just outside the building point-defense perimeter. They flashed across the red-orange ball, their deadly silhouettes outlined for a split second.

Millions of people lived in the city below this lofty perch. Millions who would be impacted by Anthony Taulke's announcement tonight. They might watch on their data glasses, but more likely they would consume it encapsulated in some other newsfeed or comedy show. Many of them wouldn't even care. They would tell themselves that what was said here tonight would not change the trajectory of their lives.

And they would be wrong.

They were like the proverbial frog being boiled alive on the stove, unable to sense the heating water until it was too late. Graves grimaced. With climate change, baked alive might be a better analogy.

"Is this a private party, General, or can anyone join in?" Cora's dark eyes flashed with humor. "You look very handsome in your dress uniform."

Graves grunted a reply, unwilling to acknowledge her. With the speed of political will, the incident at Fort Hood had disappeared in favor of a more palatable narrative where Graves and Corazon Santos had unified the Neos and the government objectives. The ten dead were collateral damage.

Cora moved closer and rested her hand on his arm. Her fingernails were painted deep red, the same color as her dress. "I'm very sorry about your soldiers, William. They did not deserve what happened to them. My people did not deserve it either. But you and I, we were able to move past that. It could have been much worse."

Graves gritted his teeth. It could have been so much worse. Their trust in each other had averted potentially hundreds of casualties.

"Please," she said. "I want your friendship, William. Perhaps we can start over."

Graves sighed and nodded at her empty glass. "What are you drinking, Cora?"

"Soda water. I feel like I need to keep a clear head in this pit of piranhas."

Graves chuckled to himself as he refilled their glasses. When he turned around, he saw Cora for the first time. She was dressed in a long crimson gown that hugged her slender figure. The slash of color across her chest left one shoulder bare. The muscles of her upper arms rippled under her skin when she reached for the glass. Her long sliver hair had been curled and drawn into a chignon at the back of her neck, exposing her Neo tattoo for all to see.

"You look beautiful," Graves said.

Cora's red painted lips parted in a dazzling smile. "Thank you. I feel like a fool in this dress, in this room ..." She let her words trail away.

"I know what you mean." Graves returned to his post against the column. "I don't belong here."

"Where did you grow up, William?"

Graves mentioned his family's home on the outskirts of Boston, then an anecdote about his late sister Jane. That led to a description of the family lighthouse in Maine and his fear of heights, which he somehow connected to an appointment to West Point and his service in the Sinai Wars. Before he knew it, Graves had been speaking for twenty minutes, captivated by Cora's dark eyes. He stopped himself, blushing.

"I'm sorry," he said. "I don't normally talk this much. It's not what I do."

Cora's fingers found his and she gave them a quick squeeze. "It's okay. Your secrets are safe with me, William."

"What about you, Cora? I know nothing about you."

"Oh, come now, General. Military intelligence has been watching me for months, years even. I have no secrets from you."

"No," Graves said, and it was true. Their dossier on Corazon Santos was uncomfortably thin. They suspected she was a doctor, but there was no record of medical school anywhere in her background. She had no police record under her name or any other. They weren't even completely sure of her country of origin. The intel community was split between Brazil and Argentina.

"Where did you grow up, for example?" Graves said.

A tritone sounded. "Ladies and gentlemen, please move into the adjoining room for the next part of the evening."

Cora laughed, a sound that made Graves's pulse race. Had he ever heard her laugh before? Had he ever even seen her with her guard down?

"I believe you Americans call that 'saved by the bell,'" she said, touching his hand again.

An usher showed them to their assigned seats in the front row, where Graves learned he was sitting next to Cora. "Looks like you're stuck with me," he said.

"I can think of worse places to be."

The chairs in the ballroom were bunched close together to allow as much room as possible on either side of the stage for the press pool. Floating screens along the wall showed a looping video, a promo for the Taulke Renewal Initiative. Graves could have linked his data glasses in, but he didn't bother. It was the normal baloney about "fixing" disasters made by people who had no idea what it took to recover from a disaster.

Instead of air transports filled with nonperishable food and tents, the vid showed grinning children playing tag in a grassy field and a woman handing out fresh bread to well-groomed young men and women in native dress. Their eyes were friendly and full of hope.

Graves had been to the front lines where hope was a commodity in short supply. The people he'd met were dirty and desperate. Dirty with the kind of ground-in grime that comes from weeks without a chance to bathe. Desperate for one thing—anything, really—in their life to be the same from one day to the next. That was what life on the edge looked like.

Cora's bare left shoulder pressed against his uniform. She pointed to the screen. "That's what he's really after."

The vid had changed again. The Earth viewed from space, the sun line creeping across the globe. Animated dots like a grid checkered the surface. The image zoomed in on one to show a satellite with a comms array facing downward, toward the planet. A pretend signal shot downward to the ground and a newly planted field received a gentle rain shower. The sun came back out and morphed into a flare with the Taulke family logo zooming back out into space.

Weather control. What was it with Anthony Taulke and his weather control obsession? He'd tried twice and failed twice—why not just go live on Mars and be done with it?

"He thinks he can pick up where the New Earth Order left off," Cora said, her tone scornful.

Graves looked at her in a new light. "You don't agree?"

"Cassandra's teachings have been perverted by men like Anthony Taulke and his council. The New Earth Order in its purest form is about restoring our planet to health, not controlling the weather." She gestured at the screen. "This is a distraction from their real goal."

"Which is?" She had Graves's attention now.

"Domination, of course. People are expendable. What they care about are the resources. Food, mostly." Cora leaned in close enough that he could smell her faint perfume and feel the gentle pulse of her breath against his cheek. "In the past year, Taulke's council has launched pilot operations on Titan, Callisto, and any number of asteroids. What do all those operations need to be successful? Resources. Smart people, skilled labor, and most of all food."

Graves sat back in his chair. Why had he never seen an intel assessment on this concept? "So you're going to launch a rebellion?" he said.

Cora offered him a quizzical look, then shook her head. "Not me, William. The Child. I serve the Child of Cassandra. She will set her people free."

Graves stared at her. She had sounded so sane—up until the Child nonsense. It was all he could do not to snort. How could a baby stop the Council of Corporations?

"You do not believe me, but you have a part to play, William. A big part. I have seen it."

She faced the stage, her profile in repose. Beautiful, charismatic, and completely out of her mind.

A ripple of applause distracted him from Cora.

Anthony Taulke's son, Tony, was at the podium. Graves had seen the young man in the newsfeeds and on YourVoice, but never in person. Now that he was a scant eight feet away and above them, Graves was able to make a close study.

On the surface, with his square jaw and curly dark hair, he looked remarkably like a younger version of his father. But on closer inspection, Graves saw subtle differences. It was in how they held themselves, Graves decided. A chin-out, face-the-world attitude versus a bob and weave. The old man, for all his foibles, was an idealist, who said what he said because he believed it to be true. Anthony was the height of hubris. *I want this thing to be true, so it must be true.*

But the son ... Tony was a realist. A guy who believed not only that he could take whatever he wanted, but that he was entitled to whatever he wanted. He would never say that, of course. Tony was the kind of man who would smile sweetly at a baby even as he stole her candy. Not because he was hungry, but just because.

The young man's gaze swept over the quiet audience, lighting on Graves for a split second, then moving on. Behind him, Anthony sat flanked by Adriana Rabh on one side and Teller and the UN secretary-general on the other. Tony's vacant seat was next to Adriana. The wall behind them was all windows. The sun was nearly gone, leaving a dusky glow on the horizon. The pair of security drones flashed by like a reminder that all was not well in the world at large.

The cloud of tiny indoor news drones ebbed and flowed as the networks jockeyed for the best angle on Taulke the younger.

When Tony spoke, it was with an intensity that startled Graves. "Tonight I have the distinct pleasure of introducing a man who means everything to me. A man whom I have looked up to my whole life. My hero, really. My father, Anthony Taulke."

Thunderous applause. Graves and Cora got to their feet along with everyone else. Not because they wanted to clap, but because everyone behind them had already gotten to their feet.

Anthony Taulke hugged his son and kissed Adriana Rabh on the cheek before he moved to the podium. He gripped the sides like he was commanding a ship. Behind him, the security drones flashed by, their navigation lights blinking in the darkening sky.

Graves had worked with Anthony up close and personally when they'd outfitted missiles with the nanites of the Lazarus Protocol. He'd studied the man's mannerisms and seen him under pressure.

But the Anthony Taulke before him now was a man brimming with heartfelt emotion. His knuckles turned white under the strain of his grip on the podium and the crowd hushed. Even the press pool seemed subdued. When Anthony looked up, tears glistened in his eyes.

"I have led a fortunate life," he began, his voice husky with emotion. "A life of privilege and wealth and opportunity. I have tried to apply my skills and my resources where they could best serve my fellow humans." He took a break and squinted into the distance as if he was trying to think of what to say.

"When President Teller approached me about his next-generation Marshall Plan, I was enthusiastic in my support." Teller straightened in his chair and beamed for the cameras, nodding in agreement. The security drones flashed by.

"But then I asked myself: Is that all I can do for the planet that has given me so much? Is the Marshall Plan equal to the task of stopping—and even reversing—climate change?" He shook his head slowly as if the idea just came to him. Teller's smile suddenly looked plastic.

"No, it's not. I need to commit *myself*—not my money or my company, myself—to this cause. That is why tonight I am announcing the Taulke Renewal Initiative, headed by me, to solve this problem once and for all."

More applause. A single security drone buzzed behind Anthony. The thought registered in Graves's mind. Why one? They always operated in pairs to protect the other's blind spot. The people around him were standing again and he did the same automatically, but the unpaired drone floated in his head like a loose bit of information.

The noise was deafening in the high-ceilinged hall, waves of applause reverberating from every surface. Then, under his feet, Graves felt a pulsing motion.

Regular, rhythmic, like the rapid heartbeat of a small animal ... or the firing of a point-defense cannon. He stood on his tiptoes and swiveled his head to see all the windows.

There, in the final gasp of the sunset, he saw a flash of light. A drone, surrounded by tracer fire, was headed directly for the windows.

Graves reacted. He seized Cora and threw her to the ground, pushing her up against the edge of the stage.

The drone fired. Graves saw the spits of light and the windows behind

Anthony Taulke dissolved in a shower of glass. He lunged onto the stage. Adriana, Tony, and Teller were gone, but Anthony stood there, transfixed by the oncoming wave of glass. Graves saw Taulke's body stutter as one of the slugs took him in the chest. He seized the collar of Anthony Taulke's jacket and hauled him backwards as hard as he could.

19

MING QINLAO • OUTSKIRTS OF SHANGHAI, CHINA

Ming crouched in the shadow of a stone wall, letting the night sounds flow around her. A rat scampered across the faint cone of light thrown by the lamp hanging over the cobblestone street. The lights were of the made-to-look-old variety, fashioned in the shape of an ancient lantern possibly carried by some historical figure.

The building on the other side of the twelve-foot-high wall was like that. New, but made to look ancient. Except for the square, one-story structure in the center. That one was real. Once upon a time it had been the home of her Qinlao ancestors. Ming's father's grandfather had been a farmer, and the brick and stucco building with the red tile roof ornamented with fanciful dragons on the corners was real.

Everything else about the compound was a lie.

She remembered her father's amused comments about her Auntie Xi's passion project. Her aunt had found the old Qinlao homestead and moved it to Shanghai. Every brick and carved dragon head was disassembled, restored, and rebuilt in detail in her compound outside of the city.

But that was not enough for Xi Qinlao. With the three-room structure at the center, she built an entire village around it. Wherever possible, she used native materials, but when those were not available she created authentic replicas. Hence the lamps that lit her authentic alleys so poorly.

She pressed her cheek against the stone, feeling the vibrations on the other side of the wall. The heavy tread of a man's boot, an aircar passing overhead, the faint sound of music. All the sounds of a household settling in for the night.

Ming stood, pressing her back against the wall. She was wearing the skintight MoSCOW suit, the new one from Viktor. He had made many improvements. The haptic sensors embedded in the suit exterior sang with data about the night around her, so much so that she had to use Echo to manage the flow. The body armor moved with her like silk over skin. And the camouflage system worked now.

She lifted the hood and dropped it over her head so the leading edge came just to her eyebrows. A simple command to Echo and Ming Qinlao became a hole in the darkness.

Ming scaled the wall in two bounds, feeling the suit augment her muscles. She crouched atop the wall for a second, then dropped lightly to the ground.

The deserted alley around her was barely lit by more of the ancient-looking lanterns. She knew enough not to be fooled by the low-tech shell of this faux village. Any guards she encountered would be well-armed and using infrared enhancements, so the light wasn't really necessary for them to do their jobs. In her MoSCOW suit, Ming would appear like a dim silhouette of a woman-shaped ghost.

But she had no intention of meeting a guard face-to-face. With a quick leap, she landed on the roof of a one-story building. The red clay tiles looked black in the dark. She carefully climbed to the peak of the roof. These tiles were made of heavy ceramic and held in place by gravity. A false step could loosen one and cause the kind of noise that would make even the most inattentive guard look up.

She ran lightly along the roof peak, the soft tread of her suit gripping the narrow capping tiles. Auntie Xi's compound was laid out in rings like the Forbidden City, all encircling the center humble dwelling where the Qinlao dynasty had begun. At the end of the first building, Ming leaped across the space to the second row of buildings, then a third and a fourth.

Her breath sang in her throat and Ming felt the rise of invincibility in her chest. The jade medallion given to her by her mother was layered between her suit and the bare skin of her body, leaving a dead spot in her senses. Fitting, Ming thought as she launched across another row of buildings.

And then she was at her destination. Ming engaged Echo to help her assess the low-slung building at the center of the compound. Cracked stucco covered baked clay bricks. A lintel of cut stone hung over the open doorway. Golden light spilled onto the courtyard and the twanging sound of a zither floated into the night.

Ming shook her hooded head. Her Auntie Xi was a woman in conflict with herself. By day, she was the picture of modernity, the hard-bitten executive who reveled in the intricacies of finance. By night, she retreated to an ancient replica house to play an even more ancient instrument.

Another careful scan of the area showed no guards, no cameras, no drones, no security of any kind. Ming dropped to the ground. She would have expected her Auntie Xi to have better security.

The mournful sound of the zither wound into the night. A vague memory tugged at Ming. An image of her mother—before she was taken ill —playing the same instrument. It stopped her. What was she doing here?

Echo prodded her forward. She had a mission to accomplish.

Ming eyed the doorway, then flattened herself against the wall of the building. The time for second thoughts was past. She stepped into the doorway.

The square front room of the homestead house was lit by another of the faux lanterns. The rough stone floor of the entranceway gave way to thick woven mats, undoubtedly made from authentic wild grasses. The walls were dull yellow plaster, with faint trowel marks frozen in the material. Facing her on the far wall was a framed photograph. Not a modern 3-D live photo, but an old-timey printed photo in fading sepia. It showed a boy and girl, grinning madly for the camera. The boy was missing his front teeth, which would have put him at about seven years old. The girl was older and taller with long dark hair.

Although she'd never seen the photo before, Ming knew it was of her father and his older sister, Xi.

Ming peeled back her hood and disengaged the camouflage mode of her suit, making her fully visible to the woman playing the zither.

The music stopped with a discordant clang.

"Ming," the woman breathed.

Ming smiled at her, enjoying the rush of emotion that surged inside her chest. Pride at having fooled the old woman. Satisfaction that her plan had worked. And an icy rage to underpin all of it.

"Tell me about my father," Ming said in a low voice.

Auntie Xi shifted. Ming watched her every movement. Echo was on full alert. Her aunt surely had a security signal with her staff for emergencies. She'd probably already sent it.

"I don't know—"

"How he died," Ming cut in. "I want to know why you killed him."

Xi's face flushed. "Why I killed him? Your father died in an accident in the—"

"He gave you everything you ever wanted." Ming pointed at the photo. "You were poor kids and he gave you wealth beyond your wildest dreams. And yet that wasn't enough for you."

Xi struggled to her feet. She was wearing traditional dress, a long heavy robe with a woven belt. She even dressed the part when playacting history, but Echo flagged the jade brooch on her lapel as oddly out of place in this setting. The zither belched out a twanging chorus as her knee bumped it.

"I loved my brother," she said in a heated voice. "You know that, Ming. Whatever I did, I did for him and for our legacy."

Ming's gaze ran over her aunt's face. Her aging skin was stretched tightly across her cheekbones, her thin lips a red slash in her face, her deep green eyes flashed with anger, and her dark hair was pulled back into a bun.

It all looked like Auntie Xi. Except it wasn't.

Ming gripped the woman's robe and dragged her close. "Who are you?"

"Ming." The woman's voice faltered and Echo detected a provincial accent breaking through under the stress. "You're hurting me."

The brooch. Ming snatched the pin from the woman's lapel and crushed it between her fingers. The cracked shell revealed a camera.

The woman squealed in pain as Ming twisted her head to look for the transmitter buried in her ear. She tossed the impostor hard against the wall and the counterfeit Xi collapsed to the floor.

A trap.

Ming spun, whipping the hood over her head and engaging camouflage mode at the same time. She could hear the quiet tread of boots on the cobblestones in the courtyard, the suppressed breathing of soldiers, the smell of their weapons.

And they had her surrounded.

The suit, sensing the spike of adrenaline in her body, tightened around her muscles. Her mind raced as Echo searched for options. The narrow window was the obvious escape port. They would have that covered.

She spied the stone lintel over the door. It stuck out a bare four centimeters from the plaster wall. In a flash, she snatched up the lantern and hurled it out the window, then spidered up the wall and stretched her body over the door. She dug her fingers into the plaster and held on.

The lantern through the window had the desired effect of drawing their attention. She closed her eyes to concentrate on the sounds around the building. Eight ... nine ... ten people were out there.

Auntie Xi hadn't underestimated her after all.

A whispered instruction, the crunch of boots on stone. Ming knew what was coming next. She clenched her eyes shut, thankful for the protective hood over her ears.

The blast of the concussion grenade nearly dislodged her from the wall. Nearly. Ming struggled to catch her breath but hung on. Crushed plaster sifted between her fingers to the floor.

There were three in the first wave. The first man through the door put a three-round burst into the impostor's body without a second thought, the second person swept the opposite side of the room, while the third stopped directly below Ming in the doorway.

"Clear!" they all shouted.

A flurry of activity in the other two rooms sounded as the assault teams swept the tiny house.

"Where the fuck is—" the one directly below Ming started.

She dropped her legs onto his shoulders and twisted his head sharply to the right. Using the momentum of his fall, she hit the floor on her back and used her legs to hurl his limp body at the second man. They crashed back into the zither, releasing a cacophony of discord.

The third guard—a woman, Ming realized—had her weapon up, searching for a target. She sprayed the room at waist height to avoid hitting her prone companions.

But Ming, still in camouflage, was on the floor. She reached up to grip the barrel of her rifle, then swept the guard's feet out from under her. She hit the floor hard, but rolled instantly, avoiding Ming's heel strike where her face would have been.

"In here!" the soldier shouted in Mandarin.

Ming's next punch knocked her back against the wall, silencing her call for help. She pounced on the fallen soldier, but the woman would not give up. Her frantic fingers tried to find Ming's eyes and tore back her hood instead. With a final frustrated cry, Ming smashed her fist into the woman's face.

She whipped the hood back in place to find that it was torn. Ming cursed as another soldier came through the door. She took him out with a swift kick across the face, then launched herself through the broken window.

The cobblestones of the courtyard were rough across her back as Ming broke her fall with a somersault. A lone soldier was in charge of guarding this side of the courtyard. He saw the flash of movement from her damaged camouflage suit and fired immediately.

In the slow-motion processing of Echo, Ming saw sparks from two bullets hitting the cobblestones skip away from her before the third impacted her torso and she was thrown backwards into the shadows.

Ming saw the stars in the night sky winking above her. She smelled damp stone and dirt as she drew in a fresh breath. The body armor had saved her, but the camouflage of the suit was failing. Any second now, she'd be completely exposed.

The soldier called out as he advanced. "I have her!"

He turned on a light on the barrel of his weapon and the spotlight searched back and forth as he tried to find her in the shadows. Ming's hand crept to the carbon smartglass knife she kept on her calf. If she drew it too soon, he'd see the movement. Echo made her reflexes fast, but not faster than a bullet.

She could hear the others regrouping in the house, finding the bodies in the front room.

The spotlight was a meter away now ... still too far. Her grip tightened on the hilt of the knife. Any second now, he'd see the spot where her hood was torn.

A half-meter away...

Ming turned off the camouflage and she sprang into existence right at the soldier's feet. He recoiled in fright, just as she had hoped. His rifle went off, mere centimeters from her head, but she was already moving.

From between his legs, she stabbed upwards, searching for the femoral artery. She felt a gush of warmth flow over her gloved fingers and she slid behind him. He tried to spin around, to engage her again, but she nailed him in the back with both feet.

Camouflage broken, hurting from the bullet hit to her armor and covered in a man's blood, Ming shimmied up the nearest pillar and rolled onto the tile roof. Beneath her, the courtyard erupted in confusion as they discovered the dead soldier.

Ming pushed herself to a kneeling position and got to her feet.

Then she ran.

20

WILLIAM GRAVES • NEW YORK CITY

The Neo hacker den was in the Bronx. Not the nice part of the Bronx, the other part. And not in one of the high-rises in the not-nice part, but in a below-ground hovel positioned such that the best way to make a tactical approach was from below, via the old sewer system.

Graves breathed through his mouth to avoid the stench that threatened to make him gag. Although the atmosphere was technically breathable, the FBI prep team at the top of the manhole entrance six blocks away had offered him a gas mask. He'd refused out of some tough-guy machismo and now he was beginning to regret it.

He resisted the urge to touch the brick walls that glistened in the glow of his headlamp. No telling what kind of bacterial scourge lived down here. A sharp movement at floor level a few meters ahead caught his attention, made him startle.

"Just a rat, general," Special Agent Craft said over his shoulder.

"Biggest goddamn rat I've ever seen."

Craft snickered. "Yeah, they grow pretty big down here."

They both wore knee-high rubber boots as protection against the puddles of fetid water that slopped at their ankles. They would probably protect him from a rat bite, too. A normal-sized rat, that is.

"I never knew these tunnels were down here," Graves said, more to change the subject than because he cared. All this closeness was starting to get to him.

"Yeah, pretty cool, huh?" Craft reached out and stroked the wall with his gloved hand. "Some of these tunnels date from the early 1900s. You can still see the original brick. They've all been bypassed now by newer pipes and drainage systems, but some of these old tunnels are still around."

Craft, who had struck Graves at their first meeting as a no-nonsense, just-the-facts-ma'am kind of guy, had a wistful tone to his old-school Brooklyn accent. In fact, Graves had attributed their quick success in finding the bomber at Anthony Taulke's UN announcement to Craft's bulldog attitude.

"We have positive confirmation they're in the house?" he asked.

Craft paused for a breath. The smell was denser here and Graves wished again for a gas mask. The FBI agent nodded. "They're in there. As soon as we send the street team after them from above, they'll skedaddle down here. And then we've got 'em. No muss, no fuss." He made a dusting motion with his hands.

Graves still wasn't convinced. It just felt too easy. Why go to the trouble of hacking the UN security system and turning a security drone into a weapon—neither action a small feat of technical prowess—and then hang around New York? If it had been him, he'd be in Vancouver by now, maybe somewhere in Asia that wasn't flooded or being threatened by a massive storm or an earthquake ... maybe he was answering his own question. The United States was one of the better places to be, but it was a big country. He'd at least have gone to Kansas or Missouri.

Craft paused next to a ladder that disappeared up into darkness. "This is it," he said. "The assault team is up there ready to snatch them up. Easy-peasy." He made another dusting motion with his hands.

Graves wished this guy would stop telling him how simple this was going to be. He put his booted foot on the first rung and started to climb, leaving Craft steadying the ladder.

The ladder brought him to another tunnel. This one had rough concrete walls and smelled like there was fresh air being supplied from somewhere. The space was lit by intense floodlights set up in a ring, making Graves squint in the glare. Through narrowed eyes, he saw a gloved hand reach out and he grasped it, letting the man lift him the last few feet.

As his vision adjusted, he found himself standing in a circle of six black-suited agents with FBI stenciled in yellow across the front and back of their bulky body armor and their helmets. Craft clambered up beside him. "Turn those goddamned lights off," he said in a harsh stage whisper.

All the lights went out except for one, leaving purple afterimages in Graves's vision.

"What's our status, Nichols?" Craft said, less harshly this time.

"Standing by, sir," said the man beside Graves. "I can send you the inside feed if you want it."

"Do that, and send it to the general as well. He needs to let Mr. Taulke know we're taking all possible precautions to take this asshole alive."

Graves slid on his data glasses and waited for the pulsed prompt from Nichols. By Mr. Taulke, Craft meant Tony. As far as he knew, Anthony was still in a medically induced coma. He'd live, but when they finally woke him up he was going to wish he hadn't.

Graves's last-ditch effort to pull Anthony off the stage at the UN had probably saved his life. Basically, his body was one enormous bruise now, but he was alive and that was what mattered—at least that's what Tony said.

Tony himself was a hero of sorts for getting Adriana Rabh off the stage before the window blew in and shredded them both. He'd taken a few shards of glass in the arm and had a pretty nasty cut on his brow, but he'd fared okay. Adriana Rabh emerged with nary a scratch. Teller on the other side of the stage had also bailed to safety, but his seatmate, the secretary-general, was among the dead.

The rest of the audience and news corps did not fare so well. One hundred sixty-nine dead and twice as many injured. Graves found it hard to believe there were even that many people in the room that night, but whatever the number, the carnage had been horrific. The drone had plowed into the audience and then smashed right through the back wall into the room where they'd had cocktails and then into the kitchens.

Graves, Cora, and the people in the front row who had had the foresight to shelter beneath the lip of the stage actually fared pretty well. Cora was shaken up but unhurt. Graves had taken some glass when he pulled Anthony down, but he was okay after a few stitches.

The woman who'd been sitting next to Graves had stood frozen when the drone crashed into the room. The only thing they found of her was a single high-heeled shoe.

It had been Tony's idea to put Graves in charge of finding his father's assassin—as if Graves didn't have enough to worry about.

"Please, General," Tony said, refusing to let go of Graves's hand after they shook. "We—I—need your help. The council, we can't trust anyone, least of all the UN. They tried to kill my father." He finally let go of Graves's hand and pressed his fingers to his forehead. He was sporting a colorful bruise on the side of his face and a thin red slice an inch or so above his brow.

Graves let him have a moment.

"Look," Tony said finally. "All I'm asking is that you act as my eyes and ears for this investigation. I need someone I can trust on the inside."

"Why me?" Graves asked. "You don't know me."

"My father trusted you, that's good enough for me. If—when—he wakes up, I want him to know that we did everything we could to bring this assassin to justice."

That was the short version of how Graves came to be standing above a stinking, centuries-old sewer line under the Bronx waiting for his government-issue data glasses to sync with the FBI's live feed on the Neo hacker den.

The image popped into his vision. Four young people, two men, two women, sat on beanbag chairs in a rough circle. One of the girls was vaping, a cloud of smoke obscuring her face. She had her fingers entwined with the guy next to her and he seemed anxious to get a hit of whatever she was puffing.

There was another girl with her back to them, her Neo tattoo clearly visible on the slender white nape of her neck. Graves thought she looked like she was sixteen. Barely.

"That him?" Graves said. "Guy on the left?"

"That's him, sir," Craft replied.

Archibald "Spike" Lemmon. Graves studied the kid's profile as he recalled what he knew about him. Twenty-seven years old, MIT grad, summa cum laude in computer science. Ran identity scams and ByteCoin ransoms to pay for school and fund his operation. Citizens Against Weather Superiority, or CAWS, was a Neo splinter group dedicated to stopping all forms of manipulation of nature. Anthony Taulke, a two-time offender in their eyes, was public enemy number one.

On paper, Spike had the skills needed to hack the UN, but something still bothered Graves. It was a big leap from stealing ByteCoin from rich people to turning a drone into a weapon of mass murder. Nothing in his record indicated he was violent. And then there was the fact that he was still here, as if waiting to get picked up by the FBI.

"We're ready to go whenever you are, General," Craft said. "Just waiting on you."

Graves nodded. Maybe once he got a chance to talk to this hacker he could make himself comfortable with the inconsistencies in the suspect. "Okay, let's do it. Remember, I want them alive."

"Roger that, sir," Craft said. "When we hit them from the street level they will scurry to their bolt-hole, which will take them right here." He pointed to a narrow hole in the ceiling. "We wait for all of them to get down here, then we hit the lights and take them all together. No muss, no fuss. Any questions?"

The armored FBI agents retreated to form a semicircle outside the lights, weapons up. Graves stepped back until his leg touched the steel ladder he had used to climb up from the sewer below. He was unarmed. The FBI was in charge of the arrest. He was here to observe and get a crack at talking to the infamous Spike.

The last light went out and Graves put his data glasses in his pocket. Craft's Brooklyn accent said quietly: "Street team, this is mole team leader, you are a go. I repeat, you are go for the takedown."

"Roger that, mole team."

Graves held his breath, listening. Silence, then a distant thundering noise like running feet. There was the squeak of a hinge and the slapping sound of a rope hitting the floor of the tunnel. A clink and a hiss.

"Smoke grenade," someone whispered.

"Steady," came Craft's whispered reply.

Another clink and the room erupted in the flash of a concussion grenade. Graves felt himself slammed backwards into the rough concrete wall, ears ringing, eyes watering from the force of the blow. He clawed himself to his hands and knees.

"Craft!" he shouted, but he couldn't hear his own voice over the ringing in his ears. He crawled forward, his fingers finding the hole in the floor and the reassuring solidity of the steel ladder.

And something else. A hand, attached to an arm, connected to a body not wearing armor. With his free hand, Graves switched on his headlamp to find he was gripping the arm of the suspect Spike Lemmon.

The young man's eyes widened and he struggled to get away. Graves hung on.

Spike smashed him in the face with his elbow and then slithered down the hole. The weight of the man pulled Graves downward. He hooked an elbow over the rung of the ladder and held on. Beneath him, Spike struggled like a wild animal. He gripped Graves's wrist, hauled himself up, and bit Graves's hand.

With a scream of pain, Graves let go, but he wasn't finished yet. With Spike still in the glare of his headlamp, he launched his body headfirst down the hole. He hooked an arm over the kid's thin neck, using him to break his fall and take him into the brick floor of the sewer.

Graves felt his face smash into slimy bricks and the rest of his body slammed down beside him. The fall knocked the wind out of him.

Spike stirred underneath him and Graves tightened his grip. "No, you don't."

Ignoring the waves of pain, Graves got to his knees and pulled Spike upright, forcing his body back against the ladder. His headlamp flickered, damaged in the fall.

Spike's face was covered in sewer slime and one eye was already starting to swell. His eyes focused on Graves's face. "Please," he whispered. "Help me. They'll kill me."

Graves gripped the front of his shirt, keeping Spike pressed back against the ladder.

"Who? Who is—"

An explosion went off over his head and Graves felt the heat of a muzzle flash. He ducked automatically, then looked up.

Craft was framed in the open hole. In the flickering light of Graves's headlamp, he had blood running out of his nose and he'd lost his helmet. His eyes were wild. "I saw a gun," he shouted.

Graves looked back at the kid. He was still clutching Spike's shirt front, but the kid's body had gone slack under Graves's fist. Still, he looked okay. Graves shook him gently and his head lolled to one side.

When he pulled him away from the ladder, the back of the boy's head was gone.

21

ANTHONY TAULKE • OLYMPUS STATION

"Pop."

The voice came from far away, like a distant shout across a field on a windy day.

"Pop," said the voice again. *Tony? Was that Tony's voice?*

"Can you hear me, Pop? Move your fingers if you can hear me."

Fingers... Anthony considered that word for a long time. Funny-sounding word... Then, with a sound in his head like relays slamming shut, he realized what the word meant.

Fingers... the things on the end of his hand. *Hand* ... another funny word.

"There!" said the voice that was assigned in his head to Tony. "He moved his fingers. See?"

"That's a good sign," said a new voice. A woman's voice, clipped with authority. Anthony felt a new touch on his shoulder. "Mr. Taulke, my name is Dr. Langley. You've been in an accident. We're letting you wake up naturally. Move your fingers if you understand me."

It was easier to move his fingers this time and the word sounded normal in his head now.

An accident? His brain felt fuzzy, like it was packed full of cotton candy instead of synapses. The last thing he remembered was having a drink in a big room. The room was filled with people all dressed in fine clothes and talking ... so much talking that he could hardly hear himself. But it was okay, it was a good memory. He felt happy in this memory ... but why?

Anthony thought about this question for a long time and he may have even gone back to sleep. Time seemed elastic with his eyes closed.

He'd been happy in the big room with the big windows and all the well-dressed people. He remembered that much. They were all there to see him, he decided. The way the women flirted and the men gripped his hand. All of them wanted to be him—or at least be near him. He was the center of attention, that's why he'd been so happy.

Mystery solved.

"Mr. Taulke?" The doctor's voice again. She was speaking slowly, clearly, but it felt a little shouty, too. She was right next to him; no reason to shout, doc. "We're removing your eye shade. Your eyes may be sensitive to light."

The comforting blackness was replaced by a deep red glow through his closed eyelids. He winced.

A hand on his forehead. Long fingers, gentle touch. The doctor. "It's okay, Mr. Taulke. Your eyes will adjust in a few seconds. Just be patient."

The intensity of the light lessened and he tried to say thank you. His mouth was full of something.

"We're taking out your breathing tube, Mr. Taulke. This might be uncomfortable for a second or two."

Anthony felt a tearing sensation in his throat. He gagged, and then sweet, clean air rushed into his lungs. He coughed.

The bed rose up under his back, helping him sit up. Helping him breathe.

Anthony opened his eyes.

Tony was standing on his right. His son had a shadow of a bruise on the side of his face and a thin red line over his brow. The doctor said he'd been in an accident. Maybe Tony had been there too.

Doctor Langley was nothing like her voice. She was a diminutive woman of Japanese descent with a sensible bobbed cut to her electric-blue hair. When she took his hand, he recognized her touch.

"Squeeze my fingers as hard as you can, Mr. Taulke," she said. Same voice.

Anthony did as he was told and she nodded. She took his other hand and repeated the process. She nodded at Tony. "Good. Very good."

Tony gave Langley a tight smile. Anthony could tell he was worried. "Can you give us a minute, Doctor?"

Langley closed the door behind her.

Tony looked at the ceiling and sighed. "Thank God you're okay, Pop. You had me worried."

Anthony tried to speak but found his voice was not responding. He pointed at a cup of water and Tony held it for him as he sipped. He coughed.

"What happened?" he finally managed to say.

"You don't remember the accident? The drone? At the UN?"

The UN, that rang a bell. United Nations. He thought about the party where all the people were there to see him. It had been more than drinks. He was there to tell them something, something important. A wave of frustration made his eyes water. The answer was right there, but just out of his mental grasp.

Tony patted his arm. "It's okay, Pop. Take it easy. You've had a big shock, but you're going to be okay. The doc says your concussion is healing well."

Anthony pulled up the sleeve of his hospital gown. His skin was mottled with fading bruises. He pulled down his collar and found the same thing on his chest. Under the covers, his legs were also blotched with sickly yellow and green.

Tony watched him with a rueful smile. "You were basically one giant bruise when they brought you here."

Anthony cocked his head. "Where is here? Where am I?"

"Olympus Station."

The name sounded familiar to Anthony. Tony must have noticed his confusion.

"The station at the end of the Taulke Space Elevator, remember?"

Anthony nodded. That sounded right.

"How long?" he rasped out.

Tony shifted his feet. "Two weeks. The accident was two weeks ago. We've got you here and Adriana and Elise and Viktor. It's the safest place for all of us now."

"Safe from what?" Anthony asked. If it was an accident, why did he need to be safe?

Tony's eyes searched his face. "You really don't remember, do you?" He seemed to loosen up then and perched one buttock on the edge of Anthony's bed. "Someone tried to assassinate you, Pop. A radical Neo splinter group. The FBI tracked them down." He leaned closer and spoke in a whisper. "I put Graves on it. I figured he's as neutral as they come—in case it was an inside job."

Inside job. The term rattled around in Anthony's empty memory. Why would someone on his council want to kill him?

"Show me," he said. "Show me what happened."

Tony shook his head. "That's not a good idea, Pop. It's best if you let the memories come back on their own."

Anthony gripped his son's arm. "Show me."

Tony looked at the door. "Your retinal implant is deactivated so your brain can heal, so I'll put it on a tablet for you." He slid a slim piece of rectangular glass into Anthony's hands. "If it's too much for you, we can take it away, okay?"

Anthony nodded. The screen showed a drone shot of a high-ceilinged ballroom, facing a stage. Behind the stage was all glass looking out on a city —New York City, he remembered. The UN was in New York City. Below him in the darkened room were the tops of people's heads, swaying and bobbing as they jockeyed for a sight line or whispered to each other.

A handsome man was at the podium on the stage, smiling and talking with expansive hand gestures as he pointed at a holograph floating above the crowd. The words Taulke Renewal Initiative glowed and then disappeared. The drone moved higher, making the moving heads feel like a darkened sea below him. The people were standing and clapping at something the man said—

The man at the podium was him, Anthony realized with a start. He was speaking and they were clapping for him. A warm sense of fulfillment rose in his chest. These people liked him—no, these people loved him. Anthony cried tears of joy.

Tony stopped the vid. "You okay? It gets pretty bad from here on out. We can do it later, if you want."

Anthony shook his head. "Now."

Tony shrugged, still watching his father's face closely. "You don't remember any of this? Really?"

Anthony shook his head.

"Whatever." Tony handed him the tablet.

The vid started again. Anthony saw a flash of light from behind the man on the podium—him—beyond the glass. Tony was on the stage with him, and he saw his son twist in his seat. A look of horror shot across his features, he seized the dark-haired woman—her name was Adriana, Anthony knew that somehow—next to him and rolled off the stage.

A ripple of movement went through the crowd and Anthony at the podium started to turn. The glass exploded behind him as a drone crashed into the ballroom. Just before he was about to get run over by the speeding drone, a man reached up and dragged him down.

The drone smashed into the audience. Anthony saw bodies and parts of bodies spewing everywhere. He felt sick, and drops of water splashed onto the screen. He wiped at his face to find tears running down his cheeks.

Tony snatched the tablet away. "Okay, that's enough, Pop."

"Wait," Anthony croaked. "The man. Who was the man?"

Tony moved through the vid and froze on the image of the man reaching up and dragging him out of the way of the drone.

"This guy?" Tony asked. "That's General Graves."

Graves. Anthony locked the name in his head. Graves, the man who had saved his life.

"How many?"

"How many what?" Tony replied. He looked away immediately. Anthony didn't say anything. Tony knew what he meant.

"A lot. Hundreds," Tony said finally.

Anthony leaned back, deflated, feeling the tears starting afresh.

All those people dead and yet he was alive. He closed his eyes, wanting nothing more than to retreat back into darkness. He was safe there ... why had they woken him up anyway?

Tony's hand rested on his arm. "Don't worry, Pop. The Neos did this, we know it, and we'll hit back ten times harder. You just concentrate on getting better. The council will take care of this."

Anthony let sleep wrap around him. His thoughts were clearer now, the ideas coming quicker and with more urgency.

All he ever wanted to do was help people—these people needed his help—and in return, they tried to kill him.

Hit back ten times harder, Tony had said. Counterpunch. His weary brain took that idea in and then rejected it. There had to be a better way.

Anthony drifted off to sleep.

22

WILLIAM GRAVES • FORT HOOD, TEXAS

The call came in to Graves's quarters at 2 a.m., Texas time, the light from the data glasses on his bedside table flashing him awake. He considered ignoring it. If it was really important, they would send someone to wake him.

He closed his eyes again. The light on the temple of the data glasses stopped, then started again a few seconds later. Whoever it was, they were calling back.

Graves fumbled for the glasses, blinking as the screen popped up before his eyes. He scanned to accept the message.

A trim young woman wearing an Air Force uniform looked relieved when he answered. "General Graves, please stand by for the president."

The screen went blank for another second, then Teller's face popped into view. "General, sorry about the late hour."

Despite the apology, Teller was still dressed as if he hadn't been to bed yet. He wore a crisp white shirt, unbuttoned at the collar, and looked freshly shaved. Any injuries he'd sustained in the UN attack were either healed or hidden by cosmetics. The man had been extraordinarily lucky. The UN secretary-general who'd been sitting next to him was dead.

"What can I do for you, sir?" Graves said. He knew he did not look anywhere near as well turned out and he felt at a disadvantage for it.

"I have a meeting with Anthony Taulke at the UN headquarters at nine sharp tomorrow morning."

Graves sat up straighter. "He's okay? I haven't heard anything."

"Apparently he's fine, according to his son. He wants to see where the attack took place for himself. Hear about these Neo nutjobs that tried to take him out."

"Is that a good idea, Mr. President? The people who did it were all killed in the FBI raid. We don't really know why they did it or what they were trying to achieve. And why the UN building? The place is still a crime scene."

Teller sighed. "All good questions, Graves, and you can put them to the man himself when you see him. He asked for you—by name—to be there."

"Sir, I—"

"Stow it, General. You will be at the UN building tomorrow at nine with Corazon Santos."

"What does Cora have to do with this, sir?"

Teller frowned for a split second at Graves's use of the familiar name. "Don't know. He's insisted you and she be there to meet him." The president made no attempt to hide his disdain for the meeting. "He's the boss, General. Yours and mine—at least that's how it is now. Are we clear about meeting logistics, General? Any issues I should know about beforehand?"

Graves shook his head. "I've given all my updates to H, sir. I'm happy to answer any specific questions you might have—"

"That'll be all, then, General. Enjoy the rest of your night."

Graves's screen went blank again. He snatched the glasses off his face and threw them on the bedside table. He didn't need this kind of aggravation. He was a fifty-year-old—fifty-one, he remembered—one-star general who was never going to get a second star. He was resented by his peers because he'd been promoted over them and now all but ostracized by the very guy who'd promoted him in the first place.

He clenched his eyes shut. If his career was a dead end, his personal life was a wasteland. He was alone, living in a converted office next to his real office, with no opportunity to meet women, no real friends to speak of, and no family still living.

He faced the facts: he was a committed workaholic in the dead-end job of trying to save the citizens of a planet that didn't really want to be saved. If there was a definition of insanity online, his picture should be next to it.

Graves looked at his watch and did some quick mental math. If he went back to sleep right now, he could get another two hours. He slammed his head back into his pillow and closed his eyes.

Who was he trying to fool? He was way too worked up now to think of sleeping. With a sigh of exasperation, Graves threw off the covers and used the intercom to call down to the duty sergeant to send up a pot of coffee. He showered quickly and dressed, studying his reflection as he combed his hair.

He wasn't a bad-looking guy. He supposed he could date if he wanted to, but he just never made it a priority beyond a few casual flings. He paused. There was always Olga Rodchenkov. When she'd come to see him during the California wildfire recovery effort—he made a grimace when he realized he marked all the events in his life by disasters—there'd been a spark there. He'd felt it and was pretty sure she had too.

The smile faded from his face as he recalled what she had been there to see him about and his hand went to the Saint Christopher medal. A cadre of like-minded officers, she'd said. People, citizens of the world, who want to make a difference. She'd tried to recruit him to join some crazy military coup. Granted, after the events of the last few weeks, it sounded less crazy ... but still, she was talking about betraying his country. She was talking about treason.

A knock on the door with the promised coffee ended this train of thought. Nope, Olga was off the board, which left the field exactly empty of all possible retirement companionship options. He snorted frustration and then locked that feeling away, just like he did every morning.

Time to go to work.

Graves was known as an early riser, but 3 a.m. was early even by his standards. The sergeant at the main desk had let the duty officer know the CO was up and on the prowl. Graves had to hide a smile as he returned the salute of the freshly turned-out young second lieutenant.

"Anything to report, Lieutenant?" Graves asked.

"All quiet, sir."

"Very well. Have my car ready to leave for New York at six sharp. I'm going for a walk."

Even this early in the morning, the heat settled on him like a warm blanket. A pair of security soldiers started to follow him, but Graves waved them off. He liked military bases in the very early morning. Quiet, but ready to burst with energy. In another hour, there would be PT squads getting in their exercise for the day before the sun came up. Then the smells of the chow hall would take over the base. After breakfast, as the sun was breaking over the horizon, the real work day would begin. Land vehicles and aircars crisscrossing the base, transports taking off and landing at the airfield, the sounds of live fire training from the gun range.

But now, it was just a pregnant silence waiting for another day to begin. He approached the perimeter of the refugee camp, surprising the army guards stationed outside. The men snapped to attention and saluted.

"All quiet on the western front, soldier?" he asked a young woman with eyes red from lack of sleep.

She had no idea what he was talking about, so she settled for, "All quiet, sir."

Graves chuckled to himself as he made his way into the camp. A tall recruit who looked like his waistline was the same diameter as his rifle barrel fell into step beside him. "You can wait here," Graves said. "I'll handle this on my own."

"Standing orders, sir. We use the buddy system in the camp."

"Standing orders from whom, soldier?"

"The CO, sir."

"You mean me."

The young man's Adam's apple bobbed as he realized his situation. "Yes, sir."

Graves leaned toward him and pointed to a pair of teenagers watching them from the shadow of the nearest tent. "They know I'm coming, I think. I'm going to take this one alone, son."

He walked through the arrow-straight streets of the refugee camp toward the Temple of Cassandra. Around him he heard the sounds of people sleeping. The deeper snores of adults, the quick breaths of children, a baby crying somewhere. A heat exchanger kicked on with a low hum.

As always, the temple was lit from the outside, the mark of Cassandra glowing brightly against the night sky. An acolyte met him at the entrance, a young woman with raven-black hair and fair skin. "The Corazon is waiting for you, General."

Graves nodded. "I expected nothing less." His remark earned a quizzical look from the young woman.

Cora was kneeling before the altar of the Child when Graves entered the chamber. She stood immediately and came toward him with her hands outstretched. "William, what a pleasant surprise."

She wore a simple dark gray dress belted at the waist, which Graves had come to see as her everyday wear. Her silver hair hung loose around her shoulders and her brown skin had the vibrant glowing undertone that he found so appealing. To his surprise, she kissed him on the cheek. The thrill of it stopped his breath for a moment.

"Well, when do we leave?" she asked.

Cora arched an eyebrow at the surprised look on his face. "A man only visits a woman at this hour of the morning for one of two things. I think I know you well enough to guess which one it is."

Graves blushed. "I thought maybe you had another vision," he replied.

Cora's expression grew thoughtful. "I'm afraid my visions have ended, William. I haven't had one since..." She looked him in the eye. "Since you saved my life at the United Nations."

Graves pretended to study the altar. "Well, you're about to revisit the scene of the crime then. Teller wants us in New York this morning. There's a meeting with Anthony Taulke at the UN."

Cora frowned.

"I don't know why or what he wants with us," Graves said.

"It has begun," Cora whispered to herself. Graves felt the hair stand up on the back of his neck.

"What has?" he said.

Cora stared at him for long enough that Graves thought she might not have heard him.

"The heart of man will be changed and the Child be brought into a new world."

"Another vision?" Graves said, not bothering to keep the sarcasm out of his voice.

"Her words. Cassandra's words."

"The words of a computer-generated religion."

Cora smiled at him gently. "I'm surprised at you, William. You are a man of science, no?"

"Of course."

"Then you, of all people, should agree that if a computer is given the right data, it will generate the right answer." She put her hand on Graves's elbow and steered him toward the door.

"Shall we go?"

23

CORAZON SANTOS • FORT HOOD, TEXAS

Cora watched the sun rise from the back seat of the government aircar. From this height, the Texas horizon was a shallow curve against a crimson summer sun.

Red sky in morning, sailors take warning...

A lifetime ago, her husband used to say that before he took off on another job. He was a roughneck on an oil-drilling platform and she'd married him when she was barely twenty years old. In those days, she worked as a nurse for a doctor who served in the slums of Rio de Janeiro. Her lips twisted at the irony of their life together: her husband drilled for oil to make the planet sicker, while she tried to save people one at a time.

In her work beside the doctor, she saw every sort of ailment imaginable, from broken bones to babesiosis. Like an army medic, practical experience gave her all the knowledge of medicine, but not the degree.

No matter. She was young, idealistic, and most of all, in love.

Baby Pamela was born when Cora was forty-three. She had all but given up on getting pregnant until it happened. She couldn't believe it. In her mind, the long-awaited baby was all due to Cassandra. Cora had thrown off her Roman Catholic upbringing in favor of the New Earth Order and its message of healing the planet.

At that time in her life—before Baby Pamela was born—religion was just a label for people to see who was on their team. Having a baby changed all that. Rodrigo, her husband, quit his job as an oil worker, and the three of them moved to a commune to dedicate their family to the teachings of the Neos.

It was there in the deep green of the Amazon rain forest that she found Cassandra. Many converts described the feeling of being "switched on" by Cassandra, but for Cora it wasn't like that. She saw the Mother of Earth in her dreams. She spoke to Her in conversation. Corazon Santos was there for a higher purpose, Cassandra told her. She was not some pawn in a political game, she was part of the next generation of Neos. Cora would become the heart of a reborn religion.

Pamela was two when Cora first started teaching the gospel of Cassandra to the indigenous people who came in for treatment. When she had enough converts, she convinced them to build a temple for their village in the valley below her hilltop clinic. They were happy in their little village, and Cora began to think about life after Cassandra. She stopped preaching and she stopped having visions.

That spring, a flash flood wiped the village away as if it had never existed. A wall of water rushed down the valley from someplace north of them which had received torrential rains. It wasn't even raining where they lived. Cora remembered standing in the doorway of her clinic above the valley filled with rushing water. Then she looked up at the red sun rising over the scene of destruction.

Red sky in morning...

Cora shook the memories away. She drew a wrap around her shoulders against the chill of the air conditioning in the aircar—and the chill of the memories. Her own child was gone, her husband was gone, her past was gone. She had forsaken Cassandra once at the cost of everything she loved in this world. But that was behind her. The only thing left for Corazon Santos now was her mission to serve the Child of Cassandra.

Across from her, General Graves dozed, his head dipping to one side. He was a strange man. A confirmed bachelor, she suspected, but not a hard man. A man with compassion in his heart for the world around him. Not a bachelor by choice, but a bachelor by trade.

She nodded to herself. He was a man with a past as well. They shared that in common.

And yet Cassandra had chosen him for the coming trial.

As his head nodded, a Saint Christopher medal slipped out of his collar. Odd. Cora leaned across the space between them and fingered the medallion. Graves woke up.

He did not startle, but instead watched her touch the silver medal. Cora blushed and sat back again. "I didn't take you for a religious man, William."

He slipped the necklace back inside his uniform shirt. "Patron saint of bachelors and pestilence," he said. "Given to me by an old friend a long time ago."

"A woman," Cora replied without thinking. "A lover."

Graves nodded slowly. "I guess my bachelorhood was obvious even then."

"You were a man with a purpose. You still are."

Grave shielded his eyes against the red glare flooding the cab. He could have dimmed the window, but he didn't. He seemed to enjoy the unfiltered sunshine. "I grew up near the ocean," he said. "There's a saying that sailors have. It goes: red sky in morning—"

"Sailors take warning," Cora finished for him.

Graves gave her a colorless smile. "Not a great omen for a meeting with the president and the most powerful man in the known universe. I don't suppose your visions show what's going to happen, do they?"

Cora squinted into the red sun. "My visions say you will go on to do great things, William."

Graves chuffed. "I'd be happy with someone telling me what Anthony Taulke wants."

As the military aircar flew over downtown New York City, Graves told the pilot to circle the UN building.

The site of the Neo terrorist strike was still an active crime scene, so it looked pretty much the way Cora remembered it from the night of the attack. From a distance, the blown-out windows, ringed with irregular charring, looked remarkably like a bullet wound.

The ballroom was near the top of the building and Graves directed the pilot to make a close-in, slow pass. The morning sun glinted off the millions of shards of glass that still littered the scene. Where the drone had blasted through the structure, twists of tortured steel poked out, wet in the moist morning air.

Graves pointed at the gaping hole in the building. "The drone crash was devastating from the perspective of loss of life and shock value," he said. "But from the perspective of structural damage, it was minimal." He pointed to the floor above. "The UN moved people out of the floors directly above and below the ballroom, but even that wasn't truly necessary. The rest of the structure was able to compensate for the damage."

"Is that unusual?" Cora asked. "Why would a terrorist care about a building?"

Graves shook his head, still studying the building. He signaled the pilot and the aircar rose vertically to the VIP dock on the roof. A dark-haired woman with elfin ears was waiting for them.

"General," she said with a curt nod as Graves exited the car. He ignored her, turning instead to offer a hand to Cora as she got out. Graves's face was like stone, but Cora could see the flash of anger in his eyes.

"Helena," Graves replied. "I might have known the president would make an appearance."

The woman rolled her eyes. "Try to find someone who isn't here. We've got both Taulkes, Adriana Rabh, Teller, and that reporter, Nancy Watson."

Cora waited until she had finished, then said, "What about Elise Kisaan?" She had hoped to catch a glimpse of the woman carrying Cassandra's Child.

Helena smirked, an expression that seemed permanent on her. "Nope, no weather witches allowed."

Cora's anger flared at her disrespect, but she tamped it down. This woman was a nonbeliever, she had no concept of what she was saying.

Graves took Cora's elbow. "Well, let's get this over with—whatever Anthony Taulke has planned, I'm sure we'll just be pawns in his game."

After a short elevator ride, the doors opened onto a scene of destruction bathed in the glow of soft morning light. Anthony Taulke was walking on the far side of the ballroom, near the open windows and the stage he'd been standing on the night of the attack. Nancy Watson, her trademark pink curls aflame in the drab scene, was walking with him, a pair of camera drones floating around them. Anthony, outlined in blue sky, steepled his fingers in front of his chest and was making a point to the reporter who was nodding back at him, her brow furrowed in concentration.

The rest of the group stood in a knot a few meters from the elevator, watching Anthony and the reporter talk. President Teller, Adriana Rabh, and Tony Taulke broke off a whispered conversation as Graves and Cora approached.

Graves nodded at Teller and shook hands with the three of them. Cora did the same.

"What's our timeline, sir?" H asked Teller.

Teller blew out an exasperated breath. "Damned if I know," he said.

Tony, still watching his father and the reporter, answered. "Pop wants to finish his interview with Nancy Watson, then use her platform to make a live announcement. He wants to show people that he is still alive and fighting."

"I wish he wouldn't keep us in the dark like this," Adriana said. "We're council members. We deserve to know what he's saying before he says it."

"Don't worry about Pop," Tony said. "He knows what he's doing."

"Your father has suffered a near-death experience," Cora found herself saying. "That changes a person."

She hadn't meant to say anything. It just slipped out. She didn't even know what she was doing here and certainly had no business commenting on the mental health of the most powerful man in the universe.

The rest of the group stared at her.

Adriana spoke first. "You've seen a lot of death, Ms. Santos." It was not a question.

Cora lifted her chin. "I have. It has changed me ... made me who I am."

"And who are you exactly?" Tony Taulke asked. His dark eyes glittered in a way that made her skin crawl. "My father asked for you to be here with General Graves. Why?"

Why was she here? She felt Graves tense up beside her as if to protect her, but from what? She was here because she was brought here.

"They're coming back," Adriana hissed, then turned to where Anthony and Nancy Watson were walking toward them. She flashed a bright smile at the elder Taulke. "Ready, Anthony?"

Even with makeup, the older man's face still showed the effects of the accident. His jawline was soft with residual swelling and a bruise crept up from his neckline. Anthony ignored his peers and walked straight to Graves and Cora.

"Thank you for coming," he said, taking her hand in both of his. Cora recoiled slightly at the sign of intimacy, but then relaxed. Anthony's gaze was intense but friendly. He released her hand and turned to the rest of the group. "Nancy and I had a nice chat already, which I've given her permission to use as background for the announcement—"

"Pop," Tony interrupted his father, "what announcement are we talking about? We should discuss this first—"

Anthony returned the interruption. "Son, I came here a few weeks ago to make an announcement and I plan to finish the job. I'm going back on that stage and I'm going to finish what I started." He pointed toward what was left of the stage and the gaping hole in the glass. Cora noticed his finger trembled.

"So you're going through with it then?" Teller spoke now. His face was tight with anger. "The Taulke Renewal business? I would have thought we'd stay with the Marshall Plan. It is polling well." Helena nodded her agreement from Teller's side.

Cora noticed Graves silently following the conversation, his gaze flicking from person to person. Seeking information, processing. He saw it too, Cora realized. The change in Anthony Taulke's demeanor rattled his closest advisers.

"Pop," Tony tried again, his tone softer this time. "I hardly think this is the time to be making big announcements. Let's take a day or so and talk through the whole plan—"

Anthony ignored his son. He turned to Nancy and smiled brightly. "Ready?"

To Cora's surprise, Anthony took her hand and slid it into the crook of his elbow. "I'd like to have you close by, Ms. Santos," he murmured. He looked over his shoulder at Graves and called out, "Coming, General?"

There was a rough path cleared through the debris in the room, but Cora could still feel the grit of broken glass and pulverized plastic shards under her shoes. She cast a quick glance behind her and saw the rest of the group strung out along the path as if the sheer force of Anthony's will was dragging them along.

One of Watson's camera drones flashed by, reminding Cora that she was being recorded. Nancy Watson herself ranged a few paces ahead, muttering into her comms about camera angles and her own commentary on the scene.

Anthony reached the stage and climbed to the space where the podium had been, then turned to face them. It was an incongruous, compelling scene. Shattered glass and chunks of debris lay all around him, yet behind him was clear blue sky and a cityscape bathed in morning light. The present and the future, Cora realized, seeing the scenic metaphor.

Anthony's eyes were bright and quick as he waited for the group to line up at the base of the stage. Because they had gotten there first, Cora and Graves were directly in front of Anthony. No one asked them to move and it felt right to her somehow.

With a quick nod at Nancy, Anthony began to speak.

"A few weeks ago, I nearly died on this very spot." His voice was low and husky, intense with emotion. He spread his hands to encompass the destruction on the floor.

Cora saw Tony Taulke straighten up, then he leaned toward Nancy Watson and said in a fierce whisper, "This is going out live?"

Watson nodded.

"Why? Who gave you permission?"

Watson pointed at Anthony, who resumed speaking.

"I came here to announce what I thought—no, what I believed—was the best possible thing for this planet. I called it the Taulke Renewal Initiative, and I truly believed it was what this world needed." He paused for so long that Cora wondered if Anthony had forgotten what he was going to say. He looked directly into the camera.

"I was wrong." Another pause, just as lengthy. "Not just wrong. Arrogant. Filled with conviction that I was the only person who could heal this planet." Anthony's gaze found Cora's, then slipped away to find the camera again. "To the young man who tried to kill me—and to all the members of the New Earth Order out there—I have a message for you."

Tony's voice rose above a stage whisper as he ordered Nancy Watson to stop the broadcast. "My father has been in a terrible accident. He does not know what he's saying..." Tony realized his father had stopped speaking and was staring at him like a schoolteacher waiting for an unruly member of the class to quiet down.

Anthony slowly lowered his body until he was kneeling, the knees of his uber-expensive suit in the white dust. "You have opened my eyes. The Earth is not mine to control. To every man and woman on this planet, I beg you to forgive me for my sin of hubris. Whatever race or gender or creed you might be, you have all suffered at my hand. I ask for your forgiveness." He bowed his head. "And your support."

His head snapped up again and Cora saw the light of conviction burning brightly. He leaped to his feet.

"I will change—I pledge this to you. We will change." He smacked a closed fist into an open palm. "What we need is fresh leadership, fresh ideas. Today I am announcing that the Council of Corporations will include two new members." His hand swept down to point at her. "Corazon Santos will represent the New Earth Order on the council and General William Graves will represent the United Nations of Earth."

The camera drones swept in to catch her reaction. Anthony dropped off the stage in front of her and hugged her like they were best friends. The rest of the group, pinned under the stares of the live-action cameras, made their show of congratulations, but their eyes were steely with anger. All of them.

Cora smiled through it, but her free hand sought Graves's fingers. When she squeezed his hand, he replied in kind.

She looked out at the blue of a cloudless sky.

If it is your will, Cassandra. I am yours to command.

24

ADRIANA RABH • NEW YORK CITY

Adriana closed her eyes and brought the tips of her index finger and thumb together, seeking the first sensation of touch in the sensitive skin and trying to hold that position. Concentrating, stilling the chatter of her mind with the focus exercise.

But thoughts intruded.

Adriana snapped her eyes open. Normally, the stylistic decor of her New York sitting room brought her some level of peace, but not today. All she kept thinking about was Anthony's pathetic live broadcast ... on his knees, begging forgiveness like some weeping martyr from history.

All he needed was a few arrows sticking out of his chest, she thought savagely.

Was it possible that Anthony Taulke, renowned for his unflappability under pressure, able to navigate any business deal with the nonchalance of the truly blessed, had lost his nerve?

Her mind rejected the idea. He was playing the long game, that was the only explanation, but what was it?

Her virtual pulsed her with a notice of her next visitor. Of all the members of the council, Viktor Erkennen was the one most likely to hold the answers she sought.

The Russian moved slowly in full-gee, each step a shamble, making him seem more like a bear than normal. She met him at the door, kissed him on both cheeks, and tucked his arm in hers as they made their way to the sofa.

Viktor collapsed into the cushions and let his head loll backwards. He groaned. "I cannot do this anymore, Adriana," he said.

He really was suffering. The whites of his eyes had gone pink with ruptured blood vessels and the skin of his fleshy face looked drawn. The fact that he had made the trip to the surface just to speak with her spoke volumes.

"I appreciate you coming, Viktor," she said, patting his knee. "I know this must be hard for you."

He raised his head, blinking like an owl. "This topic ... is too sensitive for communications channels."

"Yes." She would let him broach Anthony's behavior and what it meant to the council. To all their plans. She rose to her feet. "Drink?"

Viktor gave a ponderous nod. She let the silence fill the room as she fixed the drinks. Adriana could have called for a butler, but she fixed them herself. Vodka martinis, heavy on the vodka, especially for him, poured into a massive crystal glass.

"Olives?" she asked finally.

Viktor shook his head and did not look up as she sat down next to him and handed him his glass. "*Na zdrowie,*" she said, touching the rim of her glass to his.

He said nothing, but hoisted the glass and drained a quarter of the contents in one sip. His eyes widened in appreciation at her generous hand.

"I do not know what has happened to Anthony," he said.

"Meaning?" she said.

His eyes met hers. "Are we being recorded, Adriana?"

"No," she lied. She recorded everything, of course, but this conversation had no significance—yet.

Viktor shrugged. "Makes no difference either way. I have nothing to tell you."

"Then why are you here?"

The Russian took another gulp of his martini. "Same reason as you. Information. I do not know Anthony's plan, but I can count votes. When he adds the general and the Neo woman to the council—"

"He can't be allowed to do that!" Adriana interrupted.

"For now, he can. Anthony made a public appeal; if the council refuses to seat them, think of the public backlash. LUNa City is already threatening to shut off He-3 production, we still need food from Earth … what do you propose we do?"

Adriana took a moment to try her calming technique, but her hands were shaking too much to permit the tips of her fingers to touch. It was more like Morse code.

"So we allow them to be seated, then what?" she said.

"Anthony will have a lock on the council. Graves, the Neo woman, Xi, and himself. Our votes don't matter."

"Why are you so sure Xi Qinlao will vote with Anthony?"

Viktor set his empty glass down with a thump on the coffee table. "That I can answer. For the last six months, I've been working on a new weather nanite system for Anthony. Qinlao Manufacturing is producing it for us. When these satellites are in place, Elise Kisaan's cryptokey will be useless. Anthony will remove Elise from the council. We will be outnumbered four to three."

"Can you stop it?" Adriana asked.

Viktor blew out a long breath. "The summit is in two days. That's when Anthony will make his move. Deploy the satellite network, seat the new members. The first vote will remove Elise." He looked at her with a mournful gaze. "When that happens, he has a free pass to do whatever he wants."

"Then we can't let that happen."

Viktor heaved his bulky body to his feet and swayed a moment as he found his balance. "It's out of my hands. The satellites are being deployed even as we speak. The weather network will be complete in the next forty-eight hours and nothing can stop the summit meeting now."

He plodded to the door without waiting for her to get up and left. Adriana kept her seat, still holding her nearly untouched drink. With her free hand, she touched the tip of her forefinger to the tip of her thumb.

No shaking, calm breath, clear head.

The door reopened, but she kept her attention fixed on a spot on the far wall. From behind her came the sounds of someone fixing a drink, then crossing the room. Tony Taulke flopped into the sofa cushions next to her.

"Viktor is always such a downer, isn't he?" Tony said.

Adriana broke her concentration and took a sip of her martini. The drink had warmed to room temperature during her conversation with Viktor. She set it on the table with barely a ripple on the surface of the liquid.

"We need to act," she said.

"It's under control." Tony sucked at his drink.

Adriana's temper flared. "The last time you controlled something, I took the blame for the LUNa City uprising. We need to change the narrative, distract people from this summit business. That gives us breathing room to makes things happen."

Another insolent slurp from Tony. "I told you, it's being handled. That's all you need to know."

Tony's reluctance to share his plans with her both infuriated her and concerned her at the same time. Most of all, she didn't trust him. Didn't trust any of them, really. Except Anthony. She had trusted Anthony—the old Anthony, not the new one. Look where that had gotten her.

"Okay," she said finally. "I trust you."

Tony smirked. "No, you don't, but that's all right." He stood. "Good work with Viktor. I figured Pop was trying to pull a fast one with the weather network, but it's good to have it confirmed." He leaned over and kissed Adriana on the cheek. "I'll be in touch."

She did not walk him to the door. Instead, Adriana returned to her thoughts.

Two days. In two days, Anthony would make his move. Take control of the weather. Take control of the council. Sideline her, possibly for good. After all, did he really need her if he had that much power?

Teller, she decided. He would use Teller instead of her, thinking that Teller would have connections and influence equal to hers. The very idea made her quake with suppressed rage.

Tony might have it handled in his own mind, but where did she fall in his pecking order? Certainly not above Elise Kisaan, that was for sure.

No, she couldn't rely on a self-absorbed prick like Tony Taulke to keep her best interests at heart. She needed to take matters into her own hands. The satellite network, the new council members, these were all actions designed to keep her unbalanced.

Well, two could play that game. It was time for Adriana to spring her own set of surprises. If Tony was unwilling to stir things up, then she would ... but how?

Adriana walked to the window and stared down at the city. Her eye was drawn to the faraway park where a group of children were playing a game in the open field. Bright-colored jerseys clustered around a ball, then dispersed like a group of flies. Parents watched from the sidelines.

The idea formed in her head slowly. She turned it over and over, looking for flaws. There were many, but in every flaw was a latent opportunity for someone who was willing to seize the initiative.

She pulsed Eugene Fischer, the fixer Tony had lent to her. He would do nicely. He might inform on her to Tony, but that would only add to the confusion. More opportunity for her.

Her instructions to young Fischer were short, concise, and pointed, leaving lots of room for freelancing. She was interested in the results, not the methods. If the power center of the council was to be a math problem, then she could change the calculus better than any of them.

His eyes studied her face as she spoke. Intelligent eyes, she decided, capable eyes. As usual, he had a book tucked under his arm. The author's name peeked out. Kafka.

"Any questions?" she asked Fischer.

He shook his head.

When the hit man left, Adriana returned to her sofa and took a sip of her warm martini. She lifted the glass to an imaginary companion in mock congratulations.

The council was about to have a baby.

25

WILLIAM GRAVES • DARWIN, AUSTRALIA

The idea of taking the space elevator up to Olympus Station seemed inefficient to Graves. After all, a military transport would get them there in a fraction of the time.

But Anthony Taulke had insisted Graves and Cora ride in his private elevator car as his personal guests. It wasn't until they arrived in Darwin, Australia, to board the elevator that Graves realized the point of Anthony's insistence: it wasn't about the destination, it was about the journey.

A crowd filled the airfield when they disembarked the transport in sun-drenched Darwin. Anthony had literally rolled out the red carpet for their arrival, and at the end of the carpet, Graves spied a tall woman with a towering pile of bright pink curls. Nancy Watson was back for more exclusive interview footage. Banks of camera drones made a wall of eyes behind Nancy.

Anthony strode ahead, his ego drawing him to a camera like a moth to a flame. By the time Graves and Cora caught up to him, he was already chatting with Nancy like old friends.

"I meant what I said in New York. I'm here to atone for my sins of hubris. I will use my resources to place real people"—he drew Graves and Cora forward—"on the council and develop real solutions to save this planet." He turned to Cora as if she was supposed to pick up where he left off.

From his position on Anthony's other side, Graves could see the impromptu news conference was being broadcast onto large, virtual screens to the crowds on the airfield. As Cora's face showed up on the screens, a chant went up: "Cor-a-zon, Cor-a-zon."

Cora cocked her head like she didn't quite understand what she was hearing.

"They're chanting your name," Anthony said to her with a grin. "What do you think of that?"

Cora blushed and looked away. Her eyes sought Graves, who shrugged at her. He was making this up as he went along, just like her.

"I am here to serve the Child, nothing more." Cora's voice was soft, but strong. Amplified out to where the screens were, it created a ripple of excitement in the gathered people. She had regained her composure but was still obviously out of her element.

"And what about you, General?" Anthony asked. He seemed to enjoy putting them on the spot by treating their conversation in front of millions of people like it was some kind of off-the-cuff conversation. The Anthony Taulke Graves thought he knew was a calculating man whose every public utterance was scripted. This Anthony's dark eyes flashed with good nature as if he'd been freed of all the responsibilities of his former life.

Graves did his best to keep his expression neutral. He'd been in news conferences before, he knew what a stray comment could do to a mission. "I'm here to serve the greater good. I still work for the United Nations and I'm happy to accept all the help the council can provide."

Anthony cocked his head as if to say, That's the best you've got, Graves?

Turning back to Nancy, he shrugged and pulled a face. "Well, there you have it, Nancy. Your new representatives on the Council of Corporations. Ms. Santos and the general are here to keep us honest and I'm glad to have them."

"What about President Teller, Anthony?" Nancy said. "Doesn't he deserve a seat on the council?"

"Why, Nancy, I'm surprised at you." Anthony affected an expression of mock horror, drawing a smile from Watson. Graves noticed how everyone seemed to be enjoying themselves. This was fun for them. "You blast the United States nightly on your broadcast, but you seem to have a soft spot for the American president." His expression hardened into sternness. Even the drones seemed to take notice.

"The political apparatus has failed this planet. It is time for a new form of governance. One that can be nimble and effective. Ms. Santos represents a religion that covers nearly a third of the world's population. William Graves stopped being a soldier a long time ago—he's been a humanitarian, fighting for the betterment of his fellow humans for as long as I've known him. We have big problems to solve and no time left to do it." He released a blinding smile. "Now, if you'll excuse us, we have an elevator car to catch."

"Why Olympus Station, Anthony?" Nancy pressed. "Why not at the UN or someplace planetside?"

Graves could tell the implied barb stung Anthony. He swung back toward the news gathering.

"A few days ago, I was nearly assassinated. Someone could be targeting me right now, in fact." Graves saw the news people exchange uneasy glances. Anthony laughed. "No need to worry. I've had this area secured. But we need to take my personal safety and the safety of the council members out of the equation. Olympus Station is protected by my personal security forces. No one is getting in"—he threw a wink at Graves and Cora —"or out without my say-so."

The rest of Anthony's words about big decisions and world-changing ideals faded away. Graves and Cora were about to be locked in a space station with some of the most powerful people in the world. A place that he was ill-equipped to handle, if he was being honest with himself. His fingers found the Saint Christopher medal around his neck. Anthony's humorous remark about getting out took on a whole new significance. He tuned back in to the rest of his speech:

"I will be surrounded by people I can trust and who trust me. You do trust me, right, General?" Anthony said. He said it with a smile playing to the crowd, but Graves felt the prompt all the same.

"Of course, Mr. Taulke," he said.

"Anthony, General." Taulke slid him arm around Graves's shoulders. "We're colleagues now." He drew Cora under his other arm and smiled at the cameras.

The new suit provided by Anthony's tailor fit Graves's frame like a glove. He admired his new look in his new data glasses as the tailor's drone spun around his body. The cut of the charcoal gray suit made him look sleek and trim, his shoulders broader, chest deeper. Hell, it even made him feel taller.

"Acceptable, sir?" The tailor was a wizened older man with a fringe of gray and kind eyes. A tape measure hung around his neck but Graves had not seem him touch it, so he guessed it was just part of his outfit.

"It's ... magnificent. I've never had a suit like this before."

The old man chuckled. "Few have. It's smartfabric. It reads your surroundings and adjusts to suit your needs." He laughed at his own pun, then leaned in. "I even upgraded you to the bullet-resistant jacket. It's a little heavier material, but your frame can handle the extra bulk." He ran his hand across Graves's lapel in a way that felt oddly intimate.

Graves took a step back. "Bullet-resistant?"

The old man pursued him, hooking his finger into the V where the suit jacket crossed Graves's body and the snowy white shirt started. Graves felt the suit tighten against his ribcage.

"That's better." The tailor nodded. "The suit fabric is blended with the same polymer used to make bulletproof materials. Depending on the caliber of weapon, you'd survive."

"A handgun?"

He shrugged. "Probably. We don't do a lot of testing. I think it's more of a marketing pitch, honestly." The tailor fussed with his lapels again and Graves stepped back.

"Thank you. I think we're good here."

He waited for the tailor to leave, then turned to the window to admire himself again. Part of him couldn't wait for Cora to see him. He did a turn and looked at his backside in the window.

Graves stopped. What the hell was he doing? Six hours into living like one of the elite and he was checking out his own ass in the window.

He swiped his hand across his freshly shaven chin. Anthony had spared no expense in his treatment of his guests. Cora and Graves were separated as soon as they boarded Anthony's private elevator car. "Car" made it sound mundane and small. It was more like an eight-story apartment building attached to the Darwin space elevator.

He hadn't seen Cora in three hours, but if her experience was like his, she'd started with a hot shower, a massage, then a haircut. They took everything, his clothes, his government-issue data glasses—the only item he'd been able to salvage was his Saint Christopher medal and even that was an argument. The implied symbolism was clear to Graves: your old life is gone. You are one of us now.

After a light lunch, the tailor came next for a brand-new outfit. He couldn't help but admire himself one last time in the mirror. A knock at the door interrupted his thoughts.

Cora wore a white silk shirt that hung loosely to the tops of her thighs and a shimmering dark blue pant suit with a coat that reached to her knees. The thin layers of material worked together to cling suggestively to her body as she moved, her muscles outlined by silk for a moment, then disappearing inside the loose material. A simple gold chain was around her neck and her hair was pulled back into an elaborate braid that she wore pulled over her shoulder.

They stared at each other for a few seconds. "You look amazing," she said.

"So do you."

She crossed the room and embraced him. He could feel her body through the thin material. "What are we doing here?" she whispered.

Cora broke away and stood at the window. The elevator was well out of the atmosphere and the curve of Earth's horizon was a fuzzy line of clouds and haze. "How much longer?"

Graves looked up at Olympus Station. It was the size of a bright marble now. "Few hours maybe."

"What does he have planned for us?" Cora said, her voice low. It was possible, even likely that they were being watched right now. "I still don't understand why we're here."

Graves watched an armed spacecraft bearing the Taulke logo pass by the window. It looked like a full-fledged, purpose-built fighter, not a shuttle with backfitted railguns. A chill ran though him. Private companies with weapons in space. Probably better armed than any Earth-bound nation's asset. He was watching—no, participating in—the privatization of his world.

"If I know Taulke, he's got a plan. It's not us he's after, it's power. We're just pawns in his game."

"I don't believe that, William," Cora whispered. "We are here—you and I—for a reason. It can only be us ... I have seen it."

"Visions again?" He studied her and she looked back at him with nothing but openness in her face. "You believe that?"

"I do."

"So how does this end?" She really was a remarkable woman, the kind of person he would have liked to have met under other circumstances.

Cora smiled, but it was a sad smile. She shook her head. "That's not how Cassandra works. We are placed at this point in time. Together. But the outcome ... is not preordained."

"So it's up to us then?" Graves said. "What could possibly go wrong?"

They laughed together, but the undercurrent of tension never left. Cora took Graves's hand, laced her fingers into his. "I think a straightforward approach is best."

⸻

They found Anthony in his personal quarters of the space elevator car, lying on his back, eyes defocused. The room had a span of infinity windows affording a breathtaking view of the receding Earth and Olympus Station growing nearer. From this vantage point, Graves made out a four-fighter escort for the elevator car.

"Expecting trouble?" he said, nodding at a passing fighter.

Anthony broke off from whatever he was studying in his retinal implant. "You two look amazing," he said, getting to his feet. "Like you were born to wealth."

"It's never been an aspiration of mine," Cora replied with acid in her voice.

Anthony either didn't notice or didn't care about her tone. "Nevertheless, we all have parts to play, and you look the part, Ms. Santos."

"And what is my part, Mr. Taulke?" Cora's spine had stiffened.

Anthony energized a holograph in the center of the room. An image of the Earth, not unlike the one outside the window. As Graves watched, bands began to circle the globe, each one consuming a few degrees of latitude.

"This is what your Cassandra is doing to our planet," he said to Cora as he stalked around the holo. "Weather patterns appear random, but they're not. Slowly, humanity is being pushed to the margins." He overlaid a map of population density over time and Graves could see a slow migration of people from the latitudinal bands to the interstitial spaces.

"I don't understand," Cora said, her voice tight.

"We're trying to solve the wrong problem," Anthony continued. "Look closer. The weather patterns are subtle but persistent. Weather is being used to clear bands of the planet. Either people are exterminated or they become refugees who eventually settle in a more acceptable zone. It's—"

"Terraforming," Graves finished for him. He touched the holo, blowing up a section of Africa. "These are agricultural zones. Food production on a grand scale, a planetary scale."

Anthony clapped. "Very good, General. Very good."

Cora's voice shook. "Cassandra would never—"

"There is no Cassandra, Ms. Santos. Never has been. The New Earth Order was a religious movement that was coopted by an artificial intelligence. The mass indoctrination of people into a mind control experiment unlike anything in the history of mankind. Given enough time, Cassandra would have made the Third Reich look like a tea party." Anthony's eyes landed on Graves. "But thanks to the general here, she was stopped." He turned back to the holo. "But her evil plan continues."

"Who's behind it?" Graves asked.

"Who has the most to gain?" Anthony shot back.

"You," Cora said.

Anthony shook his head slowly as if it pained him to do so. "Not me."

"Then who?"

"That's what you're going to help me find out." Anthony paced now, his steps quickening as he spoke.

"There are six on the council, including me. My son, Tony, Elise Kisaan, Adriana, Viktor, and Xi Qinlao. One of them is a traitor."

"Why would we help you?" Cora asked.

Anthony came to a sudden stop. He pointed to the holograph. Graves watched a grid of dots appear in the space above the globe. "This is a new satellite network being put in place by the council to give Elise Kisaan fine control over the weather. At least that's my cover story." He offered a wolfish grin. "Viktor has designed a little surprise for the satellite launch. New nanites. Nanites capable of killing the Lazarus Protocol. Nanites under my complete control."

"I cannot go against Elise Kisaan," Cora said. "She carries the Child."

"It's not Elise," Anthony replied. "In her mind, the satellite network is for her."

"Xi Qinlao is building the network for you, and Viktor designed it," Graves said, watching Anthony's response. The other man did not acknowledge him, he just stared at the holo, his expression a mask of concentration.

"That leaves Adriana Rabh. And your own son."

Anthony Taulke nodded.

"And you're going to help me find out which one it is."

26

CORAZON SANTOS • EN ROUTE TO OLYMPUS STATION

All the primping and attention from Anthony Taulke's cosmetics staff felt unnecessary at first. But somewhere along the way, Cora surrendered herself to the process and found her bliss. The baths, the skin treatments, the hair and makeup, the massage ... it all felt so decadent and so wonderful at the same time.

And then there was the new outfit made of silky material that slid along her treated skin as if to remind her of how wondrous the day had been.

As she and William left Anthony's quarters on the elevator car, Cora took William's hand as if it was the most natural thing in the world. "He's crazy, you know," she said.

Graves put a small pressure on her hand, but said nothing in reply. He was thinking, strategizing. For her part, Cora rejected Anthony's words. The Cassandra of her heart, of her belief, would not be a party to forced migration of people. She was a goddess of life and goodness. The Cassandra she worshipped wanted to save the world.

On the other hand, Cora had seen the devastation caused by the weather. She had buried men and women and children, hundreds of them, on her own migration from South America to Fort Hood. She had been called to go north—Cassandra had made her wishes clear to Cora—but all those people who had followed her...

Her heart wanted to fall back on the old saws—*It is Her will. Everything happens for a reason*—but her head rebelled. William had seen and agreed with Anthony's conclusions about the weather patterns as if he already knew it.

"It's true, isn't it?" she said. "What Anthony told us about the weather patterns and the people? Cassandra is behind it."

Graves refused to meet her gaze. "What you know as Cassandra is gone. Taulke is right, she was a construct, a computer program used to dupe millions of people. She's behind this terraforming, there's no other explanation." He paused, and she felt the warmth of his hand more acutely. "Computer programs are created to do work, to change things. Cassandra was no different. She's remaking the Earth into ... I don't know what."

Cora's mind reeled at the idea that her entire reason for being was a lie. "No, I believed in something better than myself. She talked to me—"

"When?" Graves demanded. "When did these visions start?"

"Last year, before I left Brazil..."

"Cassandra was dead by then. The AI running the whole New Earth Order was dead, blown out of the sky."

"How do you know for sure?"

"Because I killed her. I was there when the space station went ka-blooey. There was no Cassandra, you didn't have visions, there is no religion. It's a lie, a big fat lie."

"But the Child. The Child is the second—"

"Elise Kisaan is pregnant by a man named Remy Cade. They did it the good old-fashioned way—by fucking." She flinched when he cursed. "Remy was just a grunt in love who got dumped and he blew himself up." Graves's face clenched for a second with passing emotion. "And I let him."

They were outside the room where Cora had received her spa treatment. There was a bed in there, a place to rest. She released William's hand and pushed at the controls for the door. "I need to be alone."

He caught her arm. "Listen to me, Cora. There is no Cassandra, there is no child going to save the world. It's all a giant hoax by someone on the council who wants to call the shots. Anthony's plan is the best thing for the planet. We back him and we get out of here."

She shook off his hand. "I need to be alone now."

The room was empty and cold. Her hands shook as she cleared the window, allowing a view of the planet below. She laced her fingers together and squeezed as hard as she could to still the trembling.

If she pressed her forehead to the glass and looked down, it felt as if she might fall into the swirling clouds below. The patterns changed ever so slowly, like an ancient stop-motion movie. It seemed hard to believe that something so beautiful could be so deadly.

Graves claimed he had killed Cassandra. As if her god was resident in a space station. If faith was the act of believing without proof, then she was being tested. Anthony Taulke and his models, Graves and his bombs—they lacked faith.

Cora settled into a chair, feeling the gossamer trappings of her lovely dress caress her skin, and she closed her eyes.

Darkness, the roar of angry water rushing past. The smell of churned earth and crushed greenery, an undercurrent of raw sewage.

She knew these smells, these sounds. She had been there.

When Cora opened her eyes it was a day of bright sunshine, the heat of the Brazilian rain forest cloaked her skin like a wet towel.

Home.

Behind her was the clinic. The walls still new and white, the scars of red earth not yet healed. Inside were clean smells—antiseptic, plastic, ozone—safe smells.

But out here, outside, the violence of rushing water. Somewhere under that water was a village, and her house. Ricardo and the baby were there.

She was alone on the hill. Safe. Cora opened her mouth to scream but no sound came out. All her breath had been stolen away.

It's a dream. Not real. Wake up.

An entire tree floated by in the waters of the flash flood. It rotated slowly, like a child's toy in the river of water and mud and debris.

And then, improbably loud over the roar of the river, the cry of a child. Cora whirled around, frantically searching for the sound. A tree had snagged on the bank and high in the branches she spied a speck of white.

Another wail, louder this time, filled with pain and hunger and fear. Cora raced to the tree and threw herself into the wet branches. She slipped and slid among the slimy, muddy leaves. She found footing and hoisted herself higher just as the tree trembled in the grip of the water. It was breaking loose. It would sweep away, taking her and the child with it.

The rational side of her brain told her it was all a dream. There was no baby, no child stuck high in a tree, but she didn't stop. Cora dug her claws into a clump of soggy leaves for a handhold and came away with a fist full of mud. Another hand found a branch, she moved a few feet higher.

The child cried, even more insistent, and she called out. "I'm coming. Mama is coming."

Her native Portuguese slipped from her tongue. She knew that was the language the child—her child—was used to.

There was no response from the baby and that caused Cora to climb faster. She broke through the canopy to find the bundle of white a scant body length away, caught in a cleft at the end of a long branch that hung over the river of mud.

Cora threw her leg over the main branch and shimmied out as fast she could. The rough bark clawed at her thighs, the sun hammered down from above, and the taste of mud filled her mouth.

"I'm coming," she called again.

No response.

And then she was close enough to reach the baby. Her hands left streaks of mud on the snow-white cloth that swaddled the child. She lifted the bundle from the cleft in the branch and pressed it to her chest.

The child's face was round with a fringe of dark hair peeking from the cloth wrapped close to her head. The angry red was fading from her cheeks and the tiny lips twitched in imaginary feeding.

Cora touched the baby's face and her eyes snapped open.

Eyes the color of pure gold stared back at her. Eyes that seemed both wise and curious at the same time.

The tree branch between her legs quivered, jostling the baby and forcing her to hold the child even closer. Cora felt the tree shift as it disconnected from the riverbank and entered the main stream again.

Cora nearly lost her leg grip on the tree branch. She could hold on to the baby or the tree, but not both.

Behind them, another enormous tree bore down on them like an ocean liner. Cora hooked her ankles together and crushed the child against her chest. She freed one arm and wrapped it around the thick branch.

It was all for naught. When the collision happened, Cora and the child were flicked from their perch like a bug from a blade of grass. She screamed as she fell, rolling her body so as to protect the baby when they landed in the water. The mud swallowed them whole, the viscous liquid closing about. She tried to swim with one arm—

Her arm was trapped. She pulled and pulled but she could not free it.

"Cora!"

A man's voice. Concern. Warmth. She tried to push the child toward the sound. Her breath was almost gone.

Hands on her shoulders, shaking her whole body. The baby was gone, lost to the mud. A sharp slap across her cheek woke her.

William Graves had hoisted her to her feet, one hand clamped on her arm. The other raised as if to slap her again.

"Cora..." His tone was soft and full of concern. "We're here. We've docked on Olympus Station."

She nodded, allowing herself to lean into his chest, just for a second.

"The child," she whispered.

"The what?" With her ear pressed against his chest, she felt as well as heard the response.

"Nothing," she said. "It was nothing."

27

MING QINLAO • QINLAO MANUFACTURING HEADQUARTERS

Ming paused in the entrance of her former quarters in the Qinlao building. The heavy wooden door was made of teak, salvaged from a temple somewhere in the north. Her father had loved this door, arranging the lighting above so it played off of and deepened the carvings.

He had taken care with the details of his life.

Ming stripped the hood off her head, not caring if the cameras detected her. If her aunt really wanted to find her, let her come. She pressed her gloved hand against the security lock on the door, feeling the haptics probe the circuits. With a whisper of oiled steel, the door unlocked.

The interior was dark and still. Ming did not bother to turn on any lights. She paused in the foyer until her eyes adjusted, then made her way into the study. The walls were bare, unskinned, and she left them that way. Outside the windows, the city of Shanghai was shrouded in fog, lights from nearby buildings no more than glowing blobs of mysterious illumination. A low-flying aircar passed, its navigation lights leaving a streak of red in the mist.

She took a framed picture from her pocket and placed it carefully on the desk. Ming watched her younger self chase a butterfly, her father watching, smiling. It was the only possession she had taken when she left.

Now returned. Like the last piece of a jigsaw puzzle getting locked into place.

She faced the window to wait. Ming considered lighting a fire, maybe reskinning the walls to something cozier, but that would only remind her of simpler times. Happier times. So she stared at the fog instead.

She did not have long to wait. The sound of the lock on the front door releasing came to her ears only a few minutes later.

"What do you hope to see out there, Ming?" Marcus's reedy voice, his faltering steps. Her father's oldest friend was failing in health, she could sense it even without the help of Echo.

She smiled in spite of herself. "I seek perspective." It was an old joke they shared, another common link with the man who bound them together, Ming's father.

"Hmm." The old man stood beside her at the window. She could hear the rattle of his breath, the racing of his pulse.

He is afraid, Echo said.

"Quiet, you," she whispered to herself.

"Did you say something?" Marcus asked, peering at her through thick data glasses.

Ming stiffened. "No."

Marcus turned back to contemplating the swirling fog. "I know you intended the perspective remark as a joke, but I have to say, it is an apt metaphor for the situation we find ourselves in."

"We?"

"I am still your lawyer, Ming."

She spun away from the glass. "You're here to stop me."

"You tried to kill your aunt, Ming. That will solve nothing."

"She killed my father—"

"It won't bring him back. Your father is the last person in the world who would want this. He was a man of the future, not the past. He would not want you to throw your life away like this, Ming."

She let silence settle in the room.

"You knew," she said finally.

"I suspected. After you disappeared, your mother told me the whole story. She's worried about you. Sying, too, and Ruben. All of us are worried about you."

Just hearing the names felt like she was opening a door in her heart that she had welded shut. Sying ... Ruben ... the syllables fell like body blows on her.

"Do they know?"

"Know about your father? No. But the attack on Xi's home? I think they suspect you did not die in a fiery aircar accident." He eyed her. "The illusion was well done, you know. Well planned and executed. Your father would have been proud."

Ming found that when she smiled, the voice of Echo grew softer. "Ito helped."

"Hmmm." Marcus walked to the leather sofa and turned on a light. Then he gently lowered his slight body into the cushions.

Ming hesitated, then took a seat at the far end of the couch.

"There is another way," Marcus said. "A better way."

"An inquiry." Ming didn't bother to hide the bitterness in her voice.

"An investigation, conducted by me. With the security tape as evidence, we can—"

"You had your chance, Marcus. My father's death was already investigated once. You did nothing." She hissed out the last words.

Marcus shook his head. "You need to listen, Ming-child. Listen with your head, not your heart. Your mother suppressed the security tape. She knew it would tear the company apart. It was going to be hard enough for you to take over from your father, but to add a murder investigation to the mix? And then..."

His voice trailed off, but Ming could fill in the blanks. She got mixed up with Anthony Taulke and the disastrous Lazarus Protocol. She ran for her life. She melded her brain with a supercomputer and nearly died. Ming felt the skin of the MoSCOW suit clinging to her body and all she wanted to do was strip it off. This was all her fault. Every step that led her to this room and this night was a direct result of her choices.

Ming felt a roiling in her gut. She swallowed hard.

"What do you propose, Marcus?"

He steepled his fingers. "An investigation, a new one, run by me. We call a board meeting for tomorrow morning. You show the board the security tape. You ask for a real investigation into your father's death. They will have no choice but to agree and your aunt will get the punishment she deserves. I'll see to it."

Ming flexed her gloved fingers, considering. Echo assured her Marcus was telling the truth, but still she hesitated. Not because she didn't trust Marcus. To turn the tape over to him meant turning over control to him. This was personal. For months, revenge had been her driving force, and now to give it up meant ... what?

"Ming," Marcus said softly. "It's what Jie would have wanted. He never intended for his daughter to become his avenger."

Her gaze found the butterfly picture and for a second she lost herself in the innocence of the moment.

"Okay."

Marcus waited. Ming let the seconds tick by.

"Are you going to make me ask for it?" he said.

Ming pulsed him the security vid. Marcus used the arm of the sofa to get his body upright.

"You're doing the right thing."

Ming said nothing, just stared at the blank wall.

Marcus let himself out, his footsteps tracking down the hall and out the front door. Still, Ming stared ahead, her mind blank.

The door whispered open in the empty room behind her and Ming spun, arms up in a defensive stance, her senses at full alert.

Sying Qinlao stood in the doorway. "Ming? Is that you?"

Ming's arms dropped. She vaulted over the couch and closed the distance between them in two strides.

Sying wore a thin dress that seemed to melt under Ming's touch. Her lover's body was firm and warm. Ming shook with pent-up emotion.

Sying cupped Ming's face between her hands, her grip deceptively strong. She forced Ming to look at her and Ming felt her reason melt under her gaze. Sying's finger traced the faint outline of the scar where MoSCOW had mated with her cheek. She brushed back the newly grown hair.

"What have they done to you?" she whispered. "My sweet girl, what have they done?"

Ming tried to speak, tried to tell her that she had done it to herself. It was the only way. If she wanted to come home, to be in this moment, she needed to take risks...

But her voice stuck in her throat. Her lips found Sying's and her knees grew weak.

Sying's fingers stroked Ming's chest, sending the haptic sensors into overdrive. She arched an eyebrow. "I'd like to see what's underneath this catsuit."

Ming had been wrong about one thing: the haptic sensors were no match for bare flesh.

Ming paced in the study, waiting for a pulsed message from Marcus before she left the apartment for the boardroom. Sying had left her bed shortly before dawn, but if Ming closed her eyes she could still feel the brush of Sying's hair on her cheek, the hot flush of skin against skin, the taste of her soft lips.

She sucked in a sharp breath and held it to re-center her emotions. It made no difference. She felt alive in a way she hadn't felt in a year, like peeling off the MoSCOW suit had shed every past mistake. Marcus was right. She would put the evidence against Xi in front of the board and let them decide how to handle it for the good of the company. Her father would have wanted that, she knew that now.

Ming left the MoSCOW suit folded on her bed, choosing an outfit for the board meeting from what she had left in the closet of her former apartment. She selected a dove-gray cashmere suit and a dark blue blouse with black pearl buttons. Unlike the MoSCOW suit, these garments fit her loosely; it seemed she had lost weight in the last year.

In the background noise of her thoughts, Echo lurked. Her companion seemed uncomfortable with the onslaught of emotions unleashed by her night with Sying. The voice feedback felt contradictory and self-serving. Almost as if Echo was jealous.

Ming smiled at the thought.

By the time Marcus's pulse arrived, she had circled the room at least a dozen times, alone with her thoughts. Outside the windows, the fog was gone and it was a clear day over Shanghai. The midmorning sun etched the details of the buildings below the Qinlao tower, making the crowded city feel shiny and clean. Air traffic crowded the sky, casting fast-moving shadows over the cityscape. Inside the room, the scent of Sying lingered, keeping Ming's emotions on edge.

It all felt like a fresh start.

She tried not to rush as she made her way to the private elevator that would take her to the boardroom. Her retinal implant connected to the elevator and ordered the floor.

When the door opened, all eyes were on her. She could tell from the stares that Marcus and Sying had not told the rest of the people in the room that she was coming—or even that she was still alive.

Danny Xiao, her one-time suitor, was facing the elevator as it opened and nearly spit out a mouthful of tea. JC Han twisted in his chair. His face went slack with shock. Sying and Marcus shared a secret smile. At the sight of her, her mother's lips twisted into her version of a smile. The rest of the room, lower-level board members and those who were holoing in—they were going to regret missing this meeting in person—all started talking at once.

But Ming had eyes for one person only: Auntie Xi. Her aunt's eyes narrowed, telling Ming she had expected her niece to show up. The older woman wore a dress of dark green that hugged her spare frame and a silver scarf. Her makeup was perfect and her long dark hair was pulled into an elaborately-wrapped bun at the nape of her neck. She threw a sharp glance at Marcus, then stood.

"Welcome, niece," she said in an acid tone that suggested anything but. "I see the reports of your demise are greatly exaggerated." She smiled then. "As are the reports of my own."

Ming felt a fury then. It grew in her gut and raged up her body, making her neck flush with anger. If she'd been wearing the MoSCOW suit at that moment, her aunt might have ended up in pieces on the expensive carpet.

Sying vacated her seat next to Auntie Xi and stepped close to Ming. She gripped Ming's forearm, the touch of her hand bleeding away the anger that threatened to consume her.

Ming formed her lips into a smile. "Thank you, Auntie. I'm feeling much better now." She dug her fingers into the back of the leather chair and drew it toward her in a slow, controlled manner. Then she took her seat the same way. Slow, in control.

Her aunt glared at her, trying to decide if she should call security or play the situation out, Ming guessed.

Marcus cleared his throat. "Ming is here for a reason, Xi. She has a proposal for the board."

Xi's perfectly formed eyebrows went up a notch. "She does? She has no place on this board, remember?"

"I would like to hear what she has to say," Wenqian's amplified voice rang out in the room.

"I would, too," Sying said. Ming saw nods all around the table. Marcus had prepared the room well.

"We can make a motion or you can just let her speak, Xi," Marcus said gently.

Ming watched the warring emotions in her aunt's face using Echo's enhanced capabilities. Confusion, uncertainty, but no fear.

She doesn't know why I'm here, Ming realized.

Xi took her seat and made a great show of pulling in the chair and arranging her tablet and stylus on the table. She picked up her teacup and took an exaggerated sip. Then she nodded at Marcus. "Proceed."

Marcus threw the security vid to the main screen in the room and dimmed the lights. The frozen picture showed a smiling Jie Qinlao, hair mussed from a hard hat. Marcus nodded at Ming.

"Last year, I came into possession of this security vid." Ming paused. The words seemed stuck in her throat. She swallowed. "It shows ... it shows the death—no, the murder—of my father."

Marcus started the fifty-nine-second vid. Ming watched for the thousandth time the comforting sound of Jie Qinlao laughing with his work crew, then the scream of fighters, and the explosion of incendiary bombs. Each frame was seared into her brain.

The room was still when the vid finished. Auntie Xi's face was slack and pale in a way no makeup could conceal. "I thought..." she began.

Ming ignored her. "My father did not die from a rogue virus. His body was not lost when the authorities firebombed the camp to stop the spread of the virus. He was murdered."

JC Han's face was purple with rage under his iron-gray pompadour. "Who?" he said in a voice that cut through the room.

Ming manipulated the vid to the final seconds, stopping on the shot of the last fighter just as it released the final incendiary bomb. The one that killed her father.

She zoomed in on the cockpit, enhancing the image so the room could see the reflection of the pilot's helmet logo. She heard her aunt gasp, then the rest of the room follow suit.

The logo on the helmet was the Qinlao seal.

"Our own people?" JC Han demanded. "We did this?"

"We," Ming spat out. "This was the work of one person. A traitor."

Auntie Xi's chin was high, her eyes flashing. "Why are we just seeing this now?"

"It was my choice," Ming's mother's amplified voice broke in.

"I should have known," Xi replied. She swayed, the first sign of weakness Ming had seen in her, and gripped the edge of the table to steady herself. Xi took another sip of tea. "There must be an investigation."

"There will be," Marcus assured her. "I'll see to it personally."

"Good," Xi said in a breathy tone. "I—I don't feel well." She started to get up, then sat back down immediately. She looked at Ming with a softer emotion in her eyes.

"My brother..." She caught her breath, her hand fluttering to her throat. "My brother was a great man."

Then she pitched face forward onto the table.

28

WILLIAM GRAVES • OLYMPUS STATION

Graves knew politics—or at least he thought he did. But these people played the game at a level so far above his skill that he might as well have been holding a pacifier instead of a drink.

He hoisted his flute of champagne, undoubtedly a rare and expensive vintage that was utterly wasted on him, and took a sip. The drink had a fruity aftertaste and the bubbles made him clear his throat. He reminded himself to go slow. The last thing he needed was to drink too much in this room.

Anthony Taulke and his partners reminded him of sharks. Predators circling the space, wary eyes looking for a weakness, waiting for a drop of blood in the water to spark a feeding frenzy. He recalled seeing a vid a long time ago about how female praying mantises ate their partners after mating. Maybe that was a more apt analogy.

Before Olympus, when he envisioned a space station, Graves had painted a mental picture of steel and formed plastic walls. Efficient and functional. True to form, Anthony Taulke defied those expectations. The room he stood in could have been transported directly from a European salon—probably was. The polished parquet floor under his feet had the springy feel of real wood, and when he knocked discreetly on the butter-cream-yellow panel walls, they were most certainly not made from formed

plastic. An elaborate, vaulted ceiling that looked like real plaster was tastefully illuminated with hidden lights and a magnificent crystal chandelier
the size of his desk in Fort Hood completed the illusion.

Graves spied Cora across the room speaking to Adriana Rabh. Like him,
she held a champagne flute and seemed to be drinking sparingly as well.
Her eyes met his for a second and he raised his glass a few millimeters to
acknowledge her.

He was worried about Cora. When they docked at Olympus and he'd
gone to find her, he expected to find a woman devastated that Anthony
Taulke had revealed her religion as a sham. What he found instead was a
woman in the throes of a bad dream, twisting and crying out. At first he'd
thought maybe she was having a seizure, but when he woke her she acted
normal.

No, better than normal. Focused, driven, and capable of handling
herself in any situation. Come to think of it, she was handling all this way
better than he was.

"General? Are you finding everything to your liking?" Tony Taulke's
tone was professional and courteous, but with the subtle undercurrent of
you-don't-belong-here. Graves gave an inward sigh. If he didn't want to be
buttonholed into an unwanted conversation, he shouldn't have been acting
like a wallflower.

"Amazing," he replied. "Not like any space station I've seen."

"Been on many space stations, have you?"

Graves took note of the sharpness in his voice. "Just one, actually, the
Neo station. And that didn't work out so well for the Neos."

Tony drained his glass and snagged another from a passing waiter. Even
the waiters were dressed in short, dark jackets and ruffed shirt fronts, in
keeping with the European drawing room theme. He quaffed a long swal-
low, then forced a smile.

"So I've heard," Tony said.

Graves changed the subject. "I haven't seen Ms. Qinlao tonight."

Tony made a face like his champagne was sour. "The Qinlao faction will
be joining us for your induction ceremony tomorrow. I'm afraid the Qinlao
organization is tied up with other matters at present."

"I was sad to hear of Ming's passing," Graves said. "She was quite a young woman. We worked together on Lazarus."

"Hmm." Tony nursed his glass. "The Qinlaos are consumed with their loss, I'm told."

"And Ms. Kisaan?"

Tony studied Graves's face, his dark eyes scanning for clues of Graves knew not what. Somehow, the mere mention of Elise Kisaan had touched a nerve. "Our lady in waiting. I'm afraid her condition doesn't agree with her, but I suspect she'll make an appearance at dinner."

Graves offered up a tiny prayer of thanks that there was going to be food to counteract all the alcohol he'd already consumed. "And the baby? When is it due?"

"Ah, the blessed Child of Cassandra!" Tony said it just as there was a lull in the overall noise level in the room and everyone heard him. All eyes turned to Tony and Graves. Graves's face went warm, but Tony seemed not to care about the attention.

Instead, he pointed to the door at the far end of the room. "Speak of the devil!"

Elise Kisaan stood framed in the three-meter-high drawing room doorway. She was clad in a flowing robe of white that hung on the curves of her very pregnant body. She wore no makeup and her straight dark hair was drawn back in a simple braid over her Neo tattoo. Her long face was drawn.

The room stood still and silent. Then Cora advanced cautiously. Elise's smile lit up her face, making the lines and tiredness evaporate. She held out both hands to Cora. "Corazon, I'm so glad to see you again."

Graves watched Cora's shoulders quiver at Elise's words, knowing his friend was crying tears of joy. Elise guided Cora's hands to her belly.

From his vantage point at the back of the room, Graves could see everyone's face in profile as they watched the scene play out before them. Tony had a smirk on his face, the edges of his lips twitching. Anthony and Viktor were standing together wearing nearly identical sympathetic expressions. Graves shifted his gaze to Adriana. Her eyes were cold and piercing and her sharp features were twisted into an angry scowl. This was a woman with an axe to grind.

A young man stepped close to her and she whispered into his ear. The man was Adriana's height with thinning brown hair brushed straight back and a slight but wiry frame. The most notable thing about him was that he had an old paperback book tucked into his back pocket.

Their encounter lasted all of two seconds, so quickly that if Graves had not been staring at Adriana at that moment, he might have missed the meeting entirely. Graves swiveled his head to look around the room, but the man was gone.

Anthony stepped forward to put a fatherly hand on Elise's shoulder. "Now that Elise has joined us, let's go in to dinner, shall we?"

The wall to Graves's left retracted to reveal a dining table set for seven. Anthony shooed his guests forward, using a pat on the back here, a gentle arm squeeze there. When he got to Graves, he guided him to one of two settings on the long side of the rectangular table. Graves surveyed the battlefield. Across from him were three places, then one on either flank. He and Cora would be on display—and surrounded—for dinner.

Cora touched his hand briefly as they all stood behind their chairs. Anthony took the center place directly across from Graves and Cora, with Adriana and Tony on either side. Elise and Viktor took the short ends of the table. Cora had secured her place closest to Elise.

Graves heard the doors close behind him, shutting out the European drawing room decor. In contrast, the dining room was uber-modern, all sleek glass and sculpted steel. The chair when he dragged it back was heavy and resembled a steel torture device. But when he sat, Graves felt the chair mold to his body and lift off the floor.

Anthony watched his expression change when he sat. "Happens every time," he laughed. "The Mollet chairs are the most comfortable seat money can buy."

Graves was inclined to agree. The lighting in the ceiling was hidden, but arranged so that the table glowed, illuminating the faces of the diners but leaving the rest of the room around them in deep darkness. Waiters passed like shadows behind them. Disembodied hands placed seven oblong plates in front of the diners all at exactly the same moment.

The white plate was mostly empty, except for a squirt of something that looked like Dijon mustard and two squares of bread with a curlicue of deep green on top. Years of practice told Graves to watch Anthony for his dining cues.

The elder Taulke picked up one of the triangles with his fingers, dipped one tip in the yellow sauce, and popped the whole thing in his mouth. Graves followed suit. His eyes snapped open at the explosion of taste on his tongue. Sweet and hot at the same time. A glass of white wine appeared in front of him and he took a careful sip. The taste expanded and deepened, making Graves think of a day at the beach.

"Well, what do you taste? Good?" Anthony asked.

Graves nodded. "Very. I guess I'm not very good at this, but I tasted the ocean."

Adriana's eyes widened. "You have a very sensitive palate, General. The pairing with the wine is designed to bring out the essence of sea urchin, but it's very subtle. Most people miss it."

Graves noticed Elise ate only one of the triangles and left her wine untouched.

In spite of himself, Graves enjoyed the meal immensely and scored several more appreciative nods from Adriana and Anthony. Tony slouched in his seat and ate his courses in spiteful bites without seeming to savor them. Viktor spent more time drinking than eating. To his right, Cora spoke in low tones to Elise, mostly talking about her migration experience to the US.

Graves caught Adriana's eye. "Who was that man you were speaking to in the other room? The one with the book in his pocket."

Adriana froze. Anthony sensed the change in her demeanor and turned in her direction. To Graves's surprise, Tony answered his question. "You mean Fischer. Man only reads real books, says he can feel the words coming off the page. Can you believe that?"

"What's he doing up on this level?" Anthony asked. "Fischer is security, right?"

Tony sat up in his chair. He waved his hands dismissively. "I lent him to Adriana as a body man back in New York. Just temporarily."

Anthony nodded and was about to ask another question when dessert arrived. He smiled at Graves. "Now, General, this you will truly appreciate —" He broke off when Elise sat up suddenly.

"You will have to excuse me, Anthony." Her voice was pinched and her face twisted with discomfort. "I think I need to lie down for a bit." She put a hand on her belly and grimaced. "I don't think the meal agreed with me." She stood up, still gripping the edge of the table.

Cora was on her feet. "I'll be happy to help—" She gasped.

The lower half of Elise Kisaan's white dress was covered in blood.

29

MING QINLAO • QINLAO MANUFACTURING HEADQUARTERS

Auntie Xi was dead.

Ming had built up the moment in her mind for so long and to such an extent that when dream met reality, reality suffered.

She expected elation. Or maybe satisfaction. But she felt none of those things. A scant twelve hours ago, she might have snapped her aunt's neck without a second thought and now she felt ... nothing.

The poison had been in her tea, or to be more precise, her teacup. Auntie Xi had a favorite teacup, an ancient, ceramic bowl replete with cracks and dings that she carried in her purse wherever she went. It was a slow-acting poison, which meant it could have been applied anytime over the last eighteen hours and could have been attributed to as many as a hundred people or more.

Marcus acted quickly. The sudden death of a CEO of a major corporation could be a catastrophic event, and Auntie Xi's participation on Anthony Taulke's Council of Corporations only made the potential impact greater.

"I propose we appoint Ming Qinlao as interim CEO," he said to the assembled board later that day. "This needs to be kept quiet until we can determine who is targeting the company. We are now investigating the murder of two chief executives."

"You're sure they're targeting the company and not Xi herself?" Danny Xiao's normal playboy nonchalance was gone. The slim-cut suit emphasized his lean frame and he secured his stylish hair away from his eyes with gel. His face was hard and his gaze locked on Ming. He was all business today.

"Exactly what are you implying, Danny?" Ming kept her tone neutral. She was getting what she wanted, no need to settle old scores with scorned boyfriends. She let her gaze travel around the room, meeting each set of eyes with frank openness, letting Echo tell her what she needed to know. They were frightened. Even JC Han, who had seen his share of boardroom coups, looked more than concerned. She saved Sying for last, letting herself savor those dark eyes a second longer than was prudent in front of this audience. But no one seemed to notice. They were all thinking about their own skins.

"Well, Danny?" she said. "Let's have it. You think I killed Xi. You saw the vid. She was the one person who had the means and the motive to kill my father and I wanted her dead. She lied to me about his death and everything else. But I didn't do it." She looked at Marcus. "Tell them."

"Ming met with me last night. There's no way she could have poisoned Xi."

"All night?" Danny challenged, the hint of a leer on his face.

"No," Sying broke in. "She spent the rest of the night with me." Spots of color appeared on Sying's cheeks as she faced the board, her gaze defiant. "We were—are—together."

Ming didn't need Echo to interpret the room's reaction to the revelation that Ming and her stepmother were lovers. JC Han, Ming's former father-in-law, had an expression carved from stone.

Marcus cleared his throat. "The important thing is that Ming is not a suspect, which makes her an ideal candidate to take over as interim CEO. I've already called in Ito to take over the investigation. In my estimation, we have perhaps twenty-four hours to find whoever killed both of these people. We will need complete cooperation from all of you." His lips were set in a firm line and his back was ramrod straight. "Now, we are wasting time. I renew my proposal for Ming Qinlao to take over as interim CEO."

In the end, the vote for Ming was unanimous. Even Danny Xiao voted for her.

When she turned around, Ito was there. He nodded at her and pulsed her a message: *"Welcome back, Little Tiger."*

Marcus took her arm, steering her to the private elevator back to the apartment. "We need to talk," he whispered. She tried to speak to him in the elevator and he cut her off. It wasn't until they were back in her father's study and had set up a jamming device that he uttered another word.

"The suit I saw you in last night," he began. "You have new ... capabilities? Ito said..." His voice trailed off.

"What are you asking, Marcus?" she said.

"Xi was working on something for the council. A secret project at the factory in Suzhou."

Ming's ears perked up at the mention of Suzhou. That was where she had developed the Lazarus nanites. "There's no records of what she was working on?" Ming asked.

"There's no records on any external device that I can find." He peered at Ming, eyes narrowed.

Now she understood what he was asking her. Could she use MoSCOW to access Xi's onboard implant?

"Where is she?" Ming asked.

Whatever poison was used, it must not have been painful. Apart from a bruise the size of a coin in the center of her forehead from when she slammed face first into the table, Xi's perfectly maintained countenance was relaxed as if she was merely asleep.

Ming shut the bedroom door and locked it. Whatever happened, Marcus didn't need to be part of this. She clenched and released her gloved fists, feeling the MoSCOW suit meld with her skin. All over her body, her amplified senses came alive, forcing Ming to take a deep, steadying breath.

Working quickly, she turned the corpse so that her head was at the foot of the bed. Her aunt was loose and light in her arms, almost like a sleeping child. She arranged the body in repose, smoothing her dress with care and placing her arms to her side.

Ming knelt on the bed, taking Auntie Xi's head in her lap. She looked down on the older woman's face. Her chin had slackened and Ming carefully pressed her mouth closed. It stayed in place.

She placed the tips of her fingers on either side of Xi's head and closed her eyes.

When the haptics of the suit merged with the dead flesh, it felt like she was pressing her fingers into marshmallow. She told herself it was just a sensation, but she kept her eyes closed anyway.

The fingers of her right hand found the implant and energized it. Her left hand shook as the suit pumped energy into the decaying brain. Ming's lips trembled from the effort of establishing the connection. Echo was by her side, merged with her consciousness, pushing with her...

And then, like stepping through a curtain of water, she was on the other side. Ming had become her aunt. She sucked in a deep strangling breath, fighting to maintain control. The room around her spun and she felt darkness leaking into the corners of her vision.

Ming clenched her eyes harder and refocused.

Data files. She needed to find the Suzhou factory data files.

Echo navigated her through the maze of personal storage that existed in her aunt's implant. The Suzhou file was massive, filled with snippets of recordings, invoices, designs, notes...

Find conversations with Anthony Taulke, she instructed Echo. *Private conversations.*

Images spun by her in a kaleidoscope of color and garbled sound, stopping on a crystal-clear screen shot of Anthony Taulke.

"Viktor will get you the designs, Xi," he said. "I need to know if you can manufacture them in sufficient quantity in time for the launch."

"Are you sure they will work as advertised?" It was creepy to hear her dead aunt's voice in Ming's own head. "After all, Viktor's track record on this is not the best. Neither is yours, Anthony dear."

Anthony flinched as if he'd been slapped. "These nanites are designed to kill the Lazarus bugs and put us back in charge of the weather. Now, can I count on you?"

"It depends." Ming knew Auntie Xi's negotiating voice.

"What do you want?"

"My niece." Ming felt a ball of icy rage build in her stomach. "I want your assurances that she will be safe after all this."

Ming's brain slammed to a halt. She paused the recording and listened again. *I want your assurances that she will be safe after all this.*

Anthony frowned. "Are you sure? I have doubts about her loyalty to me. I can make her disappear for you."

"I made a promise to my brother that I would protect her. I failed to protect him and I failed to keep her out of the company. The company was always Jie's blind spot. He could never understand that a family legacy is not about an invention, it's about the people you leave behind. All Ming ever wanted was to be left alone to live her life in peace. Now she'll never have that chance."

"As long as you side with me on the council, Xi, I will do whatever you want," Anthony said.

"And I will side with you as long as it is in my family's best interest."

Ming felt the connection to Xi's implant fading. In the final few seconds, she downloaded the design specs from the Suzhou file.

The bedroom in the apartment snapped back into focus. Ming blinked as if emerging from a dream.

Auntie Xi ... was trying to protect her? It made no sense. She tried to remember each interaction with her imperious aunt, trying to place them in a new frame of reference.

She had been in her Auntie Xi's head, heard the words, felt the intonation, sensed the intention behind each syllable. There was no faking that kind of emotion, especially with Echo looking over her shoulder.

And then there was the way she had spoken about her brother. Those were not the words and feelings of a murderer.

Ming placed Xi's head gently on the bed. She could feel a slight tension in the corpse's muscles. Rigor mortis was beginning to settle in.

Ming swayed as she stood, feeling both sick and hungry at the same time. She fumbled with the door lock and plodded to the study where Marcus waited for her. He looked up when she entered. "Well?"

Ming nodded. She spied a tray of food left over from her breakfast and unceremoniously stuffed a Danish into her mouth, then another and another. Marcus waited. She washed down the carbohydrates with a luke-warm cup of tea from the ceramic teapot. Then she collapsed onto the couch next to her lawyer.

"It worked. I—I..." She hesitated. How could she explain what it was like to be inside her aunt's head? Hear her thoughts, experience her point of view? Her stomach turned with a mixture of guilt and half-chewed food as Marcus waited patiently.

Ming took a deep breath. "First thing, I want the Suzhou factory shut down and the nanites they're building destroyed."

"But what about—"

He stopped when Ming held up her hand. "Destroy it all. Designs, work product, prototypes, everything. Destroy the entire building if you have to. Next, we have a new problem: Auntie Xi did not kill my father."

She let that sink in. Marcus stared at her owlishly. "Then who did?"

Ming got to her feet. She felt strong again, steady. The final piece clicked into place in her head like the completion of a massive jigsaw puzzle. She stepped back and saw the full picture for the first time. A now-familiar sensation of cold rage settled like a stone in her gut.

Ming Qinlao had been used for the last time.

"I'm going to the council meeting."

30

CORAZON SANTOS • OLYMPUS STATION

Cora caught Elise Kisaan as she fell back into the chair. As she eased the pregnant body into the adaptive cushion of the Mollet chair, Elise gripped her hand. Her fingers were cold and clammy, like being touched by a sea creature.

"It's not time," Elise whispered. "The baby is not ready. Something is wrong."

Cora turned to Anthony Taulke. "I'll take her to her quarters if someone will show me the way."

"I'll get the medical staff—" Anthony began.

"No!" Elise cut him off, then winced in pain again. "No one but Corazon."

Cora placed her hand on the woman's belly and felt rock-hard muscles. Elise Kisaan was going into premature labor. "We're wasting time. She needs to lie down now."

As she turned back, her gaze took in the rest of the people around the dining room table. All the men had looks that ranged from fear to compassion, but Adriana wore a hard, impatient expression, as if Cora dared to interrupt a perfectly good party. She locked eyes with Adriana. "Show me her quarters. Now!"

The order snapped Adriana out of whatever reverie she was caught in.

She helped Cora spin the chair around and push it away from the well-lighted table. The hallways of Olympus were wide and covered with short fiber carpet that deadened their footsteps, leaving only the sound of Elise breathing in short, sharp bursts. Cora put a comforting hand on her shoulder and felt the other woman's body ease into relaxation.

"That was a long contraction," Elise whispered. She leaned over her belly, eyes half-closed, face flushed.

A door on Cora's right opened as they approached and she instinctively steered the chair through the open doorway. Lights came on as they entered, revealing a large bed at thigh height piled high with pillows and blankets. She looked back to find Adriana still standing in the entrance.

"Come in and close the door," Cora said.

Adriana shook her head, her eyes locked on the dark red stains on Elise's dress. "I—I ... this is not for me." She let the door shut on her.

Cora helped Elise out of her dress and into bed. Her hand touched Elise's thigh and she drew back. Her leg was hard as steel.

Despite her pain, Elise laughed at her reaction. "Bionic." She rapped her knuckles on the limb and put Cora's hand just above her hip. The flesh there was warm and pliable. "From here down, I'm all machine." She smiled at Cora, her face still flushed and sweaty from her last contraction.

"But the baby..." Cora began.

Elise put her hand up as another contraction began. As Cora helped her breathe through it, she checked the time. Less than ten minutes between contractions. This was progressing fast, too fast. And the bionics added complications.

She adjusted the bed and Elise leaned back into a stack of pillows. "There's something wrong," Elise said finally. Her voice was husky.

Cora had delivered hundreds of babies. The heavy bleeding, the rapid onset of contractions, Elise's lethargy. The symptoms didn't add up for her, but she kept her thoughts to herself. "Rest," she said. "Let the baby come in her own time."

Elise looked at her sharply. "You're a believer, aren't you? A true believer, I mean."

"I am."

Their conversation was interrupted by another contraction. Four minutes apart. Cora needed help and she needed it now. She slid on her data glasses and pulsed a message to William. *"Send medical team to Kisaan quarters now."*

Elise took Cora's hand. "This baby is special."

Cora squeezed her hand, feeling herself choke with emotion. "I know. I am here to serve the Child."

Elise's head lolled, but she managed to catch it and refocus on Cora. "I need your help."

"Anything."

"Stay with the baby. Do not let anyone hurt her." Her eyelids dipped. "Promise me. In Her name." Elise's head drooped.

Cora felt her heart race. This was not normal.

The door snapped open and a two-person team entered pushing a med pod. While one opened the pod, the other elbowed Cora out of the way to gain access to Elise.

"How long has she been like this?" asked a bulky woman with short red hair who appeared to be in charge.

"A few seconds. She was just talking to me." The pod had opened into a full medical bed with a diagnostic hood overhead and an adjoining neonatal warmer. They moved the contraption next to Elise's bed and transferred her inert, naked body underneath the hood. A virtual screen popped up showing Elise's vitals and the baby's. The red-haired doctor draped a sterile cloth over Elise and did a quick examination.

She squinted up at the diagnostic screen. "I don't like it," she said to her colleague. "Doesn't add up."

"What doesn't add up?" Cora asked. Then she added, "I'm a midwife."

The doctor answered her question with one of her own. "What has she had to eat or drink in the past few hours?"

"We were at dinner. She didn't eat much, drank less. Some fruit juice, I think. You think this is a reaction to something she ate?"

"I think she's been given something to induce labor and she's having a reaction to it. Whoever gave her the dose probably didn't know about the bionics and she's OD'd. I've given her something to counteract it, but I'm guessing at what she's been given..."

A red light flashed on the diagnostic and a soft, insistent pulse sounded. The doctor swore.

"Dammit. The baby's in distress. We're going to have to do a C-section. Prep her."

The tech punched at a console and whipped off the sheet covering Elise. Cora was treated to a glimpse of Elise's swollen stomach writhing from the movement of the baby inside.

"Engaging the air curtain," said the tech, and Cora felt a gentle flow of air pushing away from the operating table.

"Begin UV sterilization," the doctor ordered. A faint blue glow showed over the mound of Elise's midsection.

"UV is on, Doctor."

The doctor selected a laser scalpel from the tray as the tech moved the neonatal incubator inside the air curtain. Cora saw a flash of the scalpel and the warm, rich smell of open flesh reached her nostrils. Then a cry and the doctor was hoisting a tiny, wriggling form out of Elise's open body. When she handed the baby across to the tech, the man almost dropped the infant.

"Holy shit, her eyes are open!" the tech said.

"Hold still while I sever the umbilical," the doctor snapped back. Then she busied herself with Elise.

Cora moved to the side of the medical bed where the tech was wrapping the child in warm blankets. "Give her to me," she said to the tech.

The fresh blankets warmed her chest as Cora held the child gently. The baby had a shock of thick dark hair and a round face still spotted with drying flecks of mucus and blood. The child opened her eyes and stared directly up at Cora.

Cora froze. The baby had eyes the color of gold, just like the baby in her dream. The child studied her face. Normally babies kept their eyes mostly closed at first and were unable to focus for the first few days outside the womb. But not only did this baby seem to be able to focus, the gaze felt like that of a much older person.

Cora shivered. This was *the* Child. Cassandra's Child. Here, in her arms. The tech tried to take the baby away and she resisted. "Ms. Kisaan gave strict instructions that I was to take care of the Child. Only me."

He shrugged as he placed an electrode on the baby's forehead, then looked up at the diagnostic screen. His eyes widened. "Doc, you need to see this."

The doctor was just finishing up with Elise. Cora could taste the acrid smell of fused flesh in the air from where the doctor had closed the incision.

"What is it now?" The doctor said in an impatient voice. She stared at the diagnostic panel, then looked at the baby, then back at the panel.

"You ever seen anything like that, doc?" the tech said. "That's off the scale."

The doctor just shook her head.

On the operating table, Elise stirred and opened her eyes. Her focus ping-ponged around the room until she found Cora holding the bundle. "Give her to me."

Cora moved to the side of the bed and transferred the child to her mother's arms. Elise's hair was limp with sweat and her movements were languid. The doctor appeared on the other side of the bed.

"We think you had a reaction to something you ate at the dinner—"

"I was drugged." Elise stated it flatly, like she was saying the sun was up or the sky was blue.

The doctor stammered. "I don't like to jump to conclusions."

"I'm not asking you to, Doctor. I'm asking you to leave. Thank you for everything you've done so far." She spoke without looking up from her baby's face. "We owe you everything."

"I'm sure the baby will do much better in the medical unit—"

Elise's eyes were dark and fierce. "That will be all, Doctor."

The medical personnel helped transfer Elise back to her own bed, then packed up the med pod and left. The bedroom still smelled like an operating room. When she was situated, Elise beckoned to Cora to give her back the baby. She exposed a breast and let the child nurse.

Cora started to back away to the door.

"Stay," Elise said. Her voice was choked with emotion and Cora realized she was crying.

"Can I do anything?" she asked.

Elise shook her head. The only sounds in the room were the baby suckling and the broken breathing of her mother.

"You had children," Elise said. A statement, not a question.

"I did. A girl ... she died in an accident with her father."

"So you know what it's like then."

Cora swallowed. The last thing she wanted to do was talk about that.

Elise continued as if Cora had answered. "Losing a child."

The baby finished feeding. "The general is outside. Bring him in."

She found William in the hallway and brought him in. Without thinking, she slipped her fingers into his. She got a gentle squeeze in return.

Elise cradled the baby, whispering something. Finally, she tore her gaze away to look at Graves and Cora. She saw them holding hands and said nothing.

"It's Remy's baby, isn't it?" William said.

Elise looked like she might lose her composure for a second, then regained control. "A child was never part of the plan. I promised Remy, but I never meant it. I was using him. I was—" She broke off and squeezed her eyes shut. Fat tears leaked out. "I was a different person then."

"You were being used," William told her. "Controlled."

"I know," Elise said. "It doesn't make it any easier, General." She looked down at the sleeping child and took another deep breath. "They changed the child—my child, Remy's child. Made her different. I let them." She held up her wrist where the black cryptokey dangled. "They will use her. Just like they used me. I can't let that happen."

Cora stiffened. "You want us to take her."

Elise sniffed. "You're a believer. I was too once, but I've strayed far from the path of Cassandra. There's no going back for me. But they can't have my baby."

Cora took the sleeping baby from Elise. "I serve the Child," she said.

"I know you do," Elise replied. "Now get her far away from here."

31

ADRIANA RABH • COUNCIL CHAMBER, OLYMPUS STATION

The corporate logos of the five families gleamed on the walls of the newly-built chamber for the Council of Corporations on Olympus Station. The Rabh seal, an ancient Egyptian pyramid topped by an all-seeing eye, was especially well rendered with the embossed R on the pyramid done at exactly the right pitch. Forgers of the Rabh logo rarely got the pitch correct. Her father had taught her that trick early in life as a sure way to spot a fake Rabh seal.

The room was shaped like a hexagon, with one wall consumed by the grand double doors and the other five sides each carrying one corporate logo. Five families, five logos. No room for interlopers from the planet surface. Graves and that Corazon woman had no family seals, no corporate backing, no reason to be seen on these walls. They were outsiders.

The new room had been appended to the very top of Olympus Station, like a jewel on the top of a king's crown. Above the walls was ... nothing. A clear bubble of plastisteel. This was the very end of the space elevator tether. The top of the room faced directly away from the Earth's surface, so there was no stunning view of the planet to distract Adriana's gaze.

When council members looked up, they saw nothing but space. Opportunity. Asteroids to mine, planets to exploit, power to be had—all theirs for the taking.

When had Anthony ordered this built? she wondered. It had only been a few days since he'd come out of the coma, and even with his considerable resources, a room of this design and quality would take longer than that.

She followed that thought. Anthony had planned to shift his base of power from Mars back to Earth long before his sudden conversion to a humanitarian. Adriana flicked her gaze to Viktor, who was dozing in his chair, probably still drunk from dinner. Anthony sat stone-faced in his own chair, the one that was just a shade taller and wider than all the other ones parked around the translucent round table. *First among peers* was how he once described his position in the council.

Adriana said, "This new council chamber is beautiful, Anthony. How long did it take to build it?"

Anthony roused himself, automatically engaging his smile. "Oh ... a while. I always liked the idea of a round table, like King Arthur, you know?"

"Of course." Adriana nodded. She could barely contain the sneer that threatened to break out across her face. King Arthur, indeed. This was not Camelot they were building. This was Las Vegas in the desert.

Where the hell was Tony, and what was going on with Elise?

She pushed the thought of the baby out of her mind. She was not a baby-killer, she was doing what needed to be done. The drug that Fischer had slipped into Elise's drink could never be traced back to her. The child would die in labor. Unfortunate, but a fact of life even in these modern times.

Still, the sight of Elise's bloody dress at the dining table had turned Adriana's stomach. But not enough to make her rethink her plans. She was doing what needed to be done. Anthony had his angle and Tony had his. Ming was dead, Xi was pliable, and Viktor was an idiot. If she injected enough uncertainty into that combustible mixture, it might just create enough of an opening for her rise to the top of the heap.

First among peers. That had a nice ring to it.

The double doors opened and a woman strode in. Red hair, a little on the chunky side for Adriana's liking, but with an air of purpose. A professional of some kind.

Anthony was out of his chair and across the room, shaking her hand in both of his. Ever the people pleaser. "Doctor, thank you for coming. How is she?"

"Ms. Kisaan is fine, sir. Resting in her quarters."

"And the baby?

The doctor smiled. "A healthy girl."

Adriana sat up so suddenly that even Viktor roused himself to look at her. "A girl?" she said to cover up her surprise. Inside, she boiled with rage. Fischer had screwed up.

The doctor had a genuine smile, the kind that spread all the way to her eyes. "Yes, a girl. She's with Ms. Santos now. If she hadn't called for the medical team, Ms. Kisaan might have died."

"That's ... remarkable," Adriana said through clenched teeth.

"I wanted to come see you personally, Mr. Taulke," the doctor said. "The baby is not normal—not sure how to describe it, actually. She's healthy, no physical issues at all."

"Then what?" Anthony said.

The doctor shook her head. "She shows brain activity that is off the charts. And her eyes are open, too. If I didn't know better, I'd say she could understand what we were saying."

Anthony laughed. "That sounds like science fiction, Doctor."

"I know what it sounds like, sir, and I know what I saw. I don't know the circumstances of Ms. Kisaan's pregnancy, but this child is not normal." She hesitated. "I know there's a lot of talk about this child having religious significance to the New Earth Order. I'm not a believer, but I'm here to tell you as a doctor for over a quarter century, I have never seen anything like this child."

Anthony seemed cowed by the news. He pinched his lip. "Thank you, Doctor."

After she left, Anthony sank down heavily into his chair. Where the hell was Tony? she wondered again.

"Adriana," Anthony said. "There's something I need to tell you."

She leaned back into chair cushions, crossing her legs, arranging the folds of her dress carefully across her knees. Using her retinal scan, she pulsed a message to Eugene Fischer.

"*The child is still alive. Finish the job.*"

Then she looked up at Anthony and gave him a soft, friendly smile. "I'm here for you, Anthony. Tell me what's on your mind."

32

ANTHONY TAULKE • COUNCIL CHAMBER, OLYMPUS STATION

The chair groaned as it took Anthony's full weight. His buoyant mood evaporated as he tried to sort through this flood of new information. The doctor's assessment of Elise's child rattled him. Had he underestimated the Neos again? Whoever was behind this cult had outsmarted him once and he had the sinking feeling he was behind the power curve again. He needed allies now more than ever. If this Child was a new Cassandra, a new weapon, his plans were in danger—again.

But could he trust Adriana? He studied his old friend. With her web of influence and bottomless resources, she was his biggest threat to power on the council. The ambassador to Earth position was a way to keep her busy, off the scent of his plan to take back control of the weather.

Anthony remembered waking up in the medical suite here on Olympus Station after the assassination attempt. Like he was resurfacing after too long underwater and dragging sweet air into his hungry lungs.

He had survived his brush with death, but it had changed him. It was a reminder of his mortality, of who he was—or should be—as a human being. All his power, all his money, all his influence were pointless unless he left a mark on history. Unless he left the world a better place for having been part of this universe.

When he knelt in the shattered glass and dust of the United Nations room where he had nearly lost his life, Anthony made a pact with himself: his fellow human beings would remember him for his good works.

The Savior Network that he had designed with Viktor and Xi was all that and more. The satellites would provide coverage over every square millimeter of the planet. Viktor's new nanites would seek out and destroy the Lazarus Protocol bugs, removing the stranglehold that Elise Kisaan and the New Earth Order had over him.

And then he would give it away. He hadn't told anyone that part yet—not even Viktor.

The Savior Network was to be his gift to humanity. The United Nations could set up a commission to decide how best to modify the atmosphere. Agriculture would flourish. Cities would be safe. Prosperity for generations.

All because of Anthony Taulke. The Savior Network would be his crowning achievement as a human being. All his. Forever.

He blinked to hold back the tears that threatened to spill over. The assassination attempt had been a sign, a sign for him to refocus on what really mattered: what he, Anthony Taulke, could give back to his fellow travelers on this journey of the human race—and getting the recognition he so richly deserved.

Adriana cleared her throat. Anthony flushed, realizing he'd been lost in his own thoughts.

Adriana sat upright in her chair, her shoulders thrown back, head at a slight tilt as she waited for him to spill his secrets. Her dark eyes raked over him, leaving Anthony feeling as if he was being assessed as a business property and his partner still had not decided if she wanted to invest.

He shot a look at Viktor but got no help from his Russian friend. Viktor had made it clear from the beginning that he was the creative side of the partnership. He would make the tech possible, but it was Anthony's responsibility to deploy it. He wondered how Viktor would respond when he found out Anthony was planning to give away the Savior Network lock, stock, and barrel.

For free. Not a cent of profit in the venture. How would Tony react? He dismissed his son. Everything that boy had in this life came from his father. Tony owed him.

The thought of his own son made Anthony think about the Child again.

He was not in the clear yet. Cassandra was still reaching from the grave to foil his plan.

First things first, he still had to deal with Adriana. She was the traitor on the council.

"Anthony," Adriana said in a sharp tone. "You had something you wanted to tell me."

Anthony tried to corral his thoughts. His mind felt slippery, his thoughts like hummingbirds zipping in all directions.

"I haven't been completely transparent with you," Anthony began.

"Do tell, Anthony." Her gaze made him feel like a naughty schoolboy sitting in the principal's office.

His head was beginning to hurt again. Maybe he'd pushed himself too hard in the recovery. Too late now. He'd set this train in motion and he was either the conductor or about to get run over.

"The satellite network that Xi Qinlao is building for the council is more than just a new platform to control the Lazarus nanites. It will deploy next-generation nanites." He shot a glance at Viktor, whose lips were sealed shut. No help there. "Nanites that are capable of killing the old Lazarus version and taking over permanently."

Adriana frowned, creating a delicate furrow in the center of her forehead. "But that would mean..."

"That Elise Kisaan is no longer needed," Anthony finished for her.

He watched Adriana sink back into her chair. "How long have you been planning this?" she asked.

Anthony looked at Viktor, who shrugged like a bear coming out of hibernation. He refused to meet Anthony's gaze.

"Since the beginning," Anthony said finally. "Since you broke me out of jail."

Adriana's frown deepened. "So your plan all along has been to cut Elise Kisaan out of the network? Why didn't you tell me?"

"The less people that knew, the better," Anthony said. "It was Viktor and myself—and Xi, because she had to build the system for us."

"Tony? Surely you told your own son."

Anthony shook his head.

"Ming? Did she know?"

Anthony sighed, his expression softened. Ming's name set off another chain reaction of emotions in his head.

"No, not even Ming."

Viktor roused himself at Ming's name and seemed like he was about to speak, then thought better of it.

"And now?" Adriana asked. "This nonsense with Graves and the Neo woman, what's all that about?"

Anthony rested his forearms on the table and leaned forward. The glass of the tabletop was cool against his skin. It was almost time to share his vision with his closest friends. The Qinlao shuttle had docked. He would wait for Tony and Xi to join them.

The double doors to the council chamber opened and Tony entered. Instead of his normal saunter, his son strode with purpose and took his seat at Anthony's right hand. Anthony waited for him to say something. As the silence deepened, he said, "Is Xi coming?"

"I'm afraid my aunt will not be joining us. Ever." A new voice. Anthony spun in his chair.

Ming Qinlao stalked past him. Her maglev chair was gone and she looked healthy—no, deadly. Anthony experienced a rush of conflicting emotions in his throbbing brain: joy that she was alive, anger at her having put him through the pain of her death, and dread at the expression on her face.

She wore the black MoSCOW suit Viktor had made for her, the matte-black material hugging her curves. Ming served a nod to Viktor, who smiled back at her. Then she pulled Xi Qinlao's chair out from the table and seated herself. The Qinlao family logo loomed on the wall behind her.

Anthony's brain processed the look exchanged between Viktor and Ming. And she was wearing the suit from the Russian's lab.

For the first time, Anthony felt a tickle of fear run up his spine. Viktor was his friend. Viktor was his confidant. Yet Viktor had helped Ming fake her own death. He looked around the room, seeing only blank faces now. What else did he not know?

"Pop," Tony said, interrupting the freight train of thoughts racing through his head. "I think you need to call the meeting to order. We have issues to discuss."

"I'll decide when and how we call—"

Anthony broke off when the empty chair under the Kisaan corporate logo filled with a holo-figure of Elise Kisaan. She looked drawn and worn, but also very angry. "I move we open the meeting, Anthony." Her voice, amplified by the speakers hidden in the headrest of her chair, was terse.

"Very well." Anthony reached under the table for the polished Mars rock that he used as a gavel. He rapped the baseball-sized chunk sharply on the table. "This meeting of the Council of Corporations will come to order. In attendance are—"

"I think we can dispense with roll call, Pop. We're all here."

"Fine." Anthony left the heavy rock in front of him. "Let's move on to new business."

Ming spoke: "Let's discuss the satellite network my aunt was building for you, Anthony." Her words were razor sharp. "The satellites were more than just transmitters for the Lazarus Protocol. My aunt was producing nanites. I reviewed the design myself—and consulted with Viktor, of course. You were planning to destroy the Lazarus nanites and replace them with your own design, a design that only you could control."

Anthony searched for a measure of compassion in Ming's gaze, but found nothing. His head throbbed. He needed to stop this madness. "If you ask Xi what she—"

"Xi Qinlao is dead," Ming snapped. "The nanites are destroyed. The satellites are being reconfigured back to their original purpose."

Elise spoke next. "You were going to betray me, Anthony." Her amplified voice crackled. "What then? Have me eliminated? I joined this council in good faith, I held up—"

"You forced your way onto my council!" Anthony shouted. He knew he needed to keep his cool, but the pain in his head was almost unbearable. He shouted again. "You and your Neo scum. And this child of yours, this half-breed mutant. Do you deny you were going to take over again? The Neos rise up and retake Earth. She put this council in danger." He looked around the room for support, but found nothing.

Surely they had to know the truth: the Neos were reshaping the Earth.

"Don't you see?" he said, pleading. "The Neos want to turn the Earth into some kind of greenhouse for the solar system. Think of the impact on the human race. I was going to stop them. I was going to put the future of humanity back in the hands of the people. We are a Council of Corporations, what do we know about the good of mankind? Who are we to decide?"

"So you were going to kill me?" Elise said in a heated voice. "And my baby?"

Anthony felt the whirlwind in his mind slam to a halt. The baby?

"No," he said. "Never. Who do you people think I am? I'm in the business of saving people—hell, I even called my project the Savior Network. It'll go down in history..." His voice trailed off. They didn't believe him. "I would not hurt a child. You know me."

"Do we, Pop?" Tony said. "Do we know you?"

Tony got to his feet and paced around the perimeter of the room. "Let's review the facts. You launched the Lazarus Protocol, planning to give your invention to the United Nations, but you lost control of the project to the Neos. You went behind our backs to help General Graves, who went on to destroy the very space station the Neos were using to control their masses. Still, for some reason, we gave you a third chance to do the right thing. Adriana even broke you out of prison. All you had to do was run the council and still you can't help yourself. You hatch another harebrained—and expensive—plan to take control of the weather on Earth."

He passed behind Anthony and kept walking. "Did it ever occur to you that there were larger forces at play? Did you ever stop trying to save the world and notice that the New Earth Order was working toward the goals of the council all the time? The weather patterns on Earth are doing just fine. Cassandra preprogrammed the nanites to continue even after her demise."

Tony stopped behind him and sighed, resting a hand on his father's shoulder. "She was a fine piece of work, if I say so myself. It was really a pity she got blown up. Such a waste of resources."

Anthony kept trying to follow Tony's words. The Neos were working for the council?

"I don't understand, son," he said.

Tony spun his father's chair around, looming over Anthony. He could feel the puff of Tony's breath in his face, taste his last meal, see the rage in his son's eyes. And it made him squirm back into the cushions of his chair.

But there was no escaping Tony.

"No, you don't understand, Pop! You don't understand anything. It was me, all me, the whole time. The Neos, the space station, Cassandra—I built it all. I built it because I couldn't trust my old man to do the right thing for the Taulke family business. How do you take over the world without a little genocide, Pop?" He slammed the chair back into the edge of the table, jarring Anthony's teeth together.

"You don't!" Tony screamed. "You. Don't. And yet every time I turn around, my old man is fucking up our business. This has to end, Pop."

Anthony saw a gleam of deep red in Tony's right hand. The Mars rock flashed down at his face. He felt an explosion of pain in his right temple. He blinked, but his eyes were gummed with liquid. He swiped at his face and his hand came away red.

Blood. His blood.

"Tony..." he managed to say. "Son."

The rock hit him again in the same place, but he had lost feeling in that side of his face.

He tried to speak again, but the words came out as a hiss.

The last thing he saw was his son's face. Lips peeled, teeth clenched. It might have been an expression of rage. Or maybe a look of horror.

Or it might have been a smile.

33

ADRIANA RABH • COUNCIL CHAMBER, OLYMPUS STATION

Adriana never saw Tony palm the Mars rock from the table in front of his father—until it was too late. She watched the young man stalk around the room like a wild animal, each step seeming to amp up his anger to a new level.

Tony has this under control, she told herself. Tony told her not to worry.

But she hadn't done that, had she? Adriana Rabh didn't take orders from a kid half her age, no matter what his last name was.

She listened with growing horror. Tony was working *with* Elise and the Neos. Tony was behind the meteoric rise of the New Earth Order. Tony Taulke took a third-rate, tree-hugger religious movement and turned it into a global juggernaut bent to his own purposes. She took a fresh look at the younger Taulke, so like his father and yet, obviously, so unlike him as well.

Adriana had made a horrible miscalculation.

Her shoulders tightened into anxious knots. Tony was blaming everything on his father, but how long before Anthony spoke up about the child? How long before Tony started looking for someone else to blame for the death of Elise's child?

She tried to send another pulse to Fischer, but his comms were off.

For his part, Anthony seemed behind the power curve of comprehension. His movements were slow, his reactions distant, and he seemed unable to process what his son was telling him. In that moment, she pitied him.

By the time Tony made his second circuit of the room, his face was scarlet with anger and his movements precise, almost robotic. He paused in front of the Taulke family logo, spinning the older man's chair around and leaning in with a rigid ferocity to his frame.

She heard Anthony say something in an urgent whisper, but the words made not a dent in his son's expression.

Tony's arm flashed down in a piston strike. When his hand came up again, a splash of red flew across the table. The moment froze in time, all eyes fixed on the streak of bright red. The blood contracted on the smooth tabletop into crimson globules, like rain beading on a windshield.

Tony stood, breathing heavily, his eyes wide as if he was unable to process what he'd just done. Then Anthony made a wheezing noise and the spell was broken.

Tony lost control. Again and again, he pummeled the figure in the chair with the heavy rock. Strings of blood whipped up and all around, painting the walls, the floor, even the bold Taulke logo behind them.

Finally, Tony stopped. He let the weapon drop to the table where it rolled away from him, leaving a bloody track in its wake. He gulped air, swayed on his feet, then collapsed into his own chair, pressing a shaking hand to his forehead.

The only sound in the room was the hiss of the air system, the only movement the stars above them. The stillness dragged on for seconds, then minutes. Adriana's gaze flicked around the table. Viktor stared at the tabletop, his eyes locked on a drop of blood the size of a dime. Elise's face in the holo image was still, unreadable. Ming Qinlao watched Tony through narrowed eyes, a ghost of a smile on her face. She was a dark one, Adriana thought.

"We needed a change in management," Tony said abruptly. His voice made Adriana startle in her chair. "I—we—have waited too long and invested too much to just give our competitive advantage back to the people who fucked it up in the first place." He grinned, a feral smile, made all the more ghoulish by the streak of smeared blood on his cheek. "Imagine.

Giving our most precious asset to the United Nations? What was he think-ing? That planet—once we're done remaking it—is our asset base. Skilled engineers, labor, food, it's all there for the taking and Pop just wanted to give it away."

He kicked Anthony's chair, making it spin slowly to face the table. Adriana tried not to look. Anthony's square jaw and firm, cosmetically enhanced lips were smashed beyond recognition. The divots where his eyes used to be were just battered pools of mush. She clamped her hand over her mouth and locked her eyes on the table.

"Too soon?" Tony laughed at his own joke, then spun his father's corpse to face the wall. He pushed it away from the table, sliding his own chair underneath the Taulke logo. He looked around the room with approval in his gaze. "Say what you will about my old man. He was a shit businessman, but he knew how to do interior design. I like this place. Five families, five council members. Simple. Bing-bang-boom."

"What about General Graves and the Neo woman?" Adriana said, trying to keep her voice calm. She needed to buy time to find Fischer and stop him. "They're supposed to be placed on the Council of Corporations in the morning. Can you imagine the public backlash if we don't follow through?"

Tony yawned. "First things first, Adriana. I propose that we disband this Council of Corporations and reform as a new entity, the Syndicate Corpo-ration." He scratched his chin. "SynCorp, for short. I like it. All in favor?"

There were no dissenters.

"I hardly think the UN will let us go back on our word just because we changed our name, Tony," Adriana said. "Public opinion will—"

"Public opinion will be what we say it is," Tony finished for her. "This shit about asking people what they want and voting on options is no more. We decide what the future looks like. We lead. We take what we need when we need it and the people follow. Simple, efficient."

Adriana guessed her job as ambassador to Earth had just been made redundant.

Tony energized the holograph station in the center of the table. After a few seconds, the head and shoulders of the Taulke security head came into view. "Mr. Taulke, what can I do for you, sir?"

"Good evening, Mr. Quince, I need you to take care of a few things for me."

"Of course, sir."

"General Graves and Corazon Santos. I want you to kill them for me."

"Sir?"

"Kill them. Liquidate, eliminate, whatever you guys call it. Shoot them, throw them out an airlock, I don't care, I just want them terminated."

"Sir...? Can I speak to your father?"

"No, you may not."

"Sir, I—" He stopped speaking when Tony spun Anthony's chair around to face the camera.

"My father is not with us anymore, Quince. I'm in charge."

"I understand, sir." Quince recovered his composure remarkably well. "Anything else?"

"Yes, there is. I want you to put Ms. Kisaan's child under armed guard in the hospital."

Quince cleared this throat.

"Problem, Quince?"

"The baby is with the general and Ms. Santos, sir."

Tony sat up in his chair. "What?"

"Yes, sir, they—"

"Find them and get that child back. Do not injure the child, do you understand?"

The room trembled, making the holograph glitch. Tony stood, leaning into the screen. "What was that?"

Quince was looking offscreen and nodding. "Sir, we have possible intruders. Deck six ... and seven."

"Go!" Tony killed the holo. He turned to the holographic image of Elise Kisaan. "What did you do?"

"My child was never part of the bargain, Tony." She smiled wryly. "You have me. That's enough."

"That child is SynCorp property. We spent—"

"The child—*my* child—is not part of the deal." Elise's holo image disappeared.

Tony threw himself against the back of his chair. "We'll see about that."

Adriana frantically tried Fischer again with no answer. If the child was killed by Fischer and traced back to her... She stood. "I'm going to see what I can do to help."

Tony laughed. "Sit down, Adriana. You'd be worse than useless." He cut his gaze to Ming. "You on the other hand are quite a badass, I'm told."

Ming got to her feet in a blur of motion. To Adriana's eye, her black suit seemed to absorb the light.

Viktor made a noise that distracted Adriana for a second. When she turned back, Ming was gone.

34

WILLIAM GRAVES • MEDICAL DECK, OLYMPUS STATION

Graves didn't like the feeling brewing in his gut one bit. A twisting knot of unease born of years in high-risk situations gave him a sixth sense of when things were about to go sideways—and he was rarely wrong.

Graves followed the medical team at a wary distance, watching Cora with the baby. The tech had insisted she put the child in the warming incubator for the trip to the medical deck. She walked close to the incubator, her hand always touching the clear plastic, her eyes on the bundle of snowy white blankets.

The baby returned the favor, watching Cora with her calm, golden eyes. It occurred to Graves that he hadn't heard the child cry, not even once. He was the farthest thing from an expert on infants, but that just didn't seem right to him.

The hallways of Olympus Station were wide and carpeted with thin material that flexed under his feet. The latest in fixed and drone security cameras were everywhere and the security people he'd seen were all openly carrying sidearms. He knew this station had been built over a decade ago, but everything looked brand spanking new to him. It looked to him like Anthony Taulke and his council were settling in to a new home base.

The knot twisted tighter.

It wasn't just the newness of the place that bugged Graves. It had been hours since dinner and not a single person had even called to check up on Elise and the child. Judging by the reaction from the medical team, a live birth on Olympus was a rarity. Surely Anthony the Showman would want to work this miracle birth into his sales pitch for the new council that was expected to go live in the next few hours. Even Graves could see a PR angle on that story.

They passed a narrow window, affording Graves a clear view of the planet. He could see the space elevator tether run all the way down to the tip of Australia, the brown continent uncluttered with cloud cover. He paused. The station was much higher than most of the orbiting traffic around the planet and he could see the normal buzz of small craft zipping around like fireflies in the larger tableau below him. Something about the scene bothered him, but he could not put his finger on it. Like searching for a temporarily lost word, the idea was obvious, but just out of reach of his mental processes.

Cora was getting farther away—too far away for comfort. He wanted to keep her close. If the stuff hit the fan, she was the only one he could trust. He hurried after them and was rewarded with a quick smile.

"She's beautiful, isn't she?" Cora whispered. "Even more beautiful than I ever dreamed of. She's the one, William. I can feel it."

Graves stopped in midstride. Security, or rather, lack of security. That's what was missing. Graves spun and rushed back to the window he'd just left. He pressed his face against the glass to get the widest possible viewing angle.

On the way up, in Taulke's private space elevator car, he'd seen multiple security patrol craft. Anthony had even commented on how they were taking no chances with external threats.

But now, he couldn't spot even one. Graves waited as the seconds ticked by. Nothing. The roiling in his stomach churned into high gear. Why would someone remove the security patrols?

An attack.

As if on cue, a pair of shuttles veered from the traffic pattern toward Olympus Station. That wasn't odd, he told himself. They could be supply ships or any number of innocuous other craft authorized to approach the space station.

Then they changed course, exposing the far side of the shuttle, and Graves swore under his breath.

A half-dozen space-suited marines clung to the side of the shuttle. As he watched, the line of armored soldiers broke off from their carrier ship, using the ship's momentum to carry them toward the lower levels of Olympus Station.

The marines called the maneuver the Pain Train. Assault teams of six marines in armored space suits, deployed at high speeds from shuttles with the goal of getting inside a station's point defenses. Once on the skin of a space station, a single marine could wreak all kinds of havoc, from venting airlocks to placing shaped charges on cannons. If they got inside the station, things got even worse. The armored suits carried a small arsenal and the soldiers inside were well trained on how to use the enhanced power of their battle mechs.

Graves raced to catch up with Cora. He slid inside the elevator just as the doors were closing. The tech sighed that he had to wait for the door to cycle closed again. Graves ignored him. Cora saw the look on his face. "What?" she mouthed with an accompanying frown.

He gave her a slight headshake.

When the elevator door to the medical deck opened, a security guard met them. "We have a security situation. I'm here to escort the child."

The tech hesitated. The guard grabbed the edge of the med pod and yanked it forward. "Move!" he said.

Inside of the medical unit was all chrome and glass and blinding white. The security man walked them to an exam room as far from the single entrance as possible and indicated they should get inside.

"What's going on?" Graves said to the security man.

"Not at liberty to say, sir." Graves could see the updates flashing on his data glasses and the steady pulse of a red alarm in the corner of the lenses.

"It's an assault, right?" Graves insisted. "Who is it? Are they inside yet?"

The security man paused. "I'm here to guard the child, sir. That's all I can tell you."

Graves tried to get Cora to stay out of the room, but she refused. "I'm staying with the baby," she whispered when he took her arm.

The tech, clearly annoyed with being ordered around by security, steered the incubator unit into the room and left. Graves followed Cora and the baby into the tiny exam room. The door shut behind them, cutting off his view of the hallway outside.

As Cora busied herself cleaning and feeding the infant, Graves tried to reason with her. "We need to get out of here. There's an assault going on and we're going to be caught in the middle of it." He racked his brain to make sense of the situation. Who would attack Olympus? If Anthony Taulke held to his promise, tomorrow the governments of Earth would be getting everything they ever wanted—why attack now? The only thing that had changed in the last day was...

Cora placed the baby on her chest and rocked her gently, turning her back to Graves in the process. The child's piercing gaze studied Graves over Cora's shoulder.

The child. They were after the child.

"We need to leave, Cora. Now. I think the baby is in danger."

Still holding the baby to her chest, she turned to face him. "What do you know?" she said.

A knock sounded on the door and the door opened. A slight man with thinning brown hair entered. A paperback novel stuck out of the wide pocket of his white coat. "Hello there, I'm Doctor Eugene. Mr. Taulke asked me to look in on you."

Graves had another déjà vu moment where the doctor's face seemed like someone he'd seen before, but he could not place where. Cora laid the baby back down in the bassinet.

Dr. Eugene looked down on the child. "My, what an alert little girl we have here." He drew a small hypo gun from his pocket. "She needs a quick shot to make sure she stays that way." He reached down, but Cora stopped him.

"So soon?" she said. "I normally wait a few days before any shots."

The doctor laughed. "Well, we can't be too careful up here. Nothing but the best is what Mr. Taulke ordered."

Graves watched the conversation with a certain level of detachment, still trying to place the doctor's face. Maybe he used to be in the army? He dismissed that idea; the guy was too young to be a military doctor. His gaze settled on the paperback book. Who read real books anymore? The last time he'd seen a real book like that was...

His mind snapped into focus. This man worked for Adriana Rabh—and not as a physician.

The baby cried as the "doctor" peeled away the swaddled blanket. A plaintive cry, weak, alarmed. Graves put his hand on the man's shoulder. "Step away from the child. Do it now."

He never saw the man's foot snake around his ankle and pull Graves off balance. The wiry attacker spun with surprising quickness and hammered a fist into Graves's face. The general crashed backwards, hitting his head on the edge of the examination table on the way to the floor. He saw stars, then doubled over as the attacker landed a kick in his midsection.

It was all over in less than a second.

As the man spun back around, the hypo clutched in his fist, Cora smashed a tray across his face, opening up a gash on his cheek. When he took a knee, Graves lashed out with his foot and felt his toe connect with the man's rib cage. Cora hit him again and the man sat back on his backside, stunned.

Graves tried another kick and missed. He gripped the edge of the table and dragged himself upright, yelling for help as loud as he could. Where the hell was the security guy outside? They were making enough noise to raise the dead in here.

Cora threw away the tray and picked up a chair. As she raised it over her head, Graves saw the man reach under his lab coat for a gun.

He spied the hypo on the floor between them and leaped at the man, snatching up the hypo on the fly. The gun, a silver pistol, flashed up toward Cora, just as Graves hit him. The shot went off next to Graves's head, blinding him, making him deaf, but Graves bore down with his full body weight on their attacker. In desperation, Graves stabbed down with the hypo, hoping with all his might he wasn't just giving this guy a vitamin shot. He felt the hypo empty on first contact, then he used the snub-nosed hypo gun as a weapon, stabbing down over and over again until the body underneath his went limp.

Graves rolled off the inert attacker, his ears still ringing, his eye swollen from the blast of the point-blank gunshot. He heard a baby's screaming from very far away.

He felt hands probing his face, gentle fingers. He opened his eyes to find Cora bending over him. Using the wall, he squirmed up to a sitting position. "Get the kid. We need to get out of here."

Graves rolled the man over and found his pulse. Steady and strong, with deep breaths. The bastard was asleep. He probably had some kind of sedative in the hypo. Enough to knock out an adult would probably kill a two-kilo baby. He nicked the guy's gun, a 9 mm with a custom grip and nice balance. The weapon of a guy who knew how to use a gun. A killer.

The paperback had slid out of the man's pocket. *The Maltese Falcon*. He flipped open the cover and saw a name scrawled at the top of the first page. Eugene Fischer.

He took aim at the man's head with the gun. "Goodbye, Eugene Fischer."

Cora gripped his shoulder. "Please, William, no."

She was holding the kid, the bundle of white pressed against her shoulder. "Not in Her name, William. No killing."

Graves leaned on the wall for support. The shot or maybe the knock on the head had messed with his internal balance.

"Is she okay?" he said, pointing to the baby. He could tell from Cora's reaction that he was shouting but he could barely hear his own voice, just a damned ringing tone in his head.

Cora nodded, her face solemn. "Where should we go?" she said.

Graves opened the door. In the hallway, the security man was slumped against the wall, his head flopped at an unnatural angle. His neck was broken, but Graves felt for a pulse anyway. He took another look inside the room at the sleeping Eugene Fischer. This man was a pro, a killer who wanted no witnesses. He hefted Fischer's gun, but as if reading his thoughts, Cora shook her head again.

Graves used the security man's ID to lock Fischer in the exam room. When he woke up, that would at least slow him down.

He felt a rolling movement under his feet, a slight tremble like he was standing up in a small boat. Graves and Cora exchanged a glance. Her response confirmed that the feeling wasn't a side effect of his injury. He'd felt an explosion somewhere on the decks below them.

"We need to get off this station. Now." Graves was shouting again, but he didn't care.

He snatched the data glasses off the dead security man. The bottom of the display on the right eye flashed red.

Intruder Alert.

Good guys or bad guys? The only thing Graves knew was that right now, confusion was their only friend.

"Where do we go?" Cora asked.

Graves pointed down. They were headed toward the fighting.

35

MING QINLAO • OLYMPUS STATION

As she left the council chamber, Ming felt the MoSCOW suit tighten around her muscles in anticipation of coming action. Her senses sang as Echo came online in her head and released a rush of adrenaline into her body.

Find the child, Echo.

A schematic of the station appeared in her visual, a blinking red dot in the lower third of the Olympus. The child was on the medical deck. Echo tapped Ming's retinal implant into the space station security system and she was immediately overwhelmed by an onrush of alarms.

The station was under attack.

Give me a vid feed, Echo.

Ming lost a step at the sight that filled her display. Space troopers in full battle armor executed a flawless drop formation from a shuttle, racing toward the station in a linked line right under the point-defense systems. Clouds of vapor surrounded them as the formation broke apart and executed a decel maneuver. They slid under the field of view of the external cameras. Moments later the vid feed went blank.

She could hear Ito's voice in her head. *If your enemy is much larger, then use your speed to get inside his reach. Blind your enemy, then pick them apart, piece by piece from the inside.*

As if following her thoughts, the deck shifted under her feet. Her ears popped, indicating a sudden loss of pressure, then restabilized.

The enemy was inside the station.

Ming bypassed the elevator, heading for the maintenance shaft that ran along the outer skin of the station. She ripped off the locked access door and dove through the opening. She rebounded off the far wall, then threw herself down and across the open space to the opposite wall, leapfrogging her way down the wide-open shaft. She caught a steel girder, let the suit take the bulk of the strain off her shoulders, then pushed off again.

Down she flew like a trapeze artist, leaping, grasping, then leaping again. When she got to the medical deck, she locked her grip on a beam above the access door and kicked it open with both feet. Ming rolled into a gleaming white hallway.

A few meters away, a man dressed in an Olympus security uniform slumped against the wall. Even from this distance, Ming could tell he was dead. The door of the exam room next to him hung open. Inside, Ming processed the obvious signs of a fight—a smear of blood on the floor, a smashed hypo gun, an overturned chair—but her attention was drawn to a neonatal incubator unit.

The baby had been here.

Echo alerted her to sounds in the hallway. She heard the distinctive creak of body armor, the sound of deliberate footsteps. Ming flattened against the wall just as the muzzle of a handgun appeared in the doorway. She gripped the barrel, forcing it away from her and drawing the guard inside. The guard tried a head-butt, forcing Ming to throw her own head back.

The wall next to her face exploded into shards of plastic as the guard's partner fired through the wall. She threw herself backwards, securing the first guard in the crook of her elbow. She pressed the muzzle of his weapon against his eyeball.

"Tell your buddy to back off," she growled in his ear.

"Wilson, cease fire!"

"Show yourself," Ming called out. "Show yourself and I won't hurt him."

She could hear the near-panicked rasp of the second guard's breath.

The second man was actually a woman. She appeared in the doorway, handgun gripped in both hands, aimed at Ming's head.

"Do you know who I am?" Ming asked in a calm voice.

Quick nods from both.

"Then you know I'm on your side, right?"

Hesitation.

"Call it in," Ming said in the same calm voice. "I'll wait."

When the eyes of the female guard defocused to make the call, Ming acted. Three shots, dead center of her body armor, slammed the woman back against the far wall. She got off one shot as she went down, shattering the light above Ming's head.

The guard in her grasp struggled, but the weapon was already back poking him in the eye.

"She was wasting time," Ming said in his ear. "I'm going to let you go so you can take care of her. She's not dead, just knocked out. Her body armor saved her."

The security man nodded and she released him.

As he attended to his partner, Ming accessed the hallway camera outside the room and fast-watched it at high speed.

Graves and Santos entered the room with the child and a security man took station outside. A doctor in a white coat approached, chatted up the security guard, then put him down with a single punch to the throat. The general, Santos, and the baby exited the room, locked it, and hurried away. Minutes later, the doctor sans white coat and sporting a nasty head wound exited.

Ming paused the recording to run a face-rec on the doctor and came up empty. On a station with a controlled population like Olympus, that could only mean one thing: the man worked for one of the council in a personal capacity. The visitor was a hit man, not a doctor, and he was still operational.

In the background, Echo searched for any sign of the fleeing survivors using whatever data feeds she could scavenge. She found them in the stairwell, headed down. Graves was taking them toward the fighting.

The docks. Graves was trying to get them off the station.

This wasn't an attack, Ming realized. This was an extraction operation.

36

WILLIAM GRAVES • OLYMPUS STATION

Graves made Cora stop inside the stairwell. His head was still spinning from the gun being fired right next to his head, but his hearing was coming back. He felt a sharp jolt under his feet. Another explosion. When he touched the handrail, he could feel the rattle of nearby automatic weapons fire.

"Why are we stopping?" Cora's voice was tight and she held the baby against her chest.

Graves gripped the Saint Christopher medal and yanked it so the chain broke. He squinted at the silver disk in the dim light, then used his fingernail to peel off the back. Inside lay a clear circle of plastic about the size of the nail on his little finger.

"What is that?" Cora asked.

Graves wet the tip of his finger and touched the clear disk, which adhered to his fingertip. He held open his right eye and inserted the lens. His eye watered as the tiny disk burned into his eyeball and he grunted in pain. If the gunshot next to his face had damaged his eye, would the emergency device still work?

"William?"

The burning stopped. His vision cleared and he heard the calm, professional voice of Major Olga Rodchenkov in his ear. "Saint Christopher, this is Wildfire. Do you read me?"

"Wildfire, this is Christopher, I am online."

He could hear the relief in her voice. "Roger that, Chris, I have your location. You have a six-pack in your cooler. Proceed to the bar."

The assault team was six troopers and they were here to get him out.

"Be advised, Wildfire. We have plus one point five for extraction."

"Negative, Chris. There is no room at the inn." The troopers would have an emergency pressure suit for him, but extra passengers—especially a baby—were an issue.

"We are en route, Wildfire. Make room."

"Copy that, Chris. Join the party at the bar. We will improvise."

Graves pulled the silver handgun from his waistband.

"What is going on, William?" Cora whispered.

"We're getting out of here."

"How?"

"I'm still working on that part."

His display updated, showing Graves the path to follow. Quickly, he led Cora down the stairs to the command deck. He paused at the heavy steel door, feeling the thud of gunfire in the space beyond them.

"Standing by, Wildfire," he whispered. The gunfire ceased.

"Chris, you are clear to proceed. Area is secure."

Graves pushed open the door.

The hallway beyond was like a war zone. Bullets had shredded the walls and ceiling, spent ammunition and bits of molded plastic littered the floor, the sharp smell of gunfire hung in the air. To his right, a three-round burst shattered the stillness. The sound of heavy treads reached his ears and a mech trooper rounded the corner. Graves heard Cora draw a sharp breath of surprise.

A space trooper is a fearsome sight. The two-meter-tall figure was a soldier clad in a combination pressure suit/body armor, allowing the highly trained combat soldier inside to enhance his natural fighting skills and operate in or out of atmosphere or gravity. They also carried a virtual arsenal with them for any battle situation.

"Christopher, meet Five. He's your rear guard. Follow the route."

On his temporary retinal display, Graves saw an arrow point to the right down the shattered hallway toward the docks one level below them. He pushed Cora in that direction. The hallway curved, exposing to view the landing for the space elevator one level below them.

Cora stopped, pointing. Fischer, the man who had tried to kill them in the exam room, emerged from the elevator lift. He held a heavy black Glock in his grip. He looked up, saw Cora and the baby, and opened fire.

Graves popped off a shot in reply as he dragged Cora backwards. "Wildfire, we have a situation."

No answer.

"Wildfire, do you read me?"

Nothing.

Graves cursed and hauled Cora down the hallway faster. The layout on his display showed him that this deck was laid out like a U opening on to the space elevator docks. He paused, staring at the rectangular room on the display labeled ESCAPE PODS. He remembered seeing the row of gleaming open portals at the top of the steps from the dock landing.

He formulated a new plan: send Cora and the baby the long way around the U while he kept Fischer occupied. A fresh burst of gunfire, full automatic this time, sounded behind them.

"Chris, this is Wildfire. We have a new threat inbound to your location."

"I know," Graves shouted back. "It's a Taulke hit man. Can you vector a trooper to us?"

"Negative, Chris. You need to get out of there. Threat incoming is a ninja woman, all in black. A one-woman shit show. Unit six is down, unit five is between you and her. Get out of there now."

"Wildfire, we are being pursued by—" Graves pulled Cora around the corner and pressed her back against the wall.

Trooper Five was locked in a battle with a black-suited woman. The attacker moved with superhuman speed, kicking off a wall, vaulting over the head of the trooper. Bullets sprayed from the trooper's weapon but the mech soldier was unable to keep track of his attacker long enough to pin her down.

She dropped to the floor and swept the soldier's legs, making him crash to the ground. The trooper was good; he broke his fall and slammed a fist down where the ninja should have been.

But she wasn't there—and now he'd exposed his back to her. The ninja leaped onto his shoulders. Her arm flashed up and Graves swore he saw her gloved hand become a solid blade. She jammed the sword between the seam at the helmet-collar weld of the armor.

The trooper collapsed to the ground.

The ninja stood and turned to face Graves and he saw her face for the first time.

"Ming?" That was impossible, Ming Qinlao was dead.

She grinned. "Surprised to see me, General?"

Olga screamed in his ear. "Wildfire, Five is down! Get out of there!"

Ming took a step toward them. "I need you to give me that baby, General. You can go, and her, too. But the child stays with us. Tony has plans for her."

Graves saw on his display that two more mech soldiers were headed their way. If he could hold her off for another few seconds, there was no way she could take down two troopers.

Ming's eyes flicked past Graves.

Fischer.

"I need the kid," Fischer said, coming into view, weapon on Ming. "I don't know who you are, but the kid's mine"

Graves felt Cora step behind him and hold the baby between them. The child was quiet, as if it knew what was happening. In the silence, he could even hear tiny breaths being drawn.

Ming's voice was full of confidence. "You will not harm the child. Not while I'm alive."

For a second, there was no motion from either side, then pandemonium broke loose. Two space troopers rounded the corner at a full sprint, guns blazing. Graves felt bullets rip into the ceiling over his head and threw Cora and the baby to the ground.

Ming moved in a blur of speed toward the troopers. Fischer started firing at the incoming threat. A stray round caught Fischer in the shoulder and spun him around. He hit the wall and collapsed to the floor.

Graves hauled Cora upright and dragged her around the corner, away from the fighting.

His legs pumped. Cora's hand was tight in his, the weapon he'd taken from Fischer in the other. Most of the lights had been shot out, but Graves could see the row of open escape pods less than twenty meters away. Backup lighting in the emergency escape space had come on, making the room look all the more inviting and safe.

"Wildfire," he yelled, "we are on the move—"

Two shots rang out and a tremendous blow knocked him to the floor. The rough tread of the deck smashed against his face and it felt like someone had driven a nail between his shoulder blades.

"William, get up." Cora's voice.

Graves rolled over, gasping for breath, and put his hand behind his neck. It came back dry. The body armor in his suit, he remembered.

He tilted his head up far enough to see Fischer on his feet, staggering in their direction.

Graves got to his hands and knees. "Go! Get in the pod." He pushed her away.

As Graves looked around frantically for his weapon, another shot rang out. He spied the silver handgun and lunged for it. His fingers curled around the grip, and he spun in Fischer's direction.

Graves pointed the gun and pulled the trigger until the weapon was empty. He stumbled to his feet, grabbing the wall to steady himself.

Fischer was down, but a groan indicated he was still alive.

The oval pressure hatch labeled EMERGENCY ESCAPE called to him in lighted red letters. He lurched toward the escape pod bay.

Cora lay sprawled on the deck just inside the doorway, a dark stain growing across her back. The harsh emergency lighting was a cold white that made the white bundle of blankets peeking over her shoulder glow. The child's golden eyes were wide open, staring at Graves. Behind them, Grave could hear Ming still battling it out with at least one trooper.

He knelt next to Cora and rolled her over. She was still breathing.

"Save her," she said.

"I'm going to save you both," Graves replied. He tucked the baby under his arm and dragged her the last few meters to the nearest escape pod, leaving a bloody smear on the floor. Inside the four-person pod was a ring of standard-issue crash couches.

The sound of gunfire at the other end of the hall had ended. If Ming was still alive, she'd be here any second.

Graves fell backwards into the pod, dragging Cora's inert body with him. He threaded a leg into a harness and used his free foot to activate the launch sequence.

As the pod door slammed shut, Graves saw a flash of movement on the other side. Ming's face filled the tiny window.

The pod blew away from the station, throwing Graves in the opposite direction of the thrust. Cora's head lolled like a rag doll. The baby made a grunting noise. Graves just held on.

The bullet had hit him between the shoulder blades and it even hurt to breathe. "Wildfire, this is Saint Christopher," he said. "We're in an escape pod. Follow my signal."

"Cora," he whispered. "We made it." She did not respond. He released her body and she floated up, away from him. He kept the baby with the golden eyes secure in his arm.

"Roger, Christopher. We have your signal. Advise on medical status."

Through the tiny porthole window, Graves saw Olympus Station growing smaller. From this distance, the massive station looked like a toy on a string. He kept his eyes on the circle of glass so he didn't have to look at Cora.

"Two alive, one deceased, Wildfire." He paused, looking down at the child in his arms. "I hope you have baby formula."

When the tears finally came, the moisture lifted away from his face like little crystal beads.

37

MING QINLAO • QINLAO MANUFACTURING HEADQUARTERS

Ming set up the small table in the tiny walled garden on the roof of the Qinlao building. The gardeners had done a wonderful job turning a few square meters of rooftop into an island of tranquility. In this sanctuary of ivy-covered brick and lush greenery, she found a moment of peace. The fountain in the corner burbled happily, almost drowning out the aircar traffic flashing overhead.

Ming dismissed the staff to set the table by herself. Everything had to be perfect for Sying's arrival.

She smoothed the thick linen tablecloth across the square meter of polished oak and positioned the broad umbrella so that it blocked the sun. She placed two identical teapots on the table and two mismatched cups. While the water boiled, she walked the perimeter of the garden, reveling in the bright sunshine.

Now that the Taulke Geo-Array was online, it was sunny every day in Shanghai, with clear blue skies. When needed, an appropriate amount of rain was metered onto the city during the nighttime hours.

Tony had wasted no time after the unfortunate death of his father making sure he cemented the legacy of the Taulke family name in deeds and not just words. The satellite network, manufactured by Qinlao, had been put into orbit within days and positioned as a weather-management array. With Elise Kisaan and her cryptokey, the Syndicate Corporation was able to micromanage the weather anywhere on the planet.

Ming ran her fingers across the silky leaves of a deep purple iris. The United Nations had not taken lightly to General Graves and Corazon Santos not being placed on the council, but once Tony explained how the new council was going to operate, they said they understood. Ming had not been in that meeting, but she knew how persuasive Tony Taulke could be when the situation called for it.

She cupped a lovely black-eyed Susan flower in her hands. It was a moot point anyway. No one had seen either General Graves or Corazon Santos—or the Kisaan child—since the attack on Olympus Station. In fact, Ming herself had been the last one to see them. She could revisit the footage whenever she wanted if she engaged Echo.

It had been just a fleeting glimpse, but it told her all she needed to know. The general with Cora's body in one arm and a bundle of blood-spotted blankets in the other. Echo calculated the amount of blood in the hallway outside the escape pod and concluded with seventy-eight percent certainty that Corazon Santos was dead.

The baby? No one knew. The blood patterns on the blankets were inconclusive.

Ming was sure of one thing: Graves had held onto both woman and child as if his life depended on it. As if they were both still alive. That was what she remembered most about that split-second scene. Graves had cared. It showed in the set of his shoulders, the way one arm gently tucked the baby against his side and the other gripped Cora as if he would never let her go.

Ming tilted her face to the sun. That's all she ever really wanted. Someone who would hold her with no reservations or hidden agendas. Hold her as if they would never let go. Given the chance, Graves would have gladly taken Cora's place.

Lily was in her thoughts now more than ever. Lily had been that kind of love for Ming, but Lily was gone.

A delicate knock at the door interrupted her errant thoughts. The door was a heavy wooden affair, scavenged from a Buddhist monastery that was in a zone now dedicated to agriculture under the SynCorp global realignment program.

Sying's smile was brighter than the sunshine and Ming shivered as her lover's soft lips touched her cheek. She was dressed in a loose-fitting dark blue skirt that shimmered as she stepped into the garden, a butter-yellow blouse of the same material, and topped off with a wide-brimmed hat that made her look smart and sexy at the same time.

"Oh, Ming, this is lovely!" she exclaimed. Ming took her arm as they made their way slowly around the tiny garden and she named each of the plants. Sying played with her fingers as they stepped from plant to plant until they finished at the linen-clad table.

"Tea?" Sying said. "How sweet of you." She lifted one of the pots and sniffed. "Pu'er? Oh, Ming, that's my favorite!"

"I know." Ming poured hot water into both pots and replaced the lids, then waved Sying to her seat. She let Sying chatter as the tea steeped, happy to listen to her husky tones, the words meant only for her, laden with meaning and affection.

When she poured the tea, Sying studied her through narrowed eyes. "You have something you want to tell me," she said. "No, wait! Something you want to *ask* me. That's it, isn't it? My answer is yes."

Ming smiled at her, willing away all the feelings that threatened to break through. "You haven't heard the question yet, Sying dear."

The older woman's hand snaked across the table and found Ming's. Her fingers were strong and soft and so inviting. Ming drew back and placed a packet of papers on the white linen tablecloth. She laid a fountain pen across the top.

Sying giggled. "Another surprise from Marcus, I see. Who else uses paper contracts these days?"

"People who value traditions," Ming replied. "That's who."

Sying noticed her tone. Her dark eyes studied Ming's face. "What's gotten into you?" She flipped up the top page and her expression changed.

"I don't understand," she said after scanning the page and flipping to the next. "This is an adoption agreement for Ruben."

Ming nodded. "In the event of your death or incarceration, Ruben will become my ward."

"I see." Sying flipped the pages back and rested the fountain pen on the stack of papers. She reached for her teacup, but Ming stopped her.

"I wouldn't drink that just yet."

Sying's hand shook ever so slightly as she lowered the cup. The light drained from her face. "How long have you known?"

Ming gave her a rueful smirk. "Not long enough to save my aunt's life, unfortunately."

For a long time, Sying said nothing. Ming was content to let the silence lengthen. Time was on her side.

"I didn't mean for this to happen," Sying said finally.

"You mean you didn't expect to have feelings for me. The same kind of feelings you had for my father? How long before you would have me removed?"

Her hand found Ming's again, but the magic of her touch was gone. "It's not like that, Ming. Together—you and I—we're unstoppable. You ... are so much more than I expected." Her tone took on a pleading quality, a wheedling that grated on Ming's senses.

"And you are so much less than I expected," Ming replied. "All your talk of queens and pawns and power. I idolized you. I would have died for you —gladly. And yet that meant nothing to you. You used me."

"Used you?" It was Sying's turn to draw back. "I *made* you. I molded you into a strong, confident woman. I gave you wisdom and guidance and the comfort of my bed. And this is how you repay me?" Sying got to her feet.

"Sit. Down." Ming's voice cracked like a whip. Sying froze. For a second, Ming wasn't sure Sying would follow her orders, but she reseated herself.

"I sense a negotiation in the offing, Ming dear." Her face was like carved alabaster, her eyes black ice.

Ming resisted the urge to lunge across the table and snap her neck. Until this moment, Ming had found it hard not to still love Sying. But now, she had to hold herself back from ripping her apart. Her moral decline, what Ming had let herself become, had started when this woman killed her father. Ming could see the trail of death and destruction she had wrought under this woman's control and it sickened her.

When Ming spoke again, her voice was like glass. "The Shanghai police are in the lobby with a warrant for your arrest for the murder of Jie Qinlao and Xi Qinlao, my father and my aunt."

"Or?" Sying eyed the cup of tea.

"That cup contains the same poison you used to murder Auntie Xi. The dose is much larger than what you gave her. The poor woman dosed herself for hours before she died. This dose will kill you instantly."

"There will be a scandal," Sying said. "Your part in all this, all your weaknesses and failings, will come to light. Everyone will see you for who you are."

"I don't care."

"You're scared to kill me yourself," Sying sneered, her face twisted with hate. "Don't you want the satisfaction of killing me to make yourself feel stronger?" She leaned across the table, baring her neck. "Kill me. Break my neck. You pathetic, weak girl."

For what seemed like an eternity, Ming fought with Echo in her head. She *did* want to kill Sying with her bare hands, feel the separation of her vertebrae under her fingers...

Ming won. Echo faded away. "I am not like you."

"You are exactly like me."

Sying took the teacup with both hands and drank the entire contents in one gulp. The poison acted swiftly. She slumped in her chair, but gracefully, as if determined to be beautiful even in death.

Ming sat still, feeling the gentle breeze on her cheek, the sunshine on her face, the emptiness in her heart. Tears would come later, maybe even regrets, but she had avenged her family the only way she knew how.

Her hand was steady when she reached out and plucked the papers from under Sying's lifeless hand. She flipped to the last page and forged the dead woman's signature.

Then she took her teacup and raised it to Sying's corpse in a mock toast. "Checkmate."

38

WILLIAM GRAVES • AN UNDISCLOSED LOCATION IN THE HIMALAYAS

The hangar deck behind him was deserted and still save for the squeak of a few hungry bats. Between the cornea replacement from the damage caused by the emergency transponder, the pain of three cracked ribs stabbing him every time he stretched the wrong way, and the ongoing ringing in his ears, Graves hadn't had a decent night's sleep since he'd been brought here from Olympus Station.

The doctor told him the pain from the eye surgery and the ribs and the hearing damage would get better with time. There was no cure for the nightmares.

Instead of sleeping at night, he walked. He visited the nursery to see Cassie sleeping. He explored the underground tunnel system, surprising the young men and women on guard duty. But most of the time he ended up right here, on the edge of the flight deck, staring up at the star-studded skies.

The official name for the site was New Earth Order Assault Base Twelve, but the residents called it Shangri-La.

Not a bad likeness, Graves reasoned, as he looked out the moonlit valley. Behind him in the tunnels carved out of this mountain were enough weapons of war to start a revolution.

That's exactly what the Sentinels were planning to do—start a war to take back the future of the human race from SynCorp.

Graves gritted his teeth. In hindsight, everyone should have seen that it would be just a matter of time before the council turned their destructive tendencies on each other. Power was a hungry beast and absolute power was ravenous.

Anthony Taulke was dead and Graves felt the loss of the man. The elder Taulke had his flaws to be sure, but when it came down to it, he cared.

Graves still chose to believe Anthony's move to place him and Cora on the Council of Corporations was sincere. He was equally sure Anthony had some trick up his sleeve to benefit himself more than others, but that was just his nature. Sleep with dogs, wake up with fleas.

Now Anthony was dead and Cora was dead too.

He felt the burden of Cora's presence in everything he did. Graves was a father now whether he liked it or not and he had to start thinking like one. That's what Cora would have wanted.

He decided to call the child Cassie, because in his mind there was no running away from her future. Whatever they had done to the child in utero was done—there would be a time to deal with that. Graves's responsibility now was to help her grow up as normally as possible and face whatever the future had in store for her.

For now, they would both stay at Shangri-La. Together. That was the most important part.

"I thought I might find you here." Olga's voice was scratchy with lack of sleep. She took his arm gently so as not to tweak his ribs. The night air was cool and she moved close to him. "It'll be light in a few hours. Have you thought about what you're going to say?"

Cora's funeral. Graves had asked that her body be put in cold storage until he could decide what to do. He tried to think of what she would want him to do with her remains. Corazon Santos was a woman without a home, he finally decided. Or rather, a woman for whom the world was her home.

A funeral pyre at dawn, Viking style, was Graves' decision. No one questioned it or even looked at him strangely and the Buddhists among the cadre of rebels here even seemed enthusiastic.

"Earth to Will," Olga said. "Come in, Will."

Graves slipped his arm around her waist, ignoring the tweaks of pain from his bound ribs.

"She was special to you," Olga said.

Graves nodded. He could see a paleness spreading across the sky behind the mountains on the other side of the deep valley. "She was my friend."

"More than just a friend, Will. A woman can tell."

He squinted at the valley floor. In the daytime he liked to watch the herd of goats play in the sun. Cora would have appreciated their antics. He drew Olga closer and felt her respond.

"No," he said. "Cora had bigger things on her mind than some broken-down old soldier like me."

He expected a snarky response from Olga, but she stayed silent.

"I want you to stay," she said.

Graves started to speak but she stopped him.

"Stay with me. Fight with us. You and Cassie belong here, Will. It's what she would have wanted for the child."

"I—I...need to think about it."

"Every day matters, Will. SynCorp is consolidating their power. They will rape this planet for whatever they want. People, resources, information. There's nothing the UN or any other government can do. The Sentinels are the resistance."

Graves let her talk.

"They won't stop until they have Cassie," Olga said. "She's part of their plan and you messed with that plan."

The sky behind the mountain range across the valley had turned pink.

"I have a funeral to attend." Graves left Olga on the edge of the hangar deck.

Someone had managed to find Graves a US Army dress uniform complete with correct rank insignia and all his medals. The size was correct, but the uniform fit loosely. He'd lost weight.

Looking at his reflection in the mirror, he adjusted his tie and smiled wryly. The black eye patch over his damaged eye gave him a rakish look. A US Army pirate. How fitting for a member of a rebel faction out to save the world.

A young woman waited for him at the nursery with Cassie bundled into a ball of blankets. He took the child from her. Cassie was asleep, her tiny lips moving in imaginary feeding. Her features were delicate, her skin a light brown, the same shade as her mother's. A wisp of dark hair peeked out from under her cap.

The elevator took the three of them from the main personnel deck to the peak of the mountain. When he stepped out of the elevator car, the first rays of the sun were just creeping over the distant mountains and a chill breeze cut through his uniform jacket.

Cassie's eyes remained closed.

A group of about a hundred people gathered around a tiered pyre of wood and brush. Cora's body lay on top of the six-foot high structure. She wore a simple, gray dress and her silver hair was braided and looped across her shoulder. She had Graves's Saint Christopher medal around her neck. In life, her skin had a luminous glow. That was gone now. Her skin was dark and lifeless, more like clay than flesh.

Graves tried to picture her in life and failed.

He handed Cassie off to the nurse and stepped to the front of the gathering. His ribs tweaked when he took in a deep breath to speak.

"I didn't know Corazon Santos long, but I knew her well. Or rather, she knew me well. The first time we met, she told me she had walked a thousand miles to find me. I laughed it off. She told me I would help her save the world. I laughed again."

Graves broke off, feeling the bite of the chill breeze bring tears to his unprotected eye.

"I'm not laughing today. I mourn for my friend. I mourn for a woman who gave her life for a cause bigger than herself. A cause of human rights and freedom of choice for all people wherever they live in the universe." He looked over at Cassie and saw the child's eyes were open, watching him. The golden stare made him catch his breath. She was listening to him, hearing him. It made no sense, but he knew it was happening.

"There is no better example of her selflessness than her last act of saving a child. Cassandra is alive because of Corazon Santos. The child is her legacy—and ours."

Graves took the burning brand from the hand of a young man in a paramilitary uniform. He wore a patch on his shoulder, a crossed sword and olive branch superimposed over an image of Earth. The sign of the Sentinels.

He thrust the flame deep into the base of the pyre. The dry material caught quickly, consuming loose brush with a crackling roar. The flame burst through the top of the pyre, enveloping Cora's body in seconds. Graves took a step backwards in the face of the sudden heat.

Cassie let out a piercing wail. The sound gripped Graves's spine and shook him to the core. The young man next to him let out a grunt and dropped to one knee, his hands pressed against the back of his neck.

"Are you okay?" Graves whispered.

"Yeah, just felt a jolt. Right in the back of the neck." He got to his feet, and when he dropped his hands, Graves saw the young man had a Neo tattoo.

Graves' eyes found the child. Her calm gaze captured his attention.

"I think the fire startled her, sir," said the nurse. She bounced Cassie gently in her arms.

"Yes, I'm sure that was it," Graves said.

Cassie, the child with the golden eyes, smiled at him.

VALHALLA STATION
Book 4 of The SynCorp Saga

Harmony. Security. Obedience.

A generation has passed since Tony Taulke formed the Syndicate Corporation and took over Earth. SynCorp saved humanity from climate catastrophe. Now its citizens work the Sol system, cradle to grave.

Some call that slavery.

A new power rises to challenge the absolute rule of SynCorp's Five Factions.

But does mankind really want to be freed?

Get your copy today at
severnriverbooks.com/series/the-syncorp-saga

ABOUT THE AUTHORS

David Bruns is a former officer on a nuclear-powered submarine turned high-tech executive turned speculative-fiction writer. He mostly writes sci-fi/fantasy and military thrillers.

Chris Pourteau is a technical writer and editor by day, a writer of original fiction and editor of short story collections by night (or whenever else he can find the time).

Sign up for Bruns and Pourteau's newsletter at severnriverbooks.com/series/the-syncorp-saga

Printed in the United States
by Baker & Taylor Publisher Services